THE DUKE OF DEFIANCE

The Untouchables

DARCY BURKE

Copyright

The Duke of Defiance

ISBN: 1944576193
ISBN-13: 9781944576196

This is a work of fiction. Names, characters, places, and incidents are the product of the author's imagination or are used fictitiously. Any resemblance to actual events, locales, or persons, living or dead, is purely coincidental.

Book design: © Darcy Burke.
Book Cover Design: © Carrie Divine/Seductive Designs.
Image: © Period Images.
Image: © Susanna Herrera/Depositphotos
Editing: Linda Ingmanson.

For my bestie Elisabeth

You inspire me in so many ways,
plus you're just damn fun.

Chapter One

London, March 1817

"I WANTED TO tell you our exciting news."

Joanna Shaw's belly sank. She could well imagine what news her sister Nora had to share. "Are you expecting another child?" She was proud of how she kept her tone free of anguish or…jealousy.

Nora nodded, her lips spreading into a wide smile. "Titus is thrilled."

Happiness swelled inside Jo, and she felt horrible for allowing even a moment's upset. After everything Nora had been through in her youth, she deserved this and so much more. She'd overcome a scandal and was now happily married—to a duke who adored her—with a beautiful family. It was a dream come true.

It had certainly been Jo's dream.

Just then, three children darted into the drawing room. The three-year-old boy was in the lead, shrieking in what sounded like glee as two girls—both five years old—chased him with odd-shaped pieces of wood clutched in their small hands.

Nora smiled, uncaring that they'd burst into the room. She and her husband, Titus, doted on their children, and it showed. Christopher and Rebecca possessed a joy for life and a freedom of expression that warmed Jo's heart. When she thought of how her own children, if she'd had any, would've been treated by their father…well, it was perhaps best that she was barren.

The nurse, a cheerful woman in her fifties, stepped into the room, her gaze landing on the children, now squealing as the girls chased Christopher around one of the settees. She exhaled and looked to Nora. "Your Grace?"

Nora chuckled. "It's fine. We've got them. Evie's father will be here soon anyway."

With a nod, the nurse turned and left, no doubt having earned a respite.

Jo pivoted on her chair so that she could see the children, who were at a bit of a stalemate on the other side of the room. Christopher, his chest heaving, stood in front of the settee, while the girls were behind it, their heads bent together just visible over the back.

"Mama, they're plotting something," Christopher called. He didn't turn his head to look at his mother. Jo didn't blame him since it was clear they were plotting *something*.

Jo stood and walked toward her nephew. "Are you playing pirates again?" Since coming to stay with Nora and her family a few weeks ago, she'd come to know Christopher and Becky quite well. She recognized the "weapons" the girls carried as their pistols. They'd tried swords, but Nora had put a stop to them running around with sticks.

Becky spared her aunt a quick glance, her hazel eyes narrowed with intent. "Yes. We're deciding how to make Christopher walk the plank when we catch him."

Christopher dashed to Jo's side and clutched her hand. "I don't want to walk the plank."

Jo gave his fingers a squeeze. "Of course not. How about some cakes instead?"

His hazel eyes lit and the tip of his tongue darted

over his lips. "Yes, please, Auntie."

Chuckling, Jo guided him back to where his mother was sitting. A tea tray, stacked with cakes and biscuits, perched on the table.

Christopher climbed onto his mother's lap and reached for a cake.

Nora helped him get situated as he gleefully ate. "I'm surprised you didn't come here straightaway. Too preoccupied with avoiding your sister and her new friend, I'm sure."

"How are we to make him walk the plank *now*?" Becky wailed from across the room.

"Find something else to do," Nora said, smiling at her daughter. "Show Evie your favorite book."

The book—an illustrated guide to the plants and birds of England—sat on the table near the tea tray. Becky ran to grab it, along with two biscuits, and a moment later, the two girls were sprawled in the corner happily eating and perusing the tome.

Nora gazed at them the way a mother looks at her children: with a love so palpable that the entire room seemed to glow with it. "I'm so glad she's found a friend her age. It's quite fortuitous that we met her father."

"How did you make his acquaintance?"

"His godmother is Lady Dunn, and as you may recall, she's a friend of Genie's." Genie was Lady Satterfield, Nora's mother-in-law. "He's newly returned to England since inheriting his title and doesn't really know anyone. He left ages ago—fifteen years, I think—and never meant to return. He's the third son and is now the earl."

"Knightley?" Jo asked, trying to recall the name she'd heard in passing earlier.

"Knighton. His seat is on the Welsh border." Nora held on to Christopher as he leaned forward for another cake. "Just one more," she said softly.

"That would be a shock," Jo mused. "To be the third son and manage to inherit the title. Where has he been?"

"The tropics. He owns a sugar plantation."

"How exotic." Jo couldn't imagine such a place. She'd never left England. This was, in fact, only her third trip to London. She'd lived quite a sheltered life in their tiny village of St. Ives.

"Did I tell you he has a nickname?"

Jo plucked a biscuit from the tray. "He's an Untouchable, then?" This was the word they'd chosen in their youth to describe the men they dreamed of marrying, men that were too far above their station. They'd giggled about it endlessly. It was, of course, the epitome of irony that Nora was now a duchess.

"Probably," Nora said. "Time will tell if he's truly 'untouchable,' but he has a nickname nonetheless. He's the Duke of Defiance." These nonsensical names had originated with Nora's trio of friends who had also married Untouchables, all of whom they'd labeled the duke of something in accordance with their reputations.

"However did he earn that name?" Jo asked.

Nora glanced toward the corner. "It occurs to me that we should perhaps speak quietly. Or not at all."

Good heavens. Jo had completely forgotten that the Duke of Defiance's daughter was just across the room. Granted, she looked completely engrossed in the book with Becky. Jo smiled at them. "Reminds me of us when we were young."

They'd spent countless hours combing through their

father's library. And climbing trees. And digging in the ground. And storming the kitchen—both to eat and to learn to cook. The housekeeper had been more than happy to teach them.

Jo thought of the kind woman with her curly white hair and bright blue eyes. She'd given the best hugs after their mother had died. "I wonder where Mrs. Birch is now." She'd retired from their father's employ shortly before Jo had married.

"I have to think she's passed on," Nora said quietly.

"I'd prefer to imagine her baking pastries in a cottage in the Cotswolds."

Nora smiled. "Yes, let's do that."

"Excuse me." A small feminine voice drew both of them to turn. Evie stood a few feet away from their chairs, her gaze on the table. "May I have another biscuit?"

"Yes, you may," Nora said. She stood with Christopher, holding him on her hip. "I need to take Christopher up to wash his hands. And then it's nap time. I'll be back shortly." Nora left.

Evie tiptoed to the table but hesitated, her fingers hovering over the sweets.

"Can't decide?" Jo asked.

Evie shot her a quick glance. "I want the one I had before, but I can't tell them apart."

Jo scooted to the edge of her chair. "Hmm. They have subtle differences, I think. This," she pointed to one variety, "has lemon flavoring. I see little bits of lemon rind."

Evie made a face. "Not that one. I like them plain."

"Ah, then this one." Jo indicated a square stamped with a flower.

The girl's blue-green gaze shifted to Jo for a brief

moment before she gingerly picked up the biscuit. She held it to her lips and licked the edge. After a moment, she took a small nibble. A look of relief settled over her features, and she claimed a second, larger, bite.

"Is that one right, then?" Jo asked.

Evie nodded. "Thank you." She held her free hand to her mouth. After she swallowed, she said, "My apologies. I shouldn't talk with food in my mouth. Or so Nanny used to tell me."

"Who's Nanny?"

"My nurse in Barbados. I miss her."

"She didn't come with you to England?"

Evie shook her head, jostling her blonde waves. "Papa said it would be too much of a change for her. We're going to hire a new one. Once Papa finds his legs. So Papa says."

Jo imagined it was a big change for all of them. "Do you like it here?"

Evie shrugged. "It's cold. I miss the beach and the ocean."

A picture of this fair-haired girl dancing in the waves brought a smile to Jo's lips. "I would miss that too. Is the ocean warm there?"

The girl's eyes glowed. "Oh yes. And the sand can get quite hot."

Jo wiggled her stocking-clad toes in her shoes. "That sounds lovely. What else can you tell me about Barbados?"

"We have palm trees and monkeys. And turtles. They make nests in the sand."

"Indeed?"

Evie finished her biscuit and sidled closer to Jo. "When they hatch, all the little baby turtles run across the sand to the water. They look like crabs, but they're much cuter. I wanted to have one as a pet, but Papa said no, that it wouldn't be fair to keep them in a cage."

"I think your papa sounds like a wise man."

Evie grinned up at her, revealing a missing front tooth on the bottom. "Oh, he is."

"And what about your mama?"

The girl's smile faded. "She died."

Jo's heart squeezed. "My goodness, I'm so sorry for your loss. I didn't know."

Evie shrugged again. "I barely remember her."

"Lord Knighton," announced Nora's butler, Abbott.

"Papa!" Evie scrambled toward the door and threw her arms around her father's waist.

Jo rose from the chair, smoothing her hand over her skirt and dislodging a crumb in the process.

The earl hugged his daughter briefly. "Did you have a good time?" he asked quietly.

Blonde curls rioted against Evie's shoulders as she tipped her head back to look up at her father. "Yes. Can I come again?"

The earl looked over at Jo. His eyes were a deep, dark blue, almost indigo. His gaze was direct and intense, but only for a moment until he returned his attention to Evie. "If you're invited."

"Of course she's invited!" Becky chimed from the corner. "I found the picture of the hawk, Evie. Come see!"

Evie hesitated until her father gave a slight nod. Then she disengaged herself from him and tore back to Becky.

Jo curtsied to the earl. "I'm Mrs. Shaw, the duchess's sister."

He executed a bow. "Pleased to make your acquaintance. I am Cr—Knighton." He shook his head.

"Your daughter is quite charming," Jo said.

"Did she talk you into a soporific state?" His features were impassive. It sounded like it ought to be a joking remark, but she couldn't find a hint of humor in his demeanor.

"Er, no. As I said, she's charming. She told me about Barbados."

He kept his gaze focused across the room, toward the girls. "She talks of little else."

Again, she couldn't determine the emotion behind his statement. Did that bother him? "It sounds lovely. Particularly the warm sand."

"Yes, she misses that. She could never get enough of it, always burying her legs and rolling around in it." He glanced at Jo. "Not terribly ladylike, I'm afraid."

It reminded Jo of her adventures with Nora when they were girls. "No, but sometimes ladylike behavior is overrated. Often, actually." Jo had spent eight years comporting herself with the utmost decorum as a vicar's wife. And she'd been happy to do so. Until she'd learned what her husband had been doing behind her back.

She refused to think of Matthias. He didn't deserve any of her time or concern. Not that she meant to think ill of the dead. No, she meant not to think of him at all.

The earl peered at her a moment, his gaze inscrutable, and she feared she'd misspoken. Perhaps he was terribly strict and didn't appreciate her comments about ladylike behavior being overrated. She glanced toward Evie, who was a vivacious child. Surely she couldn't be the product of someone who was rigid and stodgy?

The silence grew into something awkward, so Jo

sought to break the tension. "Evie said you're looking to hire a nurse."

He glanced at her again, and maybe there was a hint of…relief? "Yes, I will be conducting some interviews, but what do I know of hiring a nurse?"

Nora breezed in at that moment. "Good afternoon, Lord Knighton. I see you've met my sister, Mrs. Shaw." She smiled brightly and came to stand with them.

"Yes." He only spared Nora a brief look, and Jo had the sense that he was maybe nervous. Yes, that could very well be it. Going from sugar plantation owner in Barbados with sun and beaches and baby turtles to earl in London, where there was far less sun and certainly no baby turtles except in soup had to be nerve rattling.

"If you wanted help locating a nurse, perhaps Nora can help," Jo suggested, knowing her sister wouldn't mind her making the offer.

"I wouldn't wish to be a bother," he said.

"It's no bother," Nora said. "I'd be delighted to help."

"The interviews are day after tomorrow. Would you want to join me?"

"Certainly."

"Excellent. I'll have my secretary send over the details."

Nora smiled warmly. "I'll look forward to it." She turned toward the girls, who were still bent over the book. "Oh, I hate to disrupt them. Girls!" she called. "Time for Evie to go."

This was met with a chorus of protestations followed by both asking for more time.

"I promise you'll get together again very soon," Nora said. She winced as she looked over at the earl. "Provided your father says it's all right."

"He already said I could if I'm invited," Evie said.

Nora laughed softly. "Then consider yourself invited."

The girls hugged, and when they parted, Becky's eyes widened. "I just realized… Aunt Jo isn't married and neither is your father. They could get married, and then we would be cousins!"

Jo stiffened and willed the heat that was rising in her neck to stop before it reached her cheeks and they turned a mortifying shade of puce.

Evie pivoted toward her father. "Oh yes, Papa! You did say you should find me a mother."

He frowned down at her. "Nonsense, I'm not going to marry the first woman I meet, Evie. I must ensure she meets our requirements."

Jo wasn't looking to marry but still tried not to feel slighted. It was an odd thing to say in front of her. She expected an apology or at least an apologetic glance.

He did neither.

Instead, he looked at Nora and thanked her again for having Evie over and for offering to help with his search for a nurse. He bowed to her and started to turn. Realigning himself, he gave a quick bow to Jo. "Mrs. Shaw."

Then he took his daughter's hand, and they left the drawing room.

Becky sighed. "I like her ever so much."

"Me too, dear," Nora said, bending to kiss her daughter's head and stroking her dark reddish-brown waves. "Time to go upstairs for afternoon reading."

"Yes, Mama." She skipped from the room, and Nora smiled after her. Again, her mother's love seemed a living, breathing thing.

"That was a rather odd reaction he had," Nora said,

turning toward Jo.

"Yes. You never did tell me how he got his name—the Duke of Defiance."

Nora's brow creased. "I'm trying to remember. I think it was Ivy who revealed that Lady Dunn had said he was a defiant child. Yes, that's it." Nora pursed her lips. "It's undoubtedly a biased assessment, but then I suppose all those names are. We should probably stop referring to them in such ways."

Yes, probably. But even Nora's husband was still called the Forbidden Duke. It was done with deference and even admiration, however. "The nickname hasn't gone public, has it?"

Nora shook her head. "I don't think so. Not like the Duke of Desire."

That was Ivy's husband, the Duke of Clare. He'd been known for his outrageous love affairs, but all that was in the past since he'd been happily wed to Ivy last fall.

"Well, based on my limited interaction with him, I'd say the Duke of Discomfort might be a better description. He didn't seem at all at ease."

Nora crossed back to her chair and sat down. "I gathered that also. Peculiar to say the least."

Jo sat too. "It has to be difficult returning here to a life he never expected."

"True." Nora replenished their teacups. "It's amazing how quickly things can change."

"And it's usually beyond our control." Especially as a woman. Jo had married someone out of necessity and had endured a marriage that had seemed a safe haven but had become a living hell.

Now she was in a position to perhaps find a measure of happiness. That would require good fortune, however, which was, of course, beyond Jo's control.

THE GARMENTS HE would shortly need to don taunted him from the other side of the dressing chamber. Bran Crowther, reluctant Earl of Knighton, closed his eyes, ignoring them, and focused on the deep pressure his valet was currently working into his shoulders.

Hudson had long fingers and particularly strong hands. Bran couldn't imagine starting his day without his massage techniques. He worked down Bran's right arm, finishing with his wrist before moving to the left.

While he worked, Bran thought about his upcoming appointments. Three nurses to interview. The Duchess of Kendal would be here soon to provide her assistance. Bran was glad for it, especially since he was fairly certain he'd botched things before leaving her house the other day.

"Hudson, I meant to ask you something. I'm afraid I misspoke at the Duchess of Kendal's the other day."

The valet massaged Bran's elbow. "In what way?"

"Evie's friend suggested I should marry the Duchess's sister since we are both unwed. I said I had requirements. I suspect it was insulting to Mrs. Shaw."

Hudson moved down to Bran's left wrist. "Probably. You do have a way of unintentionally insulting people from time to time."

Bran exhaled. "As you said, it's unintentional."

Hudson finished, and Bran opened his eyes. "Perhaps I should apologize."

"Like as not. However, that *was* two days ago, and she's a mere acquaintance. Unless you think you did her grievous injury."

"No." Bran stood and completed his toilette.

"You are resplendent," Hudson said, brushing a speck of lint from Bran's coat.

Bran gave him a gimlet eye. "I miss the way I was able to dress at home."

"Of course."

"And I miss my tailor. Any news on that front?"

Hudson's dark eyes lit, and he gave a subtle nod of his balding head. "In fact, I have found someone. He can start tomorrow, if that's agreeable."

"Yes. I'm desperate. You told him it would be a temporary arrangement?" It had to be in order to ensure his skills were acceptable. Bran was particular about his clothing. It seemed he had requirements about everything.

"Indeed."

"I need to get downstairs," Bran said. As he exited his chamber, his butler, a stodgy fellow called Kerr, met him in the gallery.

"There you are, my lord." His tone carried a bit of pomposity as it usually did. "Mrs. Shaw has arrived."

Mrs. Shaw? "Not the Duchess of Kendal?"

Kerr blinked behind his spectacles, appearing offended by Bran's query. "I think I can tell the difference, not to mention read a calling card."

Bran suppressed a growl. "I was expecting the Duchess." He stalked past the butler and started down the stairs. "Is she in my office?"

"No," Kerr said from behind him. "She's in the hall."

Bran turned, and Kerr had to stop short. He teetered on the stair, his small gray eyes widening as he recovered his balance. Bran ignored the man's distress—served him right for following so damn close behind him. Hadn't he explained to his new staff that he craved, no, he *needed* his space? "In the future, if I have an appointment, I should like you to show the person to my office to await my arrival."

"What if you're already in your office?"

"Then they won't need to await my arrival, will they?" Bran turned with a shake of his head and descended into the hall where Mrs. Shaw stood near the door. She didn't indicate that she'd heard any of their discussion on the stairs, but then she wouldn't have been able to hear it from this distance.

She sank into a curtsey. "Good morning, my lord. My sister wishes to convey her deepest apologies, but her son is ill, so she asked me to come in her stead."

Bran registered the tidy upsweep of her dark brown hair and the green-brown of her earnest eyes as well as the simplicity of her modest slate-gray gown. She was rather monochromatic, except for that hint of green in her eyes, and the tiny gold flecks that danced near the pupil. He recalled that she was widowed, which perhaps explained her somewhat dour appearance. Or maybe it was just that he was used to warmth and vibrancy and colors that defied possibility in England. Barbados seemed like an imaginary world now.

"I see. Do you have children of your own?" he asked.

Pale swaths of pink highlighted her cheeks. It was the barest bit of color, but he caught it. How could he not against the dull palette she provided?

Dull?

No, that wasn't an apt description. Her attire was dull, her hair a bit too severe, but she possessed an attractive, feminine form. Indeed, her breasts were perhaps spectacular. And she was pretty, with long, dark lashes framing her eyes and rose-colored lips that were just a bit too full. Not *too* full, he amended.

"I do not," she said, drawing his attention back to his question about whether she had children.

"Then how can you be qualified to help me with this endeavor?"

"My sister sent a list of characteristics and requirements you should seek." She straightened her shoulders and looked him in the eye. "She also sent me with her express confidence."

He liked her fortitude. "Well then, I suppose you will suffice. Come along."

Her nostrils flared slightly, and her eyes widened just the tiniest bit, the gold flecks seeming to brighten. As he turned to lead her to his office, he considered that he might just have offended her again. He had called her abilities into question, but why wouldn't he?

He strode toward the back corner of the house, where his office was located. It was a large chamber with a wall of bookshelves and windows that looked out to the garden. He moved behind the desk and indicated for her to take a chair on the opposite side.

She slowly sat, her gaze wary and her mouth tight.

He frowned. "My apologies if I insulted you."

"If you'd rather I didn't stay, you have only to say so." There was a steely set to her shoulders and a clipped edge to her tone as she spoke. "Nora wanted to help you, but I'll understand if you decide I won't *suffice*."

He dropped into his chair. She had cheek to go with her fortitude. He liked that too. He'd been prepared to deal with milksops and featherbrains when he'd returned to England—people like his mother and brothers. Not that they really were milksops or featherbrains, but they liked to put on as if they were, thinking it was somehow attractive. He supposed it wasn't fair to assume an entire population shared the same characteristics as his family.

"I'm afraid I must also apologize for the other day. I meant no offense. Sometimes… I speak without realizing how my words might sound."

One of her dark, slender brows arched. "Forgive me for saying so, but I've found that's a trait shared by most men."

A short, sharp laugh escaped him. "You may be right." Hell, she was absolutely right. But he knew he was a bit worse than average. His mother had spent the first eighteen years of his life telling him so. "I should advise you that I will likely do it again. Inadvertently offend you, I mean."

"Well, so long as it's inadvertent."

Yes, cheek to spare.

He glanced toward the reticule sitting in her lap. "You say your sister sent a list of requirements?"

"Yes." She opened the reticule and withdrew a piece of folded parchment. Scooting to the edge of her chair, she set it on the edge of the desk in front of her, laying it flat. "Nora recommends someone well versed in manners, sewing and mending, and medicine." She looked up from the paper. "Didn't Evie have a nurse in Barbados?"

"Yes, and she excelled at all those things." He thought of Amalie and how hard it had been for Evie to say goodbye. "Except perhaps the manners. Not that she didn't teach them—she did. It's just that things were different there. I didn't imagine Evie would need to grow up as the daughter of an earl." He bristled, the title pressing down on him like a mantle made of bricks.

"Your life has changed quite dramatically, I take it?"

In the span of eighteen months, he'd gone from third son to earl. He'd had to uproot his life, including his daughter from the only home she'd ever known. "Nothing is the same," he said simply.

Except his feelings at being back in England. Though it had been fifteen years since he'd last walked on this ground, he was still the same eccentric Bran. Only now he was expected to lead the family and be the earl. That meant dealing with his mother, his brothers' widows, and their daughters, of whom there were seven. He thought. Admittedly, he wasn't sure.

Forget a mantle made of bricks, perhaps it was lead. And granite. *And* bricks.

But first and foremost came Evie. Always Evie.

"Whoever I hire must possess patience and kindness. Evie is…sensitive."

"Plus she's been through a great change. Yes, I must agree that finding someone who will help her make the transition to her new life in England is critical."

Bran pressed his palm flat against the smooth top of his desk. His father's desk, rather. Like everything in this house, it wasn't his. How in the hell could he think of this as home—could Evie think of this as home—if everything had belonged to someone else?

"Do you know anything about decorating?"

She stared at him a moment before blinking, those dark lashes of hers briefly shuttering the sparkling hazel of her eyes. They were remarkable, he realized. How had he conjured the word dull in reference to her?

"Decorating?" she repeated. "Er, no. At least not here in London. I had to commission new drapes once. And order a new settee after the old one broke."

"And how did you do that? Particularly if you weren't in London."

She inhaled as her gaze traveled the room. "I hired a seamstress from the village to make the drapes, and the settee came from a furniture maker in Cambridge."

"I see."

"I'm sure Nora could offer assistance. Or Lady Satterfield. She's Nora's mother-in-law."

Bran had met her last week while visiting his godmother, Lady Dunn. In fact, he should ask the viscountess—he'd much rather seek her counsel than his mother's. And wouldn't that annoy his mother? She'd never cared for Lady Dunn, who'd been his father's choice as godmother.

He shoved thoughts of his mother aside. He'd have to deal with her soon enough when she arrived from Durham, where she'd been staying with her sister.

"I'll consult them, thank you." Or maybe he'd just delegate refurbishment to his secretary. Wouldn't the staid, fussy Dixon enjoy that?

Hell, what Bran really needed was a wife. And he was about as versed in searching for one of those as he was in securing nurses and furniture. It had been easy on Barbados—there simply weren't many choices.

He eyed Mrs. Shaw and realized he couldn't very well solicit her input on *that* topic.

He recalled the duchess's daughter's comment the other day, that both and he and Mrs. Shaw were unmarried. However, she didn't look as though she were ready to marry again. Indeed, she seemed to perhaps still be in mourning, given her attire.

"How long ago did your husband pass away?" he asked.

She started, her shoulder twitching slightly as she

blinked at him. "It's been about a year." She smoothed her hand along the top of her knee. "And your wife?"

"Nearly four years. She was struck by fever. Evie became ill as well, but thankfully recovered."

"My goodness, that must have been frightful. I'm sorry for your loss."

"And I'm sorry for yours." He noted she didn't offer a cause of death, and he wouldn't ask. He could be blunt and occasionally brash, but he wasn't a complete boor. Usually.

A soft rap on the doorframe was followed by Kerr announcing the arrival of the first candidate.

"Please show her in," Bran said, ignoring the perennially pinched expression on Kerr's face.

"Do you expect me to remain quiet for the duration of the interview?" Mrs. Shaw asked.

Bran hadn't actually thought about that. "No, if you have something to ask after I'm finished with my questions, please do so."

Mrs. Shaw gave a prim nod, then straightened her spine. As she did so, her tongue peeked between her lips, wetting them. She seemed completely unaware, but Bran was *not*.

The quick, innocuous gesture sent a shaft of heat straight to his groin. Of all the inconvenient times… The candidate stepped into the office, and he was forced to drive all thought of Mrs. Shaw from his mind.

For now.

Chapter Two

BY THE TIME they'd finished the third interview, Jo had a clear favorite, but she had no idea what Lord Knighton was thinking. He'd been thorough in his questioning, if a bit monotone. If she'd had to guess, she would say he hadn't cared for any of them. Which she supposed was possible.

She opened her mouth to speak and promptly froze. But just for a moment. Then her jaw dropped as he untied his cravat, pulling the fabric loose until it hung down his front in two snowy white swaths. The top of his shirt gapped open, revealing a triangle of bronze flesh.

"What are you doing?" She blurted the question before she could censor herself.

"Removing this bloody nuisance." He tugged the cravat from around his neck and tossed it atop the desk. He pulled at his collar, which widened the gap in the top of his shirt, which in turn exposed more of his bronzed flesh.

Jo realized she was staring and abruptly looked away. "Er…" She struggled to find the right words. Were there wrong words in this instance? "I don't know what you're used to in Barbados, but in England, it's improper for a gentleman to disrobe in front of a lady."

"Hell," he muttered. "I hadn't considered this *disrobing*. Things were different at home." He scowled. "I beg your pardon, but I can only wear the troublesome garment for short periods at a time.

Though it will likely offend you horribly, I can't put it back on."

Would it offend her? It most certainly should, but so far she found the earl's eccentricities curious. Plus, he'd used the word "can't," not "won't." "Why does it bother you? If I may ask."

He narrowed his eyes at her for a moment, perhaps weighing how to respond. "It's constricting. I start to itch."

She could understand that. Sometimes her corset was extremely unpleasant. She'd never remove it in an instance such as this, of course. But then taking off her corset wasn't as simple as removing a cravat. Why were things always easier for men?

Before she could respond to that, Evie ran into the room, her blue-green eyes wide and her hair a mess of straggly curls. "Papa! Papa!" The girl stopped short at seeing Jo. "It's you."

"Yes, it's me."

Evie turned from her and went to her father's chair. The earl pivoted and leaned forward, putting his face near to hers. "What is it, my sweetling?"

"I've hurt my finger." She held up her index finger and practically jabbed him in the eye.

"Let me see." He clasped it gently around the knuckle and frowned at the digit. "This little cut at the top?"

She nodded. "The parchment wounded me." She sounded as if she wanted to challenge the paper to a duel.

The earl's brows pitched low over his eyes. "Nasty parchment. Tell me where it is, and I'll toss it into the fireplace."

"Oh no, Papa. I'm angry with it, but you mustn't

burn it. I was drawing our ship, and it's quite good."

"I see. Then it has won a reprieve. What shall we do with your wound?"

She shrugged. "Foster didn't know what to do. She said I should go see Cook. I came here instead."

Knighton looked over at Jo briefly, his gaze searching. Did he want help?

"May I see it?" Jo asked.

Evie hesitated a moment, but when her father gave her a slight nod, she rounded the desk and came to stand before Jo. She stuck her finger beneath Jo's nose. "See?"

Jo focused on the pad of the girl's digit and saw the reddened cut. "Did it bleed?"

"A little. I wiped it on my petticoat." She lifted the edge of her dress to show the small red-brown streak at the hem of her undergarment. "Foster said I shouldn't have done that."

"Well, what should you have done?" Jo asked, glancing over at the girl's father who was watching the exchange with interest. Again, she caught herself staring at his exposed flesh, and again, she jerked her gaze away.

"Foster said I should have sucked on it until it stopped bleeding." Evie made a face, her tongue poking out of her mouth. "But that's disgusting."

"I agree. I think you did the only reasonable thing. Does it hurt?"

Evie nodded. "Not as much as it did at first, but it stings."

"Do you know what my mother used to do for me when I had a cut?" Jo didn't actually remember her mother doing it, but Nora had told her about it, so of course it was true. Nora, being two years older, remembered more about her than Jo did.

Evie shook her head, her gaze intent.

"She would blow on it and then seal it with a kiss."

Evie's eyes widened. "The kiss would close the cut?"

Jo chuckled softly. "No, but that would have been lovely, wouldn't it? Perhaps that wasn't the right way to say it. She would press a kiss to the wound, and it would instantly feel better."

Evie looked skeptical.

"Would you like me to try? I promise it won't make it worse."

With a nod, Evie thrust her finger forward once more, until it was mere inches from Jo's mouth. Jo lightly blew on the pad for a moment, then pressed a soft kiss to the girl's digit.

Evie slowly withdrew her hand, staring at her finger. She turned her hand this way and that, her expression one of bemusement. Then her lips spread into a wide smile, and she ran back around the desk to her father's chair. "Papa! It doesn't hurt anymore." She looked over at Jo, her grin exposing the gap in her bottom teeth. "Mrs. Shaw is magic."

"Magic," he murmured, his dark gaze settling on Jo.

Something about the way he uttered the word sent a shiver along Jo's arms. She covered a twitch by rolling her shoulders and straightening in the chair.

Knighton turned his attention back to his daughter. "Are you sufficiently recovered to return upstairs while I finish with Mrs. Shaw? We must decide on which nurse to hire."

"Oh yes, you met with some today." She looked from the earl to Jo and back again. "Were they nice?"

"Quite," Knighton answered.

"However will you choose?" Evie asked.

"I'm not certain, which is why I need to discuss it with Mrs. Shaw."

"All right." She turned and walked toward the door, pivoting at the threshold to regard them both with a serious stare. "Choose wisely. My happiness depends on it." She spun about and skipped from the room.

Laughter escaped Jo as she blinked after the girl. Quickly, Jo coughed to hide her reaction.

"I vaguely recall my younger sister uttering such dramatic nonsense," Knighton said. "Is it thus with all girls?"

Jo caught the barest twinkle in his eye. "I'm afraid so. Nora and I were quite dramatic. Everything is Vitally Important when you're nearly six years old."

It had certainly seemed that way for Jo, especially in the wake of her mother's death when Jo had been five. She recalled a deep and pervasive sadness and her sister trying very hard to make her smile at every possible opportunity. Nora would concoct elaborate schemes to amuse them so that they wouldn't be sad.

The earl was staring at the corner, his eyes glazed, as if he'd fallen into a trance.

"My lord?" she prompted.

He shook his head and blinked. "Yes, vitally important. Shall we discuss the candidates?"

Jo had the sense he'd gotten lost in his own memories. Were they sad like hers or something else entirely? She doubted she'd ever find out. "I liked the last one, Mrs. Poole."

He leaned forward in his chair and propped his elbow on his desk. His shirt shifted, allowing a greater exposure of flesh. Jo vowed to ignore it. "What did you like about her?" he asked.

"She—" The word came out scratchy so Jo coughed

delicately. "She was the most knowledgeable, I think, having reared her own children."

"You think that carries more weight than the other two who've several decades of employment in exemplary households between them?"

"I do. Mrs. Poole has a warmth that's important for Evie, I think." Jo could see that Evie craved a female connection. "She misses her old nurse a great deal, doesn't she?"

Jo had noticed that the earl had mentioned the woman several times during the interviews. He'd made comments about their former nurse doing something and then asked the candidate if she could do the same, such as sing. Apparently, Evie liked to be sung to. Mrs. Poole had promptly rewarded them with a lullaby delivered in a soft, pleasant tone.

"Yes, she does." He pulled his coat off and set it on the edge of his desk. As soon as he did it, his gaze darted to hers. "This is also unseemly, isn't it?"

"It is." Oh, but he looked divine, the sleeves of his shirt billowing out from the armholes of his dark blue waistcoat. "You're not going to remove anything else, are you?"

He drummed his fingers on the desk for a moment. "Perhaps. But I'll try not to. I do apologize, but I… It's necessary."

Because he felt itchy. She wondered how he was going to sit through a session in the House of Lords. Maybe it wouldn't matter. For all she knew, they sat around in shirtsleeves. "Which candidate did you prefer?"

"They were all qualified. The first one, Miss Chambers, certainly possessed the best recommendations."

She'd been Jo's least favorite. Approximately fifty, with dark, knowing eyes, she'd given Jo the sense that she saw *everything*. And judged. "Yes, but… Ugh."

Knighton's eyes widened the slightest bit. Then he let out a sharp laugh. "Ugh?"

Jo felt heat rise up her neck but held his gaze. "She seemed a bit…unctuous."

"That's an interesting description. She did have an air of superiority about her, and for that reason, I agree with your choice of Mrs. Poole."

"You do?" Jo was relieved. "I think she'll be an excellent addition to your household. She meets all your requirements *and* she's charming. Most importantly, she's someone Evie could love." Jo added the last softly, her throat tightening as she thought of the children she'd never have. Perhaps she ought to consider a career as a nurse or a governess.

"I think she'll be the most flexible and understanding of our peccadilloes."

"You're referring to your distaste for cravats, I presume. But you used a plural. Are there more…peccadilloes?"

"Yes, the cravats and too much clothing in general. I'm afraid I walk about the house like this most of the time. Some of the current staff clearly do not approve. Evie likes to run around barefoot, though she does it less here since it's not as warm as at home." He pushed his hand through his hair, making the brown locks stand practically on end. It was a bit long anyway, and tousled, it gave him a wild, reckless look, especially in his current state of undress. "I have to stop thinking of that as home," he muttered.

"I can't imagine how difficult a transition this must be."

His mouth ticked up in a brief, wry smile. "It was a shock."

Jo tried not to think of how shocking this would be if anyone saw them. Wait, would it be? She was a widow. Wasn't she allowed certain behaviors an unmarried woman wasn't? Not that it mattered since there was absolutely no reason to preserve her reputation. Except as it pertained to her sister. She'd never want to bring scandal to Nora or her family. Especially not after the scandal Nora had already endured as a young debutante during her second Season.

Forcing herself to recall their conversation and stop woolgathering about the condition of his hair and how attractive it made him look, Jo looked at the window instead of at him. "Does that mean you're going to hire Mrs. Poole?"

"Yes. You're right that Evie needs someone who will be patient and understand that her life has been upended." He frowned slightly. "Mrs. Poole is the only one who asked how Evie was faring."

That was true. She'd also seemed unconcerned about Evie's eating habits, something Lord Knighton had discussed with each of them. She was particular about her food, and while the other two candidates had vowed to ensure she overcame that problem, Mrs. Poole had chuckled and said that all children were particular about one thing or another. Yes, there were peccadilloes *plural.*

He folded his hands together on the desktop. "I suppose that concludes our business, then."

Jo felt a pang of disappointment. Today had been the most useful she'd felt since Matthias had died. Not that she wasn't helpful to Nora or that she didn't enjoy being with her and her family. But Jo was the sister, the aunt. Here, today, she'd just been Jo.

A thought came to her. "Yes, it does. However, you should probably hire a governess as well. I'm not sure Mrs. Poole would be able to add lessons to her responsibilities. Besides, you'll want someone who can educate Evie in the ways of Society. She is an earl's daughter after all."

He winced. "Isn't she a bit young to worry about that?"

Jo shook her head. "My sister plans to hire one soon, and the girls are the same age."

"Can't I just send Evie over to their house a few times a week?"

Jo heard the exasperation in his tone and didn't wish to overwhelm him. "Is there a reason you don't want to hire a governess?"

"Not a governess in particular, no. I prefer a simpler household. There are too many retainers here." He laid his palms flat as he cocked his head to the right and then to the left. He seemed uncomfortable.

"You're the earl. You can decide how many retainers you need. There's no reason you can't decrease your staff."

"Yes. I may do that." His gaze found hers. "But I *need* a governess, you say?"

"I'm afraid so."

He exhaled as he leaned back in his chair and contemplated the ceiling for a moment. When he looked back at her, his dark eyes gleamed with intensity. "Then you shall help me."

A jolt of surprise quickened her pulse. "Me? Wouldn't you prefer my sister?"

He pulled a sheaf of parchment from the top drawer

of his desk. "No. I'm more than satisfied with you." It was hardly a resounding endorsement.

"I'm glad I could pass muster."

He looked up from the paper he'd laid in front of him. "Did I misspeak again?"

"Not terribly. I'm teasing you a bit. My apologies."

"I see. Teasing. I didn't realize people did that here." He kept drawing comparisons, which she supposed made sense.

"Did they in Barbados?"

"Yes."

"You think England is so very different?" she asked.

He nodded once. "In my experience."

And she'd be willing to wager the difference favored Barbados—in every way. "You don't like it here."

He shrugged, but there was a tightness in his jaw that told her he was not apathetic. "It is not where I saw myself."

She was suddenly quite eager to learn his story. Why, she didn't know. "You left many years ago, did you not?"

"Fifteen."

"I heard you never meant to return." When he didn't respond, she realized she'd overstepped. She stood abruptly. "My apologies. I didn't mean to intrude."

He unfolded himself from the chair, rising to his full height, which had to be a good six or eight inches over her five feet six. He made her feel rather diminutive. It was an odd sensation after being married to Matthias for eight years. He'd had barely an inch on her.

"You aren't being intrusive. I didn't plan to ever live here again, no. That doesn't mean I hadn't planned to visit."

"So you had?"

"Would you believe me if I said I'd never thought about it? I'd neither planned for it nor discounted it. I simply hadn't considered it." He shrugged. "I will say that when I left, I didn't go with the thought that I'd never see my father or brothers again."

She caught the barest tinge of regret in his tone. "I'm sorry for your losses."

"I appreciate the sentiment, but let me also clarify that while I might've expected to see them again, I didn't particularly want to. At least not at the time of the departure."

His revelation surprised her. What had happened that he didn't care for his family?

He moved around the desk and paused at the corner. "I'll have my secretary look into governesses."

"Would you like me to ask Nora for recommendations?"

"Will she share them? We'll be competing for the best candidate."

Jo laughed softly. "I suppose you will. Although, I'd argue you aren't looking for the same person. Nora needs someone who will be able to manage multiple children. At least in the future—Christopher has a few years before he's ready to begin studies. I do know they want the governess to teach all their children until they reach a certain age."

"That makes sense; however, I'll be looking for the same."

Jo was momentarily confused. "Do you have other children?"

"Not yet. But I will marry and have more, I hope. It's apparently up to me to provide an heir to the earldom."

Yes, of course. Jo thought of Becky's suggestion that he marry her. Only Jo couldn't have children. That would absolutely preclude her from being his countess. As if he would actually consider the recommendation of a child about a woman he barely knew. Nevertheless, Jo realized the moment he'd removed his cravat, she'd begun thinking of him in a different way. And that wouldn't do.

She clutched her reticule. "I'll ask Nora for her recommendations, and if you decide you'd rather work with her, I'll understand." She started toward the door, and he joined her.

"I said I wanted you to help me. Are you trying to shirk the task? Perhaps you have something better to do." His gaze lingered on her, suffusing her with a touch of heat. "I wouldn't be surprised."

"I'm not trying to shirk anything. And as it happens, I don't have anything better to do." She winced inwardly at how pathetic that sounded. She'd been far too idle since Matthias's death. Perhaps she *did* need something to do. She suddenly thought that *she* could be his governess. Evie *was* an adorable child…

"Good. I'll see you soon, then." He gestured for her to precede him from the office and then followed her a short way until the butler met them and offered to show her out.

Jo turned to say goodbye to the earl, but he was already walking back to his office. His waistcoat was superbly fitted, hugging the muscles of his back and leaving no question as to his fitness. She'd never seen a naked male back—Matthias had always left his shirt on when he'd joined her in the bedchamber.

As she left Knighton's town house, she realized she would likely never see a nude male back, unless she had an affair or married someone who didn't want children or already had an heir. She wouldn't count on either of those things happening, however. She'd learned at an early age that life was full of disappointments. She wouldn't expect things to change now.

Chapter Three

BRAN STEPPED INTO Brooks's, feeling a bit tentative. He'd never been in a gentleman's club before. He'd left England before he'd had the opportunity. His brothers had certainly never invited him to join them. They'd gone out of their way to exclude him whenever possible, and their parents hadn't encouraged them to do otherwise. In fact, their mother had specifically told them they would do better to ignore their younger, ill-mannered, *defiant* brother.

The air was thick with the scent of candles and the sounds of conviviality coming from the famous subscription room. A footman greeted him, and Bran shook off the dark, painful memories.

"Good evening," Bran said. "The Duke of Kendal is expecting me." The duke had invited him, and while Bran might've preferred to decline, he had to accept his new role. Forming an association with a duke would be beneficial. In fact, the association would happen whether Bran wanted it or not since his daughter had decided that the duke's daughter was the only good thing about England.

It seemed important that Bran attempt a friendship with the girl's father. Because, at the end of the day, he'd do anything for Evie.

The footman led Bran through the subscription room. Around him, men sat at tables conversing, drinking, gambling. A few looked up as he passed, their features registering a myriad expressions, none of which were recognition. Bran was exceedingly glad he wouldn't be meeting the duke in here. It was far too crowded and Bran would likely grow agitated quickly.

Just before they reached the stairs, a man jumped up from one of the tables and intercepted Bran. "Knighton, isn't it?"

Bran didn't know the man. "Yes."

The gentleman, slender and dark-haired with an affable smile, glanced toward the table he'd just left. "We thought that's who you were. I'm Talbot. I knew your brothers. Good, friendly chaps. We miss them a great deal."

An instant shaft of dislike sliced through Bran. If this man—and the others—had been friends of his brothers, he wasn't disposed to want their company. Furthermore, "good" and "friendly" were not words Bran would've used to describe John and Wynn. Born a scant twelve months apart, they'd grown up inseparable, to the point of brutally excluding their six-years-younger brother. It wasn't that they'd just ignored him. They'd gone out of their way to ensure he knew he wasn't wanted, that he was outside their brotherly circle. And never mind the girl who'd come ten years after Bran. John and Wynn had been long gone by then, of course, off on their grand tour, which they'd taken together. Bran hadn't even had a grand tour, at least not in the traditional sense. Instead, he'd simply booked passage on a ship, not caring where it took him, provided it was far away from here. From them.

"Thank you." Bran could think of nothing else to say. He supposed John and Wynn may have matured into kinder men, but he doubted it. They'd never once sought to foster a relationship. While his sister had written to him intermittently, John and Wynn had continued their campaign of exclusion. Or maybe they'd simply forgotten he'd existed. Bran could well imagine that happening.

Bran made to continue on, but Talbot edged in front of him a bit more. "You've been in the tropics all this time?" Talbot asked.

Bran nodded. "Yes."

"And now you're the earl." Talbot blew out a breath between his gapped front teeth. "Lucky for you."

"Are you saying I should be happy that my family died?" Bran stared at him.

Talbot's face flushed. "Er, no. Of course not. As I said, we miss your brothers a great deal." He glanced again toward the table, and Bran caught the beseeching look in his eyes.

While Talbot was otherwise focused and before someone could leap to the man's aid, Bran neatly stepped around him. "Pleasure to meet you, I'm sure," he murmured. He inclined his head toward the footman, who'd paused to wait, and they continued to the stairs.

Bran's shoulders twitched as he reached the landing. He'd give just about anything to have his father and brothers back, and not because he felt sad. No, he'd just rather have his old life. And that made him feel unsettled. He *should* feel sad.

Perhaps he did. His brothers had passed first, over a year ago. He'd received word about two months after they'd drowned in a boating accident, and at that moment, he'd become the heir apparent. Neither brother had a son, and their father wouldn't live forever. Which meant Bran *had* to return to England. While he'd reluctantly made preparations, he'd received another letter from his mother two months after that informing him that his father had died of a combination of ague and sadness. According to her, he'd been utterly brokenhearted over the loss of John and Wynn.

Bran doubted their father had been capable of such depth of emotion. He'd certainly never demonstrated any. Until Bran had lost his wife and become the sole parent to Evie, he'd thought he wasn't capable of such emotion either.

They arrived at a door, and the footman rapped softly. A masculine voice called out, "Come."

The footman opened the door and waited for Bran to walk past him. "The Right Honorable the Earl of Knighton, Your Grace."

The duke rose. "Good evening, Knighton."

"Evening, Your Grace." Bran walked toward the seating area, where the duke had stood from his chair. He shook the man's hand.

"Kendal, if you please." The duke gestured for Bran to sit. "I'm glad you could join me this evening."

"I appreciate the invitation."

"It seemed necessary, given the apparent inseparability of our daughters." Kendal chuckled. "Every day, Becky begs to see Evie."

"It's the same at my house. I'm glad she's found a companion. This transition to England has been difficult."

Kendal's brow creased. "I can only imagine. Would you care for whiskey? Or brandy?"

"I don't suppose you have any rum?" Bran asked.

"I should've guessed that would be your choice. I'm afraid I don't."

"I'll send a case over, if you'd like. I have plenty, and more will arrive soon." He needed at least a taste of

Barbados. "I'll take whiskey. It's been a while since I had a good bottle."

Kendal stood, his lips curving into a smile. "I've just the thing." He went to the sideboard and poured a glass, which he handed to Bran. He reached to the table next to his chair, on which stood his own glass. He lifted it toward Bran. "To new acquaintances."

Bran raised his whiskey. "And happy daughters."

"Yes, *that*." Kendal's brow arched before he took a drink and resettled himself in the chair. "You said it's been a difficult transition. Nora tells me you recently hired a nurse. That should help things."

"It already has." Mrs. Poole had started a few days ago. At first, Evie had been a bit withdrawn and reluctant. She'd finally shared that she felt funny about liking Mrs. Poole, who'd been extremely kind and warmhearted with Evie. After discussing it with her, Bran had determined that Evie felt guilty that Mrs. Poole would replace Amalie. Bran had told her that no one could do that. Things had summarily improved.

"Your daughter has also helped," Bran said. "I'm quite grateful for your hospitality. Now that Mrs. Poole is in place, Becky should come visit." Just yesterday, Evie had pestered him for the dozenth time about Becky coming to their house. She wanted to show Becky all the things she'd brought from Barbados.

"I'm certain Becky would love that. I'll have Nora make the arrangements." He sipped his whiskey before setting the glass back on the table. "Who takes care of that sort of thing for you, your secretary?"

"No." Bran could see what he was thinking. Kendal had a wife to manage such details. "I oversee everything to do with Evie. Though now that I have Mrs. Poole, I can share some of that responsibility."

"I understand my sister-in-law, Joanna, assisted you with hiring her? Nora was sorry she wasn't able to help. Christopher had a bit of a cold."

Bran had thought of Mrs. Shaw several times over the past several days. Evie had been to the Kendals' house twice since they'd conducted interviews together, but Bran hadn't seen Mrs. Shaw on either occasion. In fact, he hadn't heard from her about hiring a governess. "Yes, Mrs. Shaw was quite helpful. She is to assist me with finding a governess next. I understand you will also be looking for one, so I shall endeavor not to steal the one you want."

A staccato laugh erupted from Kendal. "This is a conversation I never imagined myself having."

"You never thought to have children?"

"I hadn't really considered everything that would accompany being a parent. Not just the responsibility, but the overwhelming emotion." He scowled as he reached for his glass and took another drink. "I don't usually share that sort of thing."

Nothing he said could've put Bran more at ease. "Me neither, and I feel precisely the same." He lifted his glass in silent toast.

Kendal inclined his head as a rap on the door interrupted the moment. He glanced toward the sound. "I hope you don't mind, but I invited a few friends to join us."

Bran immediately tensed. A "few friends" wasn't a crowd, but they were still strangers, and right now he was just beginning to feel comfortable with the *one* stranger. Former stranger, he supposed.

"Of course not," he fibbed. "I won't be staying much longer." He drank more of his whiskey, not quite draining the glass.

"Hell, I didn't mean to drive you away." Kendal peered at Bran with curiosity. "I can ask them to go. They're good sorts, and they'll bugger off if I tell them to."

So far, Bran had enjoyed Kendal's company, so he decided to at least try. If he grew uncomfortable, he'd leave. "Well, if they're the type you can tell to bugger off, how can I leave?"

Kendal smiled as another knock sounded. "Come!"

The footman opened the door, and three men filed inside.

"It's about damned time," a dark-haired gentleman with an athletic build said with a grin.

"We were in the middle of a discussion," Kendal said, his eyes narrowing, but his tone laced with humor. "And how the hell did the three of you arrive together?"

"I picked them up," the other dark-haired gentleman said. He wore a sardonic smile and possessed the self-aware gaze of someone who knew precisely who he was and made no excuses. Bran had hoped to carry that same air someday, but had given up at the age of twelve when he'd been declared utterly hopeless by his family.

Kendal looked to Bran. "Knighton, allow me to present the Duke of Clare." He pointed to the confident gentleman who'd just spoken. "We call him West, and whether he gives you leave or not, you will too. And that is the Earl of Dartford. We call him Dart." He indicated the other one who'd spoken before gesturing to the third gentleman, a tall blond. "Finally, this is the Earl of Sutton. He's just Sutton. And sometimes a pain in the ass. But then they all are."

Dartford adopted an innocent stare. "I thought that's why you liked us."

Kendal rolled his eyes even as he quirked a smile. "Pour yourselves some whiskey, and refill our glasses while you're at it."

Clare—rather, West—bowed. "At your service, Your Grace." He crossed to the sideboard and prepared the drinks.

Sutton came forward and shook Bran's hand. "Pleased to meet you. I understand we should welcome you back to England."

"Yes, thank you."

"I'm sorry for the losses that led to your current situation." Sutton's tone held an earnest, thoughtful quality that had been lacking in Talbot's comments earlier.

"No one's sorrier than me," Bran said.

"Of that I'm certain. Family is the most important thing."

Bran couldn't agree more—as it pertained to Evie. With regard to the rest of his family, he felt the complete opposite. His mother was due to arrive in the next week or so, and just thinking of seeing her threatened to send him into a fit of itching. So he chose not to think of it.

West handed glasses to Sutton and Dartford, then refilled Kendal's and Bran's. The decanter came up empty. "Well, that's unfortunate," West said.

Kendal waved a hand. "There's another over there, and the footman will refill it." He shot an amused look at Bran. "Or we can send for a case of rum at Knighton's house, which he's promised me."

Dartford's eyebrows rose. "Rum, you say?"

"From my distillery on Barbados."

"If you find an extra case lying around, send it my way," West said. "Lord knows I can use the spirits right now. Ivy's wearing me out. What is it about carrying a child that makes a woman insatiable?"

The three men took various seats, Dartford sprawling on one end of a settee. He sipped his whiskey, and his mouth twitched up. "You say that like it's a bad thing, West," Dartford said. "I should think you'd *like* that, given your predilections." Dartford looked at Bran. "He has the most charming nickname. Everyone calls him the Duke of Desire."

Bran would've cringed at such a thing, but West's lips curved into a self-satisfied smile.

"He used to have a rather rakish reputation," Dartford explained. "But now he's a devoted husband with an apparently demanding wife." He arched a brow at West. "I shouldn't complain if I were you. You will get to a point where your wife is so uncomfortable that the merest indication of sexual interest will send her into a rant."

Kendal nodded. "Nora was like that with Becky, but more like West's wife with Christopher. We'll see what happens this time." He waggled his brows as his pride-filled smile unfurled.

This news was met with hearty congratulations from everyone.

"Let me understand," Bran said. "You," he pointed at Kendal, "and you," he pointed to West, "and you," he pointed to Dartford, "are all expecting children?"

"And me," Sutton said. "In fact, we're for Sutton Park tomorrow to await the birth."

"We'll be leaving the day after," Dartford said. "Although Lucy has told me more than once that Aquilla has invited us to come to Sutton Park so that they may be together." Dartford shook his head and looked over at Bran. "Our wives are the best of friends—along with West's and Kendal's wives."

"So, really, the four of you had to be friends," Bran said wryly.

They all laughed. "Yes, I suppose so," Sutton admitted. "Thankfully, they're not half as irritating as the rest of the ton."

Bran was getting the same feeling and was more than relieved. Their easy camaraderie and obvious affection for each other was heartwarming and quite foreign. Bran hadn't ever had a friend until he'd moved to Barbados, and he'd left them—a scant few really—behind. All but Hudson, his loyal valet. Could one consider a valet a friend? Bran did, damn the "rules."

"So yes, to answer your question," Dartford said, "it seems we are all on the verge of becoming fathers." He raised his glass toward Kendal. "Again, for one of us."

A pang of envy cut into Bran. He'd been completely thrown when Evie had come into his life. He'd had affection for his wife, but it was nothing compared to the love he felt for his daughter. He'd looked forward to experiencing that again, maybe with a son, but his wife had died two years after Evie's birth.

"Your lives will never be the same," Bran said.

"Thank God," West said. "I don't want my old life."

Dartford's answer was softer as he lowered his gaze for a moment. "Amen."

"Don't get all maudlin," Kendal warned. "You'll drive Knighton off, and I rather like him. If nothing else, it's imperative his daughter continue her friendship with my daughter. For that alone, you'll all behave yourselves."

Bran hadn't minded Dartford's flash of emotion—whatever it was—and bit his tongue before he leapt to the man's defense. His experience with male friendships wasn't great, but he could sense that Kendal's comment was teasing in nature. And there it was again. London seemed a kinder place than he remembered. Or maybe he was different. It had, after all, been fifteen years since he'd left. It had been another life.

The conversation moved to impending fatherhood, with Kendal and Bran offering advice, particularly as it pertained to surviving their wives' final days of confinement.

"They'll all be bloody miserable," Kendal said. "That doesn't change."

Bran cleared his throat. "Actually, my wife wasn't. In fact, she had a ridiculous amount of energy, right up to when Evie came into the world." An image of his pale wife with her wide, luminous eyes came to him. He rarely thought of her face anymore. Why was that?

"Aquilla's the same," Sutton said. "At least for now. She cleans the house along with the staff." He laughed. "I can't stop her."

"What happened to your wife?" West asked. "If you don't mind sharing."

Normally, Bran *would* mind, but he had to admit he felt at ease with these men. "She died of a fever about four years ago."

Sutton gazed at him in sympathy. "I'm so sorry. You've suffered quite a few losses." He glanced over at Dartford, who caught the look and seemed to stiffen momentarily. Bran knew in that moment that Dartford had experienced something similar. He also knew that it had impacted Dartford far more than it had Bran. He wasn't going to ask him about it.

Kendal cleared his throat, which broke the sudden tension. "It seems that perhaps our new friend here might be in want of a wife." He stretched his legs out and crossed his ankles. "Or would you prefer to remain a bachelor?"

"I should at least try to beget an heir."

"Hmm, he doesn't sound convinced," Dartford said, regaining his earlier lightheartedness.

Maybe because he wasn't. He'd wanted to marry again and have more children, but now it seemed as though he *had* to. He remembered the matchmaking his mother had performed when his brothers had wed. They'd scarcely had any input, ending up with wives who would support their standing and augment their fortune. Bran supposed he feared falling into the same trap, not that he planned to allow his mother to help him in any way. Indeed, the only reason he'd agreed to see her at all was because Evie wanted to meet her grandmother. "Marrying seems different now that I'm the earl. It suddenly feels like a requirement."

"I guess in some ways it is," Sutton said. "I had very specific requirements for my countess."

"Yes, but he's a special case." Dartford finished his whiskey. "He had *reasons* for his requirements. Some of us hadn't planned to marry but found we simply *had* to."

Both Kendal and West nodded. "Fell head over heels in love," West said.

Kendal grinned like a lovesick swain. "Nauseatingly so."

Bran hadn't experienced that. He'd married Louisa because he'd liked and admired her. And because she was the only young woman on Barbados for which he'd felt even that much. "The marriage mart in Barbados is not like it is here. I wouldn't even know where to begin."

"You may not have to," West said. "Sometimes love just finds you."

Sutton snorted. "Yes, well, we're not all as lucky as you." He looked at Dartford. "Or you." He straightened and smoothed a hand over his lapel. "Some of us had to spend an inordinate amount of time at Society events looking for just the right spouse."

Kendal shuddered. "Thank God, I didn't." He looked at Bran. "I detest Society events. I rarely go to any."

West chuckled. "It's actually rather ironic since he was quite the rakehell in his youth. But then he retreated and became the 'Forbidden Duke.'"

Bran blinked at Kendal. "The Forbidden Duke?"

Kendal inclined his head. "Just so. I think it's the most dashing of our titles, really. Far more respectable and commanding than Duke of Desire. Or Duke of Daring." He looked toward Dartford.

"I don't know, it makes me sound rather jaunty." Dartford's mouth sprawled into a lazy smile, and his eyes danced with merriment.

"You all have nicknames?" Bran asked, his gaze settling on Sutton. "Except you."

"Oh no, he has one too," West said. "He's the Duke of Deception." Bran opened his mouth to ask why, but West held up his hand. "It's a long story and up to Sutton to tell. Suffice it to say he doesn't care for it, while I adore my nickname." Again, his smile was self-satisfied.

Bran wouldn't care for it either. "Who comes up with this nonsense?"

They exchanged glances and promptly broke into laughter.

"Would you believe our wives?" Dartford asked. "They were wallflowers, and they amused themselves by labeling us. The nicknames were their secret for a while, but somehow became known over time. Although I'm fairly certain that Kendal's and West's are by far the most notorious.

"How horrid," Bran said, his neck twitching.

West shrugged. "I don't mind, particularly since it originated with our wives. I wouldn't worry if I were you, Knighton. I highly doubt you've been given a nickname. No one knows anything about you."

And Bran hoped it stayed that way. He exhaled as relief coursed through him. "I loathe notoriety."

Sutton held up his glass. "Hear, hear."

"Indeed," Kendal agreed. "Listen, lads, our new friend doesn't know where to begin to look for a countess. It's up to us to help him." He looked at West. "Apparently just you and I since those two are abandoning us."

"So sorry," Sutton said, not sounding the least bit sorry.

"And when you say, 'you and I,'" West said to Kendal, "you mean just me."

Kendal's mouth tipped up in a sharp, mocking smile. "Just so."

West rolled his eyes before looking over at Bran. "I'll help you."

"No one better for this task," Sutton said with an air of jocularity.

Bran was surprised he didn't tell them that he didn't require their matchmaking efforts. For whatever reason, he didn't feel uncomfortable. These men possessed a companionability that brought to mind his brothers, and yet these fellows were far more good-natured. Bran felt as though he were in on the joke instead of constantly outside the group. Because of that, he decided to let down his guard more than usual. "I do think my daughter would benefit from a mother." He thought of his own and quickly qualified that. "A good, caring mother."

"Ah-ha," Dartford said, eyeing Sutton. "He has requirements like you."

Kendal shook his head. "I hardly think good and caring are anything special—any sensible gentleman would want the same."

Good and caring were *very* special. And Bran wouldn't settle for anything less. "I should think I'd prefer a widow, perhaps someone with children. I'm not interested in some young debutante fresh from her governess."

"I don't blame you," West said. "Maturity is a beautiful thing." He smiled broadly.

"His wife is *mature*," Dartford said.

"None of our wives were in their first blush of youth," Sutton said. "And thank goodness for that. You're on the right track, Knighton. I hope things go more smoothly for you than they did for me. It took me years to find Aquilla. Shamefully, she'd been right under my nose the entire time."

When Bran thought of taking years to find a new wife…his skin began to itch. Perhaps this wasn't a good idea. Surely he could find a wife without attending an endless parade of balls and routs and whatever other nonsense he'd have to attend.

"I think we can forgo Almack's altogether," West said. "It's a bloody waste of time anyway." He swung his head to Bran. "The Harcourts are having a ball on Friday. Have you received an invitation?"

"I don't know." His secretary said he'd received several invitations, but Bran hadn't looked at them. "I'll check into it."

"If you haven't, I'll secure one for you. I'm sure Lady Harcourt will be thrilled to debut the new Earl of Knighton."

Bran inwardly winced. He didn't want that much attention. But he had to realize he couldn't avoid it completely. He'd merely do his best to be as uninteresting as possible. Hell, his cravat was starting to feel too tight and the shirt the new tailor had made wasn't living up to his requirements—there was that word again. The seams at the shoulders were too bulky. The tailor would have to redo them, and if he couldn't achieve the necessary result, his temporary assignment would be at an end.

Finishing his whiskey, Bran stood and set his empty glass on the sideboard. He turned to Kendal. "I do thank you for your hospitality."

"You're leaving already?" Dartford asked. "The night is young. We haven't seen how good you are at cards yet."

"I rarely play." He'd always been too busy for such things on Barbados. "It was a pleasure to meet you all. West, I'll send a note about the Harcourt ball."

West nodded. "Good evening, Knighton."

Bran made his way from the club, striding quickly through the subscription room. When he was finally ensconced in his coach, he pulled his cravat free and tore his coat off. He pulled at his sleeves but stopped short of divesting himself of the remaining clothing above his waist.

"It's improper for a gentleman to disrobe in front of a lady."

Mrs. Shaw's words drifted over him. She'd sounded

prim, but he swore there'd been a spark of heat in her gaze. Or at least interest. He may have shocked her, but he wasn't convinced she hadn't liked it.

He thought of West helping him to find a wife. Nausea curdled his gut. He doubted there was a woman in England who wouldn't find him improper or odd or outright distressing. Louisa had been uncomfortable with him at first, but once they'd established a routine, she'd come to accept his quirks, even if she hadn't understood them.

How he'd love to find a woman who could do all that.

Chapter Four

JO STRODE INTO the drawing room to join her sister. "Sorry to keep you waiting. The girls were showing me a play they wrote."

Nora looked up from the table on which were stacked several sheets of paper, likely letters of recommendation for the governess Nora was considering since that was what they were meant to discuss. Nora smiled at Jo, her eyes dancing. "Was it the one about the serving maid who marries the prince?"

"Yes. The little stage Titus had built for the dolls is wonderful."

"I love all the voices they do," Nora said. "Evie pitches so low for the king."

Jo chuckled as she sat down beside Nora. "They both have a flair for the dramatic."

"I'm just so pleased they have each other. Now I need to find a friend for Christopher." The boy was sleeping at present, but he toddled after his sister and her friend at every possible moment. Sometimes the girls were happy to amuse him—especially when he was an eager spectator for one of their doll plays—and other times, they ruthlessly ignored him. Jo supposed that was the way of things, but couldn't remember a time when she and Nora hadn't played together.

Jo flicked a glance at the papers. "Any luck with those?"

"There are a few excellent candidates." She nodded

toward a small stack to her left.

"Just a few?" Jo asked, thinking of Lord Knighton and his desire to also hire a governess.

"So far, yes. There are three I'd like to interview. One looks particularly promising—she's the youngest daughter of one of Lady Satterfield's closest friends." Nora tipped her head to the side, the light from the window catching the red tones in her auburn hair. "I sometimes wonder what might've happened if I'd taken a job as a governess instead of a companion. I did consider it."

Nora had returned to London six years ago after their father had lost all their money, forcing Nora to find an occupation. Jo would've taken her sister in, but her husband had insisted that Nora's scandalous behavior nine years prior wasn't something he could tolerate at the vicarage.

All Nora had done was allow a gentleman to kiss her. Unfortunately, someone had seen them, effectively shredding Nora's reputation. In turn, that had limited Jo's options. She wasn't able to have her own Season, and she'd been lucky to have an offer of marriage from Matthias Shaw.

Nine years later, Jo didn't feel particularly lucky. No, Nora was the one whose dreams had come to fruition. But would they have done if she'd taken another path? "You must've been destined to be a companion—Lady Satterfield's companion particularly," Jo said. For that had led Nora to meet her husband.

Nora shook her head, smiling. "Yes, I suppose it was destiny." She looked at Jo, her eyes narrowing slightly. "I always wonder about companions and governesses, whether they enjoy their occupation or if they merely had no other choice available to them. Sadly, I think it's the latter."

"Didn't your friend the Duchess of Clare choose to be a companion?" Jo had met her a few times, and had learned that she'd been quite content in her position until she'd met her husband.

"Yes, and Aquilla was going to follow that path until she met Sutton," Nora said, pulling another letter to the top of her pile and perusing it. "But I'm still not convinced that would really have been their choice—if women truly had choices," she said with a touch of scorn.

Jo knew that Nora had felt trapped by her mistake, and that it had barely affected the gentleman in question. Yes, women suffered many injustices and were typically not afforded much independence. As a widow, however, Jo possessed a modicum of freedom now, and she knew she wouldn't want for financial security. Nora had assured her of that.

Still, relying on her sister and settling in as an extraneous member of her household made Jo feel a bit useless. And bored. She'd been used to managing her own household, such as it was. As Nora had said, Jo's options were limited. She could likely set up her own small household somewhere outside of London, but that sounded lonely. She could try to marry again, but she'd have to find a husband who wouldn't mind her being barren, and that seemed unlikely. Furthermore, she had absolutely no intention of marrying someone she wasn't madly and hopelessly in love with. There was absolutely no reason for her to accept anything else. If her disappointing marriage had done nothing else, it had ensured she didn't have to make that same choice again.

Perhaps she ought to be a companion or a governess.

That wouldn't be boring or lonely. And if she were a governess, that could fulfill her desire to have children. The idea latched on to Jo's brain and took fervent hold. "What if I became a governess?" she blurted.

Nora's head came up sharply, and she stared at Jo. "Are you in earnest?"

Jo lifted a shoulder. "Why not? I love children, and I shan't have any of my own."

"What of marriage? When I asked you about it before, you said you weren't ready to contemplate that yet. It's been a year since Matthias died." Her gaze dipped to Jo's dove-gray gown. "You're still not wearing colors."

That was because Jo despised most of her wardrobe. Matthias had required her to dress in simple, severe, and truthfully *ugly* clothing. Indeed, she hadn't needed mourning clothes since most of her wardrobe was incredibly drab.

Deep creases dug through Nora's brow. "You're not still… Are you still devoted to Matthias?"

Jo hadn't shared the depth of the troubles in her marriage with Nora. Before Nora had married Titus, she'd been living an isolated, lonely life in the country. Jo hadn't wanted to burden her with her travails, not when Jo was at least married and her future was secure—unlike Nora's. Then Nora had found happiness, and Jo had been too thrilled for her sister to cause any concern. Now… Now she could tell her the truth of things. But Nora would be horrified. And she'd feel sorry for Jo, who didn't want her pity. Anyway, that part of her life was over. What good would it do to bring it up now?

"I am *not* still devoted. Or even sad. I suppose I should order some new gowns."

Nora's eyes lit. "Lady Satterfield will be ecstatic. She asked me the other day if you would be ready to go to Bond Street soon."

Jo couldn't help but laugh. Lady Satterfield's penchant for shopping was well known. "Tell her yes, and I'd be honored if she'd accompany me."

"She'll insist, and really, you don't want anyone else. Trust me."

There was no one Jo trusted more. So why wouldn't she tell her about Matthias? Because it was too humiliating.

Nora studied Jo for a moment. "If you aren't sad over Matthias any longer, what is prohibiting you from seeking another husband? I should think you would have no trouble. You're beautiful and intelligent, and there are plenty of gentlemen who prefer a mature woman."

That sounded positively ancient. Jo arched a brow. "*Mature?*"

Nora laughed. "You know what I mean. I think it works in your favor."

"I disagree. I think most men want a young, fresh-faced miss." Jo looked toward the window, which overlooked the street below. "They especially want someone who can bear children, and you know that I cannot."

The touch of Nora's hand on hers drew Jo to turn her head back to her sister. "I'm so very sorry for that. But perhaps you *can* have children—with someone else."

"What gentleman would want to risk that?" Jo asked. It was a moot question since Jo was certain she was barren. She'd been married eight years, and it wasn't as if they hadn't tried to conceive, especially in the early years. When she'd repeatedly failed to turn up pregnant, Matthias had grown increasingly angry with her and eventually more distant.

"A gentleman who perhaps already has children or who doesn't want them at all," Nora said.

Jo didn't think she'd want a husband who didn't want children. She thought of Lord Knighton and his devotion to Evie and his desire for more children. *That* was the kind of husband she wanted. Not him in particular, however, since he planned to enlarge his family. "I suppose a gentleman who already has children and isn't concerned with having more would be acceptable."

"Acceptable?" Nora frowned, but her gaze was sympathetic. "It's all right if you don't wish to marry again," she said quietly.

It wasn't that. "I simply don't think it's likely."

Nora squeezed Jo's hand as the butler came in and announced the arrival of Lord Knighton.

Nora stood. "Please show him up. I'll just fetch Evie." She left, and Jo rose to meet the earl.

A few moments later, he entered, and the sight of him gave her a start. He was an attractive man, though his hair could be judged too long. She liked the length, however. It seemed to fit him, especially since he preferred to lounge about in half-dress. That was why she'd been surprised at his appearance, she realized. In her mind's eye, she saw him in shirtsleeves. Completely scandalous and wholly alluring.

She tossed the useless thoughts from her brain. "Good afternoon, my lord." She offered him a curtsey.

He bowed in response. "Mrs. Shaw. I hope my appearance today meets with your satisfaction."

She nearly laughed at the accurate direction of his

thoughts. "You're jesting, I hope?"

"Can't you tell?" He shook his head. "Never mind. I've often been told my wit is far too dry."

She liked wit—dry or not. It was far preferable to cruelty, which was what she'd been accustomed to the past several years. "I'm getting used to it. From now on, I shall err on the side of humor if I'm not certain of your intent."

"A sound plan."

She looked him over, again appreciating his form and trying to make sure she didn't show it. "Your attire is more than adequate. You don't actually leave your house in a state of undress, do you?"

He shook his head. "Not here. I wonder if I will be able to get away with that at my estate in Wales. I detest riding in constricting clothing. On Barbados, I wore only a shirt, and I must say the wind billowing through it is an intoxicating sensation."

Jo tried to imagine the sensation, but couldn't. She could, however, see and hear the joy it had given him, as well as picture him racing across a beach like the one Evie had described. Intoxicating indeed. "I'm sure you can do whatever you like on your estate."

"I hope so. That will depend on my staff, I suppose. I'm beginning to learn that they talk. Gossip, I mean."

"Yes, sometimes. Are you having difficulty?"

"My butler doesn't seem to approve of my peccadilloes." He gave her a knowing look since they'd discussed that very term. "Suffice it to say, he doesn't seem to like me. And I must say the feeling is mutual."

"Perhaps you should replace him," Jo said.

"He worked for my father for twenty years."

"You'll provide him an excellent reference, then. There's nothing saying you have to keep him on." She blinked at him. "Is there?"

"No, there isn't. And your advice is also what my valet says. I'm considering it. However, then I'll have to hire a new one. Along with the governess. Any news on that?"

"Nora and I were just discussing that topic. She has some candidates she'd like to interview. I think there are others she can pass along to you."

"Her rejects?"

Jo chuckled. "You're joking again, but there's a kernel of truth in there. I believe she only rejected them because the ones she chose are simply a better match for her requirements. As I told you last week, your requirements may be different. You can ask Nora about it when she returns."

"I still want you to help me with the interviews."

Jo was pleased. It gave her something to look forward to, and she had little of that. "And I shall still be delighted."

Nora returned with the girls. Evie ran to hug her father and immediately told him of the dolls and the play they'd produced. "Jo said it was the best performance she'd ever seen," Evie said proudly.

Knighton looked over at Jo, and she nodded. "It was. The girls are quite good with their voices and the drama they infuse into the action."

"The best part is the costumes, Papa," Evie said. "Jo made the most beautiful dress for the serving maid when she becomes the princess."

"My favorite part is when the prince sees her for the first time," Becky said, her eyes alight with joy.

Jo's favorite part was watching them so happy.

Knighton smiled at the girls. "Well, I haven't even seen the play, but I'd say my favorite part is watching the two of you talk about it."

Jo snapped her gaze toward him as a tiny piece of her heart melted. Yes, she'd want a husband just like that.

What a foolish notion. She ought to focus on things she could control, such as this idea of becoming a governess. The idea of trying to lure a man with children into marriage seemed daunting. Furthermore, she wasn't sure she wanted to marry anyone. Not after her experience with Matthias. She suppressed a shudder at being trapped again.

The earl looked toward Nora. "Duchess, Mrs. Shaw mentioned you might have some governess candidates you'd like to pass on to me."

Nora crossed to the table with the stack of recommendations. "Yes." She looked over at the girls. "Go help yourselves to some biscuits if you like." She nodded toward where a tea tray had been laid out. The girls skipped to the sweets.

Jo and Knighton joined Nora at the table. "He thinks you're giving him the rejects," Jo said, tossing him a smile.

He blinked at her, and she caught a flash of alarm. It was quickly replaced with a glimmer of relief and then his lip ticked up in a half smile. At her. She'd seen him smile at Evie, but not at anyone else. There was something a bit rapturous about being on the receiving end. "He was joking," Jo clarified in response to his subtle reaction.

Nora exhaled. "Oh good. They aren't poor candidates. I simply chose the three who I most wanted to meet. They either have a particular skill I like, or they have a recommendation from someone I know."

"I don't know anyone," Knighton said. "But Mrs. Shaw will help me in that regard."

Nora smiled at Jo. "Yes, she will." She picked up the letters she'd set aside and handed them to the earl. "These are for you, then."

"Why not give them to Mrs. Shaw? She can narrow the field and send me a list of names for my secretary to contact."

Nora looked at Jo in question, and Jo nodded. She held her hand out for the letters. "I'd be happy to."

"Excellent." As he set the sheaf in her hand, his fingers grazed hers, and she realized he wasn't wearing gloves. She made a note to mention to him that he ought to do so when paying calls.

He turned toward his daughter and Becky. "Evie, it's time to go."

"Must I?" Evie asked, sounding quite dejected.

"Yes, you'll see Becky soon."

Evie walked reluctantly toward her father. "At our house next time, since we have Mrs. Poole now?"

"I'll arrange it with the Duchess."

"The day after tomorrow would be fine, if that suits you," Nora said, joining Becky near the tea tray.

"Indeed." He gave Evie an encouraging smile. "See? It's already set."

She hugged her father again. "Thank you, Papa." She turned and waved at Becky. "See you Friday." Pausing, Evie looked toward Jo. "Thank you again for watching our play."

Jo went over and crouched down to look her in the eye. "It was my pleasure. I shall look forward to your next visit. Remember, I promised to read Shakespeare."

Evie grinned. "Yes, you did!" She looked up at her father. "Isn't she wonderful?"

Knighton's lips curved into a slight smile. "Perhaps you should be her governess," he murmured.

She was certain he was teasing this time.

As they left, Jo wondered what it would be like to be governess in a household such as his. She wouldn't be a servant, but neither would she be a member of the family. It would be, she realized, somewhat like the way she'd felt married to Matthias. The two of them hadn't been much of a family, especially after—

She stopped the direction of her thoughts lest they lead her into a wilderness she had no desire to get lost within.

⁂

"HA-HA!" EVIE crowed as she penned in Bran's fox with her geese. "You're shut up now!"

Bran stared at the board and realized he was utterly closed off. "A well-deserved victory."

"Finally!" Evie leapt up and danced around the drawing room, chanting, "I shut up Papa! I shut up Papa!"

Smiling, Bran shook his head at her as he pushed himself to a sitting position. He'd been lying flat on his belly for some time, and his body had grown stiff.

Just as Evie neared the open doorway, Kerr stepped over the threshold. She collided with his legs and stepped on his foot.

"Ow!" Kerr jumped backward. Bran didn't realize the fifty-something man could move that quickly.

Bran stood. "Are you all right there, Kerr?"

The butler lifted his foot from the floor and moved it about. "She stamped on it rather hard."

For heaven's sake, she was a child and *barefoot.* Bran bit his tongue.

Evie had stopped her dancing and now stood near

Kerr. "I am terribly sorry, Kerr. It shouldn't hurt. I'm not even wearing any shoes." She wiggled her toes.

Kerr looked down his nose at her. "I can see that. Atrocious."

Bran's ire pricked. "Kerr, you won't speak to my daughter that way."

The butler's eyes widened, and he inclined his head. "My apologies. However, shoes should be required." He directed his attention to Bran's feet, then promptly frowned upon seeing that Bran wasn't wearing shoes either. He, at least, had stockings on. Kerr's gaze lifted, and his frown deepened. "As well as a coat or at least a waistcoat."

Bran's patience was nearly spent. "I've explained before that when it's just Evie and me, we shall wear whatever I deem acceptable. There is absolutely no reason for her to wear shoes—or stockings. And I'll dress however I damn well please."

Kerr straightened, his face flushing the color of the hibiscus flower that grew outside Bran's window in Barbados. "Well, it isn't just you and Lady Evangeline. Lady Dunn has arrived."

Hell. He'd forgotten she was coming today. He'd been having too much fun with Evie.

"I'll tell her you'll need a few minutes," Kerr said crisply.

"Nonsense," came Lady Dunn's voice from just outside the drawing room. A moment later, she appeared at the doorway, her cane clacking against the floor as she came abreast of Kerr, who was now looking at her with a tinge of horror. Bran had to assume that Lady Dunn had committed an offense by showing herself to the drawing room.

The viscountess peered haughtily at Kerr. "Why

you'd leave me loitering in the hall is beyond me. I'm family, you nincompoop."

Kerr's nostrils flared, and his face went scarlet hibiscus again. He pursed his lips together before pushing out the tightest sentence Bran had ever heard. "I'll bring tea."

"Please do," Lady Dunn said to his departing back. She turned to Bran and clucked her tongue. "You might have to let him go."

"I'm considering it."

His godmother turned to Evie with a bright smile. "If it isn't my favorite little girl. I've brought you something."

Evie became instantly shy the moment Lady Dunn had transferred attention to her. Bran could see it in the slight droop of Evie's shoulders and the curl of her toes against the floor. He went to stand beside her and put a comforting hand on the back of her neck. She'd met Lady Dunn only once before, and it often took a few meetings for Evie to become comfortable. Except in the case of Becky. They'd become fast friends. In fact, Evie had warmed to everyone in the Kendal household rather quickly, including Mrs. Shaw. Now, why was he thinking of her specifically?

Lady Dunn interrupted his wayward thoughts. "Come, my girl, let me sit and I'll show you." Bran's godmother walked to a settee and sat down, resting her cane against the side. She had a small paper bag in her hand and placed it on her lap.

Evie had followed and now perched beside her. Bran folded his arms to watch.

"Do you like sweet things?" Lady Dunn asked her. At Evie's nod, she continued. "What about castles?"

"I don't know that I've seen a real castle. Not up

close."

Lady Dunn turned her head to throw a dark stare at Bran. "You have taken her to see the Tower, at least?"

He hadn't thought of it. "Er, not yet." He'd ask Mrs. Poole for a list of things he should take Evie to see. Better still, he'd ask Mrs. Shaw.

"What's the Tower?" Evie asked.

"It's a very old castle here in London, rich with history, and there are many things to see there, including the *Jewel Office*." Lady Dunn said the last with great flair.

Evie gasped. "Jewels?" She lifted her gaze to Bran's. "Papa, may we go there?"

"Yes."

"Do you want to see what I brought you?" Lady Dunn asked.

Evie nodded enthusiastically. "Is it a jewel?"

Lady Dunn chuckled. "No." She opened the bag and lifted out a small item, which she placed in Evie's hand. "It's a castle."

Evie stared down at it, her lips curving to form a perfect O. "It's a very small castle. It's adorable."

"It's marzipan. You can eat it," Lady Dunn said.

Evie's eyes widened in horror. "Oh no, I shan't ever do that. It's far too precious!" She went back to studying the miniature building.

Mrs. Poole entered the drawing room, followed by Kerr, who carried the tea tray. He went about setting it up on the table in front of Lady Dunn.

"Lady Dunn, allow me to present Evie's new nurse, Mrs. Poole."

Mrs. Poole curtsied. "A pleasure to make your acquaintance, my lady."

"And a good afternoon to you, Mrs. Poole. What a

delightful young charge you have here." Lady Dunn inclined her head toward Evie.

Mrs. Poole beamed. "Yes, she's a joy."

Evie bounded off the settee to Mrs. Poole. "Look what Lady Dunn brought me! It's a tiny castle!"

Mrs. Poole squatted down and studied the candy. "Is it marzipan?"

"Yes, but I shan't eat it. I can't wait to show it to Becky tomorrow."

"An excellent plan," Mrs. Poole said, straightening. "Come, it's time for our afternoon reading time."

Evie started to leave, but turned to face Lady Dunn. "Thank you ever so much. I shall treasure it always." She pivoted and skipped from the room, Mrs. Poole on her heels. Kerr had left just before them, as quietly as he'd come in, much to Bran's satisfaction.

Lady Dunn clucked her tongue again, her lips curving up. "Evie is lovely. What a marvelous relationship you have." Her gaze settled on Bran. "Is your attire the reason for Kerr's pique? I see you're as defiant as ever."

He suppressed a scowl. How he hated being called that. "I'm not. I'll tell you what I told him—it's my damn house, and I'll dress as I please."

"Yes, yes, of course."

Thankfully, Hudson arrived just then with a waistcoat and other garments. He said nothing, merely came to Bran's side and held the items over his arm. Bran donned the waistcoat.

"You needn't do that on my account," Lady Dunn said. "I'm not about to be terrorized by seeing you in shirtsleeves. As I said to Kerr, we're family."

Hudson arched a brow in question, silently asking if Bran wanted the cravat or the coat. Bran shook his head slightly and Hudson departed. Damn, it was good to have at least one exceptional retainer on staff.

When they were alone, Bran sat in a chair near the settee. "Can I pour you some tea?"

"Yes, please." She watched him fill her cup. "Just a bit of sugar, thank you."

He finished and handed her the cup and saucer.

"Thank you, dear boy." She took a sip and lowered the cup back to the saucer. "I'd like to apologize for my comment earlier. I meant no insult when I called you defiant."

That description, coined by his mother, had followed him throughout his childhood. He'd rarely done what was expected or asked of him, largely because he simply couldn't. Aside from his clothing intolerance, there'd been his refusal to eat certain foods. Or sit still. Or stay in bed all night.

When his nurse failed to make him comply, his mother would lose her temper and thrash him until he'd succumbed. And in some cases, he hadn't. She'd banished him to a small closet on plenty of occasions, which had been fine by him. At least there he could wear whatever he liked. Or not wear, as was his preference.

Gradually, he'd learned to hide his...*defiance*. It had never completely gone, however.

"No apology is necessary," he said. "I'm afraid I was a bit worked up due to my encounter with Kerr."

She sipped her tea again. "I'll say it again—I hope you'll consider replacing him."

Perhaps after he hired a governess. It seemed he was to be perpetually seeking retainers. "When I can find the time."

"I imagine you must be horribly busy. And a father

into the bargain. I hate to ask, but when do you plan to make your social debut as earl? Society is abuzz wondering about you. I heard you were at Brooks's the other night."

The notion that his activities were gossip fodder was unsettling. "How did you know?"

She smiled conspiratorially, her brown eyes glowing. "My former companion, an absolute dear, is the Duchess of Clare. She told me her husband met you in Kendal's private dining room and that Kendal had invited you."

He rested his elbows on the arms of the chair. "Then I am surprised you didn't also know that I plan to make my debut at the Harcourt ball tomorrow night."

"No, I hadn't heard that, but what a brilliant plan. Would you like me to go with you?"

He appreciated her kindness, but he wanted the freedom to leave whenever he chose. He suspected he wouldn't last very long and would hate to abbreviate her evening. "Thank you, but I'll probably arrive later than you would prefer."

"Yes, many gentlemen do. How do you find London?" She sipped from her cup, then set it and the saucer on the table.

"Large. And cold."

"That must be a shock. How is Evie adjusting?"

"She also finds it cold."

She gave him a patient stare. "I meant, how are you both getting on? Are you happy to be here or do you detest it? I didn't think you'd ever come back."

"I'm not sure I intended to."

Lady Dunn turned to face him fully and clasped her hands in her lap. "I am your godmother, and to me, that makes us family. I know you didn't get on well with your actual family, and I suspect that's why you never meant to return. However, fate has decided to call you back to Mother England. This must be a very strange predicament for you." She cocked her head to the side. "Were you even sad to hear of their passing?" She waved her hand. "Never mind, what a ghastly question. Of course you were sad." She gave him a look that carried more understanding than anything he'd ever felt from anyone in his family.

To think that *she* could be family…

He gently coughed. "You seem to grasp the situation quite well."

"Perhaps. I wish I knew more, but I'm afraid I wasn't able to have much of a role in your life. Your mother didn't care for me, as you may know."

"I did know, although I never understood why."

She surprised him by laughing, a hearty chuckle that filled the room. "Oh, that's a story. She was certain I'd had a liaison with your father. Utter gibberish, of course. Nevertheless, she was adamant. I'm sorry to say she was quite skilled at preventing me from seeing you. I tried, but your father didn't wish to upset her."

Bran had no trouble imagining his mother railing at his father about Lady Dunn. And now he had another reason to dislike her—as if he needed one—she'd deprived him of a kind influence at a young age. "She's arriving from Durham next week." Just saying it aloud made him want to scratch the flesh from his bones.

Lady Dunn's face pinched. "I'm sorry to hear that. She isn't staying with you, is she?"

"No, I didn't invite her. The only reason I'm allowing her to visit is to meet Evie."

"That's for the best, I think." She eyed him with approval. "You're a good son. Just remember that you're the earl now. If you don't wish to tolerate her presence, you don't have to."

She was right. Bran hadn't thought about facing her now that he was the earl. Things were completely different. *He* was completely different. But then that really had nothing to do with becoming earl and everything to do with getting away from his toxic upbringing.

"I appreciate the advice, thank you. And the castle you brought Evie. That was incredibly thoughtful."

"I look forward to showering all manner of things on her—all the things I couldn't do for you." Her gaze turned sad, and the lines around her mouth and eyes deepened. "I hope you'll allow me to dote on her. And you. I think you both deserve it."

Emotion scratched his throat. He poured himself a cup of tea, which he didn't particularly care for, and took a sip to wet his mouth.

"That means you'll have to suffer my interference, or at least interest, in your lives. Tell me, do you plan to marry again? If so, I should be delighted to help you find a bride."

He did appreciate her thoughtfulness, but perhaps not the interference part. "I'd like to find a mother for Evie, but I'm not in a particular rush."

"Of course not. You mustn't hurry such things. The Harcourt ball will give you a nice introduction. Unless you want to set the tongues wagging, stay clear of dancing with any young misses. I'll be sure to steer you in the right direction."

That he appreciated most sincerely. "Thank you. I think I've found a formidable ally."

Along with Kendal, his wife, and her lovely sister, the bright and witty Mrs. Shaw. He wondered if she would be at the ball. He hoped so. She wasn't a young miss and therefore a safe dancing partner. Yes, he'd look for her as soon as he arrived.

"Now, let us discuss your wardrobe." Her gaze dipped to his practically bare arms. "I want to be sure you'll be attired correctly for the ball. You're not in the tropics any longer."

No, he wasn't.

Chapter Five

AS A GIRL, Jo had dreamt of her first London ball. She'd be gowned in a dress that shimmered beneath the thousands of candles, her hair adorned with pearls. She'd never want for a dance partner, and the evening would pass in a glorious, life-changing blur. She'd never imagined that she would be a thirty-one-year-old widow.

At least she had a new gown.

She glanced down at the pink silk with its sheer net overlay. It was, by far, the finest thing she'd ever worn. After discussing her wardrobe with Nora the other day, she and Lady Satterfield had decided she needed a ball gown *immediately* since they'd also decided she ought to attend the Harcourt ball tonight. That they'd been able to find a dress that was already made and required only a few alterations was a miracle.

That is not *a miracle,* Matthias would have said with a sneer. His religion was a convenience to suit his mercurial moods. If the parishioners had only known the truth…but of course, they never would.

Jo scowled as she pushed the thought away.

"What's wrong?" Nora asked.

Jo smiled brightly, probably overcompensating and thus drawing even more attention to herself. "Nothing at all."

Nora's mouth turned down. "I don't believe you. You've been nervous—or something—all evening."

She and Jo had arrived at the ball an hour or so ago

in the company of Lady Satterfield, who'd done an excellent job of introducing Jo to everyone worth meeting. Or so Lady Satterfield had described the endeavor. Now, Jo and Nora were stationed on the perimeter, not quite against the wall, but also not in the thick of things.

Lady Satterfield had gone off in search of a gentleman to dance with Jo. She felt like a charity case. But then she supposed she was, hanging on her sister's skirts.

Was that how she saw herself? It wasn't as if she had to be here. She had a small portion from Matthias and could live a modest life back in St. Ives, occupying a tiny cottage just outside the village. However, that existence sounded painfully dull and tragically sad.

Anyway, it wasn't as if her sister, or Titus, for that matter, treated her like she wasn't more than welcome. They wouldn't want her to live alone.

Nora exhaled as she turned her inquisitive stare away from Jo. "You can ignore me, I suppose, but I know you too well. If you'd rather go home, we can."

"I wasn't ignoring you. I was trying to decide what I'm doing here."

"Meeting people?" Nora offered.

"Yes, but to what end?"

"Must there be an end? Forget talk of marriage or even the future. Why not just enjoy the evening?" Her eyes sparkled. "It's your first ball, after all."

"Yes, I was musing about how different this is compared to my expectation. Remember how we used to imagine it?"

"Of course. We were going to marry Untouchables. We had such grand plans." Nora's gaze darkened. "And then I ruined everything."

Jo edged closer to her sister and touched her forearm. "You didn't."

"How can you say that? I had to return home in shame, and you weren't even allowed a Season." Even if Nora's scandal hadn't tainted Jo, their cousin who'd sponsored Nora had refused to sponsor her.

"No, but things worked out all right for me, didn't they?"

Tears formed in Nora's eyes, but she blinked rapidly and pressed her fingers to either side of her nose. "I shan't cry here." She summoned a wobbly smile. "I'd thought they had, but I know you weren't happy."

Yes, Jo had shared her discontent several years ago, not long after Nora had married. But that was before she'd found out Matthias's secrets. After that, she'd stopped talking about him altogether. "We weren't a great match," Jo said, preferring to keep things simple.

"I know, and I feel responsible. You've never said, but I think you wouldn't have married him if you'd had other options."

Of course she wouldn't have. She'd planned to have a Season. She'd *planned* to marry an Untouchable. Nora *had* ruined things for her, but Jo would never say so. She didn't blame her sister. Even so, that didn't mean it wasn't true.

Jo pivoted from her sister lest she see the truth in her eyes. She started as she recognized Lord Knighton bearing toward them.

Oh, he looked magnificent in evening wear, his dark charcoal-colored coat offset by his silver-threaded waistcoat and the snow-white of his cravat. Was he uncomfortable? She wondered how long he'd be able to endure the garments and pictured him stripping them off. The ballroom suddenly seemed overly warm.

He strode right to her and offered a bow, first to Nora as required by her rank, and another to Jo. "Good evening. You look lovely." His gaze swept over her.

"Thank you."

"I thought we could discuss the governess interviews," he said. "My secretary has arranged them for Tuesday."

Jo nodded. "Good."

"Lord Knighton, why don't you ask Jo to waltz? It's just starting."

Waltz? At Nora's insistence, Jo had practiced the steps earlier today, but she'd never actually waltzed. "I'm not certain that's necessary."

Lord Knighton held out his arm. "Would you do me the honor?"

Now she was trapped. Although if she could refuse any man and predict that he wouldn't take offense, it was Knighton. Once she explained her anxiety, she'd no doubt he would understand given his own foibles.

In the end, she simply put her hand on his arm and allowed him to escort her to the dance floor. It could be her only chance.

"I've never waltzed," she said softly.

"Me neither."

She turned her head sharply to look at him. "Oh dear."

"How hard can it be?" he asked as they stepped onto the dance floor.

He rested his hand on her waist and clasped her hand. She placed her palm on his shoulder and, despite the layers of clothing, was certain she could feel his muscle.

"See, we're experts," he said.

The couples around them began to move with the music, and for a moment, they stared at each other. Then he jolted forward, and Jo somehow managed to remember what she'd practiced earlier.

"Thankfully, this isn't too taxing," Bran said. "Provided you can count."

"As it happens, I am excellent with numbers."

"I would expect nothing less as you seem to be a woman of sharp intelligence."

Warmth spread through Jo at his praise. "Thank you."

They turned in a new direction, and his scent curled over her. He smelled of freshness and citrus.

"I appreciate you joining me for the interview on Tuesday. Is there anything I should prepare?"

She thought of their last endeavor. "No, I'll ask Nora if she has any questions to recommend. Just promise me you'll leave all your clothing on until we're finished."

"I did last time," he said, moving her effortlessly across the floor. Truly, she didn't have to do much but enjoy his touch. "And I'm completely clothed tonight. I thought I did an admirable job of it. Rather, my valet did."

"You look splendid." Her gaze dipped to his cravat and a bit lower. His silver waistcoat shimmered in the candlelight just like her dreamed-of ball gown.

"Thank you," he murmured. "I daresay I pale next to you. I'd grown accustomed to seeing you in gray. You are far lovelier in pink. I do hope you won't go back to the drabber colors."

She'd thought the same thing, but hadn't committed until that moment. Lady Satterfield had insisted that she needed a new wardrobe, and Nora had offered to pay for it. That took Jo right back to feeling as though she were in need of their charity…which she was.

Stop thinking like that, she admonished herself.

"I fear I may have just insulted you again," he said. "I didn't mean to say you looked drab."

"Oh, but I did. Between your distaste for certain clothing and my depressing wardrobe, we're quite a pair." Had she just referred to them as a *pair*? She rushed to say something else. "Speaking of wardrobes, I wanted to tell you that you need to wear gloves when you're out."

He looked at their clasped hands. "I am. Not that I'm enjoying it."

"I was referring to the other day when you picked up Evie. You weren't wearing gloves then."

"No, I wasn't. Must I really wear them to pick up my child from your house, of all places?"

"It isn't *my* house. It's the Duke of Kendal's."

He gave her a wry look. "I don't think he'd mind." He shook his head. "I'm not very good at being an earl."

"Nonsense. You just need more practice. Most men prepare to inherit the title. You didn't have that advantage."

He gazed at her in appreciation. "Perhaps *I'm* the one who needs a governess. Surely she could teach me how to be an earl."

She laughed at the image of him learning deportment. "I think you may be onto a grand idea. There ought to be a school for that, at least."

"Oh, there is. It's called Oxford. But I'd rather be lost at sea than return there."

She felt a shudder go through his frame. "Why?"

His jaw hardened. "I was…awkward in my youth."

His lips twisted into a self-deprecating smirk. "Some would say I still am, I'm sure. I didn't fit in at Oxford. My brothers had attended there before me and ensured I had a reputation for oddity. Many of my schoolmates were brothers of their friends. They were predisposed to dislike and ridicule me."

There was no pain in his revelation, but his tone held a distant quality, as if he were speaking of someone else. "How awful. Why would your brothers do such a thing?"

He lifted his shoulder, and she was aware of where they touched. She clasped him more tightly and wished that gloves *could* be optional in this instance. "Because that's the way they always treated me. They were the best of friends and I was…a nuisance."

A nuisance? How could anyone think that of their sibling? Or any member of their family? Jo and Nora's father was a dunderhead and their relationship was distant, but if he needed them, they'd be there for him.

He pivoted again, taking them in a new direction. "I think Becky had fun at our house today."

The sudden change in topic jarred Jo, but she didn't say anything. If he'd rather not discuss the pain of his brothers' treatment, especially in the middle of a ballroom, who was she to argue? That didn't alleviate her curiosity, however.

"Yes, I heard all about the miniature marzipan castle. Becky insists she have one too."

"I should've got one for her."

"While kind of you, that isn't necessary. Nora's cook is actually quite skilled with marzipan, so she's arranged for the girls to spend an afternoon with her in the kitchen."

He grinned. "Evie will love that. What an excellent

idea."

"It was mine, actually." Jo wasn't sure why she'd revealed that—it hardly mattered whose idea it was. Actually, maybe she did know. He'd smiled so enthusiastically, and she'd wanted that directed at her.

"Of course it was your idea. When I commented the other day that you should be my governess, I wasn't entirely teasing." And she'd been so certain he was. "But I think you should actually be a mother." He peered at her, his dark blue eyes piercing into her and somehow stealing her breath.

Or maybe it was what he'd said. Yes, definitely that.

She should be a mother.

The ache that was so often buried in her gut rose to the surface. She nearly stumbled, but he clasped her more tightly, one hand flattening against her spine and the other gently squeezing her fingers.

"All right?" he asked softly.

She nodded. "It was bound to happen," she said tightly, still fighting the emotion roiling inside her.

"I suppose so, given our novice state."

Thankfully, the music drew to a close. Jo was eager to escape the sudden cloying oppression of the ballroom. The heat, the eyes, the…expectation. She needed air. "You've acquitted yourself quite well." Her voice sounded thin to her ears, but hopefully he wouldn't notice.

"High praise that seems a bit flawed, but it's probably boorish of me to dispute you." He flashed her a half smile. "But then you already know I'm a boor in private."

She put her hand on his arm as he escorted her from the dance floor. "I wouldn't call you a boor, my lord."

"If we were in Barbados I'd ask you to call me Bran."

"They wouldn't call you my lord?"

"After I inherited, I asked them not to. Why bother since I was leaving anyway?"

He wasn't like anyone she'd ever met before. "You live by your own rules, don't you?" she asked.

"Rules, like cravats, are constricting. I prefer to just live in comfort and contentment." He delivered her to Nora and Lady Satterfield, who'd returned.

She withdrew her hand and thanked him for the dance. She liked his perspective, especially right now when she was feeling so agitated in the ballroom. In fact, while propriety demanded she stand there and chat for a few minutes, she couldn't bear it. A dull sound had started in her ears, and she felt as though she couldn't take a deep breath.

She needed to go outside, or at the very least, to the retiring room. "If you'll excuse me." She caught the worried glint in Nora's eye, but hurried from the ballroom without a backward glance.

WATCHING MRS. SHAW'S pink skirts flutter about her ankles as she fled, Bran was certain he'd said something wrong. Again. Was it that he'd been ungracious when she'd offered him a compliment about his dancing? He'd only wanted to put her at ease since it seemed as though her misstep had caused her distress.

Maybe that was it. She was merely embarrassed. People, women in particular, had always been a mystery to Bran. As soon as he thought he'd worked something out, he was thrown off course once more. At least he seemed to be improving. Things had been much worse in his youth. Had he really mentioned that to her?

And *that* was why he preferred to avoid things like this ball.

Along with the damnable clothing he was forced to wear. Hudson had insisted that his cravat hold more starch than usual, which was next to none, so tonight was a special torture. As a result, Bran felt as though he were suffering the hangman's noose.

Furthermore, he despised close crowds, and the throng in the ballroom had swelled while they were dancing. Torture was exactly the right word. He envied Mrs. Shaw's flight.

"Did you have a nice dance?" Lady Satterfield asked politely.

Bran could see that the Duchess was anxious to go after her sister, but she didn't. He'd give her that opportunity by leaving. "We did, thank you. If you'll excuse me."

Both women blinked at him, appearing a bit nonplussed. He could attribute that to Mrs. Shaw's abrupt departure, but why not his as well? He ought to have stayed and exchanged a few pleasantries. Instead, he'd dashed off at the earliest possible moment.

Damn, maybe he really wasn't any better than he'd been in his youth.

He made his way through the ballroom, uncertain of where he was going. Suddenly, he caught the gaze of a gentleman. He looked familiar… Bugger, it was that Talbot ass, whom he'd met at Brooks's the other night.

Desperate to avoid the man, Bran saw the open door to the terrace and revised his direction. Quickening his pace, he stepped outside. Lit with sconces, the terrace held several people milling about. Still too many people. Not to mention, Talbot had only to follow him outside.

Looking around for an escape, Bran noted stairs down to the garden. There were several pathways, each with flickering torches, but only for a certain distance. The farther along a path, the dimmer the light became until the route simply faded into darkness.

Bran practically ran for the nearest path.

As soon as he passed the last light, he tugged his gloves off and stuffed them into the pockets of his coat. Then he pulled his cravat free, letting the ends drape down his front. So much for simply loosening it.

Why had he bothered coming tonight? Because he'd allowed bloody Clare and Kendal to talk him into it. And Kendal wasn't even here. Was Clare? Bran hadn't seen him, and he no longer cared.

Had it really been a waste of time? He *had* managed a waltz after all.

Yes, a single waltz. He congratulated himself on his mediocrity.

He was supposed to be wife hunting. But he'd be damned if he could do that. He hadn't even been able to have a conversation with Mrs. Shaw without harkening back to his miserable past. It was difficult to be here in London, especially at a social event such as this, and not think of his brothers, how they'd driven him from England.

Not that he regretted it. The moment his ship had set sail, he'd felt free. And happy. He'd certainly never imagined he'd be back here.

There was enough light filtering through the garden that he could make his way along the path. But then it turned, and he was thrust into total darkness.

He heard an intake of breath as if it were the snap of a sail in the wind. He wasn't alone. Then he heard the rustle of fabric and knew it was a woman.

"I can hear you," he said softly. "I didn't mean to intrude." He belatedly realized it was possible she wasn't by herself, that there was perhaps a gentleman with her. He'd just turn and go—and hopefully find a way out without having to return to the ballroom.

"Lord Knighton?"

The voice was familiar. He relaxed even as his senses vaulted to hyperawareness. "Mrs. Shaw."

"I just…I needed some cool air."

"I did as well." He moved toward the sound of her voice. "I'm glad I found you. Now I can apologize for causing you distress. I'm not sure what I said or did, but I suspect it was my inability to accept your kind compliment."

"What?" She sounded genuinely perplexed. "You didn't cause me distress."

There was a quiver to her tone. He wasn't sure he believed her, but if she was trying to spare his feelings, he'd let her do whatever made her comfortable.

"I'm the one who should apologize," she said from rather nearby, meaning he'd managed to move closer. "Talking about your past, about Oxford, seemed to bother you. I didn't mean to cause *you* any upset."

"You didn't. I'm the one who brought it up." And he still didn't know why, except that he felt unabashedly comfortable with her. "I've spent fifteen years putting that behind me. Being back in England has brought it all to the surface again."

"If you'd like to tell me what 'it all' is, I'd be glad to listen."

He considered that, but reliving his brothers' torture and his mother's ambivalence wasn't something he wanted to do. Feeling as constricted as he had in the ballroom, he shrugged out of his coat and draped it over his arm.

"Are you disrobing again?" she asked.

"You can hear that?"

"I'm afraid so. But since I can't see you, it really doesn't signify."

He chuckled, pleased with her logic. "As it happens, I'd already untied my cravat before I arrived here."

"I can't even manage to feign shock." Now her voice held a lilt of humor, as if she were smiling.

He laughed again, and a cool, early spring breeze wafted over him. How he missed the warmth of Barbados.

"Will you tell me about it?" she asked.

Had he said that out loud—about Barbados? Apparently so. "I could stand here all night and not manage to tell you everything."

"Then just tell me *some*thing."

He closed his eyes and summoned his home. "The colors there are like nothing you've ever seen—the blue-green water, the white-gold sand, colors that not even the rainbow can do justice to."

"It sounds beautiful." Her voice was soft, almost reverent. "How did you decide to go there?"

He opened his eyes but still couldn't see her. "That was where the ship was headed. I didn't care where I was going, so long as it wasn't here."

"You must have been terribly miserable." She sounded as if she'd moved a bit closer.

"I wasn't needed here." Or wanted, really. His entire family had encouraged him to buy a commission or perhaps take a vicarage. He'd considered both ideas, but in the end had simply walked on the first ship leaving England. And he'd never looked back.

"And now?" Her question whispered over him,

lulling him with its sweet curiosity.

"Now, I'm the earl. I'm needed."

"And your brothers are gone."

He exhaled, as if realizing for the first time that they really were *gone*. That he could perhaps be here and be happy. Or at least not miserable. Still, it wasn't home. Not yet. "I miss the blazing sun."

"Especially right now, I'd wager."

He heard a tremor in her voice. "Wait, are you chilled? Where are you?" He reached out with his free hand and touched her.

Stepping forward—it didn't take much to reach her—he settled his coat on her shoulders. "Better?" he asked.

"Yes, thank you."

He didn't take his hands away. "Why did you come out here?"

"I—"

He heard the hesitation in her voice and felt a shiver in her body. He didn't think that was from the night air. "You can tell me. If you want."

"I felt…overwhelmed. As if I couldn't breathe. I just needed to get out."

God, he'd felt like that his entire life. "I was never able to sit still when I was younger. Or wear clothing. I often felt like I wanted to crawl out of my very skin. I used to scratch myself raw."

"That sounds horrid. How did you stop?"

"I don't know. Leaving here helped."

"And now that you're back? Things aren't as bad as they were?"

No, he supposed they weren't. Just as he had a few moments ago, when she'd pointed out that his brothers were indeed gone, he felt a lightness. Because of her.

Without thinking, he moved his hands closer to her neck and stroked the bare flesh above the collar of his coat, his thumbs tracing just below her jaw. He felt the muscles in her neck contract as she swallowed.

Her pulse sped beneath his touch. He moved closer until their bodies barely met. "I'm going to kiss you."

"Yes."

He lowered his mouth and found her lips, moving softly but purposefully. He realized he hadn't asked permission. Yet she'd given it.

He cupped her face, gently tilting her head. Her hands came up against his chest, but not to push him away. No, her fingertips pressed into him and then curled around the lengths of his cravat, effectively tugging him to her.

With a soft groan, he curled his hand around her neck and deepened the kiss, his lips molding against hers. She moved her hands up the cravat and wrapped them around his shoulders, all the while bringing her chest to his.

The feel of her so close ignited a passion that had lain dormant within him the last several years, since Louisa's death. He hadn't been a monk, but he also hadn't felt *this*.

Desire curled in his gut and hardened his cock. He moved one hand down her back and splayed his hand at the base of her spine, his fingers caressing the top of her backside.

Her hips pressed into his, and she gasped. Her mouth opened beneath his, and he took the invitation—prayed it was an invitation—stroking his tongue along her lips. Her fingertips dug into his shoulders as her tongue met his.

This wasn't what he'd planned. Hell, he'd just wanted

to escape the ballroom and find a moment's peace. Instead, he'd found heaven.

Their bodies came together as need spread through him like wildfire, hot and erratic and completely uncontainable. This could spiral beyond his control so easily… He eased back—just a bit—calming the kiss.

She pulled on his cravat again and took control of the kiss, her lips moving over his before opening once more. If she wasn't going to back away, neither was he.

He speared into her mouth, and she moaned, a dark, sensual sound that only fueled his desire. He didn't know how long they kissed, but by the time they finally parted, his heart was thundering in his chest and his breath came in short, fast pants.

She sounded much the same, and it was all he could do not to pull her into his arms again. "I'm sorry," she said. "I don't know what came over me."

"The same thing that came over me. Anyway, I started it."

"And tried to finish it—I think. But I wouldn't let you." Her voice wobbled a bit, and he couldn't tell if it was due to uncertainty or embarrassment or something else entirely.

"Hopefully, you can tell that didn't bother me. On the contrary. Mrs. Shaw, that was extraordinary." His body was screaming for completion, and if he were a different man, he might consider continuing their mutual seduction right here in this dark, private corner of the garden. His reaction wasn't an exaggeration. He wanted her with a ferocity he hadn't felt in years.

He drew her to him again, their bodies connecting. "*You* are extraordinary."

"I'm… Thank you."

He had the sense she was going to argue with him.

He was coming to know her—she thought less of herself than she ought, he realized. She was incredibly intelligent and wise and caring, and yet she didn't seem to know that. Or project that. In a way, it reminded him of himself when he was younger, before he'd escaped.

And watching her with Evie made him smile. His daughter spoke of her often, how she always spent time with her and Becky, whether it involved making clothes for the dolls, reading them stories, or apparently arranging for them to mold marzipan with the cook.

Yes, she *should* be a mother. Why not Evie's mother? He needed a wife, and he liked her. He sure as hell liked kissing her. He knew he'd enjoy bedding her too.

"Marry me," he blurted.

She stiffened, but even if she hadn't, he'd immediately realized he'd bungled that proposal.

She took a step back. "I cannot."

Yes, *completely* cocked it up. He clasped her hand, not wanting her to go. "I'm sorry, that was incredibly awkward. As I mentioned earlier, I'm quite good at that. Mrs. Shaw, would you do me the great honor of becoming my countess?"

"We scarcely know each other. I can't—" She pulled her hand from his. "No."

"Why not? It makes perfect sense. I need a mother for Evie, and you've developed an excellent rapport with her. Add in this apparent attraction we feel, and it's a logical match."

"Logical?" He heard the befuddlement in her tone and suspected that had been the wrong thing to say. Hell, he'd never been much of a romantic. Louisa had tried to train him. He'd at least learned to bring her flowers on occasion. Yes, he'd send Mrs. Shaw—

Joanna—flowers tomorrow.

"I mean to say that you'd make a wonderful countess—and mother."

"No, I won't." Her tone was cold. "I was married eight years, Lord Knighton, and I have no children to show for it. You say this is a logical match, but you want children—an heir—and I can't give you one. So you see, it's an *impossible* match."

Suddenly, she thrust his coat into his arms. He caught it against him as she strode past and fled down the path toward the light.

Bran stayed in the dark. That was the only place he really belonged.

Chapter Six

JO SIGNED THE last of her correspondence and folded the parchment. She'd written to her father, a friend from St. Ives, and a few of the villagers who'd started sending her notes of sympathy and encouragement after Matthias had died. Now that she'd come to London, their letters talked of missing her and Matthias's presence and how the new vicar was terribly dull in comparison. They spoke highly of Matthias, and it took everything Jo had not to tell them their faith and devotion were utterly misplaced. Matthias had been a liar and a wretch. If they only knew the truth…

"Writing letters?" Nora breezed into the drawing room, carrying a bit of sewing.

Jo twisted in her chair. "Yes, I wrote to Father." Their father was a terrible correspondent, but they made sure to write him a couple of times a month.

Nora sat near the windows, setting her sewing on her lap as she looked at Jo. "I need to coordinate his annual visit."

Jo had seen him only once in the six years since he'd relocated to Dorset, but he'd managed to visit Nora every June after she'd become a duchess. "I suppose that means I'll get to see him this year."

Assuming she was still residing with Nora. The sensation of an uncertain future was very strange. At least her marriage to Matthias had given her a security in knowing where she would be and what she would be doing. Security was, perhaps, overrated.

"Yes," Nora said. "Unless you decide to get married." She flashed Jo a wide smile.

Jo's stomach curdled, and she jerked her gaze to the windows. Knighton's proposal had been at the forefront of her mind since the ball three nights ago. Along with the kisses they'd shared. He'd called her extraordinary. She still didn't know what to make of that. He had to have been flattering her. She was the very definition of ordinary. Or even lackluster, if Matthias was to be believed. Her common sense told her that Matthias *wasn't* to be believed, that he was a callous liar. And yet she couldn't help but think there was a kernel of truth to his criticism of her. Otherwise, she likely *would* be a mother…

But she couldn't. She was, as Matthias was so fond of telling her, only half a woman. Unable to please a man in bed and bear children, she wasn't even sure if *half* was an adequate measurement.

"Jo?"

Nora's gentle query drew her to turn her head once more. "Yes?"

"You seem faraway. You've been like that the past few days. Since the ball, really. I know something had to have happened. I wish you'd tell me."

After fleeing from Knighton, Jo had found the retiring room where she'd hidden for close to an hour. By the time she found Nora again, she pleaded a dreadful headache and asked to go home. Nora had insisted on accompanying her, worried that Jo had disappeared for so long and that she apparently felt so horrid.

"Nothing happened. I told you it was a headache, nothing more. I'm merely feeling introspective as I think about the future. I can't just ride your skirts for the next fifty years."

Nora's brow creased. "You aren't doing that *now.*"

They'd had this conversation so many times, and it was beyond tired. Jo turned back to the desk and gathered up her correspondence to give it to Abbott.

"You're going to ignore me, aren't you?"

Jo exhaled in exasperation. "I don't wish to discuss it. You have to stop worrying about me."

"I'm your older sister. I've always worried about you."

Then why did you mess up my life?

The question rose unbidden in her mind, and she instantly regretted even thinking it. But it persisted. She didn't blame Nora for her lot. At least not consciously. Oh hell, she barely knew her own mind anymore.

Becky and Evie dashed into the drawing room just then, their grins as wide as the Thames.

Nora chuckled upon seeing them, and Jo couldn't help but smile too. They both looked so happy. "How was the marzipan?"

"It was ever so much fun!" Becky said. "We made animals and flowers and even a cottage. They have to set for a bit, and then Abbot will bring them upstairs so you can see them."

Nora leaned toward the girls, her eyes twinkling. "Oh good, I can't wait to see your creations."

"I tried a castle, but it was too hard." Becky's mouth tightened with determination. "But I'll work at it. Next time, I'll try for something a bit less complicated and work my way up to turrets."

"So there's to be a next time?" Jo asked.

Both girls nodded. "Cook said so," Becky said. "She said once a month if it was all right with Mama."

"It's all right with me. We'll just check with Lord

Knighton."

"Papa will agree." Evie looked at Jo. "Don't you think so?"

Jo felt suddenly self-conscious. Why was the girl asking her? "Probably."

Evie shrugged. "You've been to our house. You know what he's like."

Jo wasn't certain what that meant either or what it had to do with the conversation. She knew he liked to walk about with far too much flesh showing. And that had absolutely nothing to do with marzipan. Though she imagined it tasting just as sweet.

Good Lord, she really had *no* control over her thoughts, did she? She hoped the heat rising in her neck didn't make it all the way to her face.

Evie sat on the settee facing Nora, and Becky plopped down beside her. "Papa says he's going to take me to see some castles."

"Which ones?" Nora asked.

"The Tower of London," Becky answered. "Mama can we go too? I know you said I've been there, but I barely remember."

"Of course we can go," Nora said.

"With *Evie*."

Nora smiled. "We'll see."

Evie leaned closer to her friend and loudly whispered, "That means 'maybe, but probably not' in parent-talk. Papa says that to me all the time, and oftentimes it doesn't happen."

Becky's eyes narrowed. "You're right." She crossed her arms and pouted at her mother.

Nora laughed. "In this case, I really meant that we will have to wait and see. I'll have to discuss it with Lord Knighton and your father and see if we can find a mutually agreeable time."

Becky exhaled loudly. "I suppose."

"I hope so," Evie said. "It won't be as fun unless you all come too." She looked up at Jo, who still stood near the desk. "Including you, Jo." The girl's eyes were so clear and earnest—she truly wanted Jo's presence. That she could've been this girl's mother if she'd only said yes to Knighton's proposal…

Her stomach turned again, and her throat tightened. She couldn't have said yes even if things—*she*—were different. She barely knew him, had no idea what sort of husband he would be. She'd endured one unhappy, thoroughly horrid marriage and had no desire to enter into another.

"Mama, are there other castles we can go to?" Becky asked.

"Well, there's Hampton Court, but it's more of a palace than a castle. There's a large maze."

The girls exchanged excited looks.

Abbott entered and announced the arrival of Lord Knighton. The butler stepped out of the way, and the earl moved into the drawing room. He seemed to immediately command every bit of space and air, making Jo feel as though she couldn't breathe. He was breathtakingly handsome with his too-long hair and dark-as-sin blue eyes. Not to mention his mouth. She couldn't stop staring at it and imagining the way his lips had moved over hers, the thrust of his tongue…

"Papa!" Evie jumped from the settee and hugged him. "We made marzipan! They're in the kitchen, but I think Abbott's gone to fetch them so I can take mine home."

Knighton looked down at his daughter. "What did you make?"

"A cat, a turtle, and some flowers like we had at home. I tried a castle, but it was too hard, so I made it into a cottage instead. I'm going to work on mastering the elements for a castle next time. We're going to make it once a month."

"I see." The earl glanced over at Nora, who gave him a nod. "Well, that's most generous of the Kendals' cook to offer her time."

Evie pulled a face. "I can't see *our* cook doing that."

Knighton chuckled. "No, I can't see her doing that either."

Jo continued to stare at his mouth, despite her best efforts. Not that it mattered since he hadn't looked at her once since entering the drawing room. In fact, she wondered if he even realized she was there. Yes, why not think that? It was far less painful than thinking he was ignoring her. Could she blame him if he were? She'd turned down his marriage proposal after kissing him like a wanton.

Ugh, she *wished* she wasn't there.

In fact, maybe she could just tiptoe from the room…

"Papa, we must invite the Kendals to come to the Tower with us. And Jo." Evie looked over at Jo as she'd begun edging toward the doorway.

"That would be lovely," Knighton said, turning to Nora. "I'll see if we can coordinate something." Now he looked at Jo. And the full force of his gaze nearly took her breath away, as he'd done earlier by simply entering the room. "I'll see you tomorrow at noon?"

For the governess appointments. She'd wondered if he might disinvite her, after what had happened at the ball. "If you'd still like me to come." Perhaps he just needed an opportunity to relieve her obligation.

His brow furrowed slightly, and he blinked. "Of

course. What do I know of such things?"

"About the same as me." She didn't mean to sound tart but feared she may have.

Nora's gaze whipped to hers, and Jo felt the intensity of her silent reaction as if she'd shouted, *What is wrong with you?*

"Are you saying you'd rather not come?" he asked.

Now he was giving *her* the opportunity to withdraw. How kind. And she meant to take it.

"Of course she does," Nora answered before she could. She smiled placidly at both of them. "Joanna is delighted to help."

Knighton still looked a little unsure but ultimately nodded. "Very well. I'll see you at noon. Come, Evie."

Abbott returned at that moment with a bag containing her marzipan. "Here you are, Lady Evangeline."

She took the bag. "Thank you, Abbott. Are they all there, or did you eat one?" She winked at him, and Jo was charmed anew.

Abbott chuckled. "I was tempted, but I did not." He winked back at her.

Evie turned to her father. "Papa, we need a butler like Abbott. He's ever so much kinder than Kerr."

Jo was sorry to hear that things weren't improving with his servants. Perhaps she'd discuss it with him tomorrow.

What? She'd been trying to avoid tomorrow's appointment, and indeed all future encounters with the earl, not further embroil herself in his life.

The girls said their goodbyes, and Knighton and Evie left.

Nora immediately turned to Becky. "Time to go upstairs for reading."

Becky slipped from the settee. "Yes, Mama. Don't you want to see my marzipan?"

"Of course, dear. After reading. I'll come fetch you in a bit."

The girl nodded and took herself off.

Jo tried to follow her, but Nora stopped her with her demonstrable Big Sister tone. "You are *not* running away. You may not want to tell me what's bothering you, but if you don't, I shall suspect it's to do with Lord Knighton. You began acting peculiar after you danced with him. You disappeared directly after—*for quite some time*—and you've been in a funk ever since. Did something happen?"

Jo's grip on the letters tightened, and she had to mentally tell herself to relax her hands before she crumpled them. "No. It's just…dancing with him reminded me of Matthias."

Nora paled slightly. "I'm sorry. I didn't mean to arouse old memories. But you did say you weren't still harboring a tendre for him."

"No, I am not." Jo thrust her shoulders back and decided to let go—at least a little. "Matthias was a wretched husband. I don't miss him in the slightest. He didn't care much for me. In fact, he was often cruel." Her sister's eyes widened, and Jo could see the question in her troubled gaze. "Please don't ask me to explain. I'd rather leave everything to do with him where it belongs—dead and buried with him. Dancing with Lord Knighton, indeed just being at the ball, put me in a position to entertain a man's attentions, and I'd rather not."

Nora nodded sympathetically. "I understand. You need time."

Jo wanted to say that she couldn't possibly

understand, but that would only invite more curiosity. "I may never want to marry again. Being alone is better." If she'd had children, it would be downright perfect.

Nora clenched her jaw for a moment. "I am trying to understand," she said softly, and Jo appreciated that she was maybe beginning to realize that they'd led very different lives. They might be sisters and best friends who loved each other dearly, but their experiences were disparate, and there were some things they didn't—and couldn't—share.

"Thank you," Jo said simply. "I'm going to post these letters."

She left the drawing room before she was tempted to let down more of her guard. And once she did, she feared the dam she'd worked so hard to build up would crumble completely.

HUDSON STEPPED INTO Bran's office carrying a coat, waistcoat, and cravat just before noon. "I'm afraid it's time to dress, my lord." The valet wore a vaguely pained expression that reflected what Bran felt.

"I suppose so." Resigned, Bran stood from behind the desk and allowed Hudson to garb him. All the while, Bran silently counted the hours until he could remove everything he was currently donning. At least the tailor was working out well, after some initial problems. He'd learned to copy the way Bran's former tailor on Barbados had made his shirts. Bran was ecstatic. It was, to date, the best thing that had happened to him in London.

Right after kissing Mrs. Shaw.

Joanna.

Mrs. Shaw was so formal. In his mind, he'd decided to think of her as Joanna. After the intimacy they'd shared, it seemed only right. And yet not, since that intimacy seemed to be a one-time occurrence. Her refusal of his marriage proposal had come fast and stinging.

He'd been a bit anxious to see her yesterday, and he'd noted that she tried to escape the drawing room without even speaking to him. Then she'd clearly tried to avoid coming here today. All he could think was that he'd completely overstepped by kissing her. But she hadn't stopped him. In fact, she'd kissed him right back. *Enthusiastically.*

He frowned.

"My lord?" Hudson asked.

Bran gave his head a shake. "Nothing." He told his valet about most things, but hadn't revealed the encounter with Mrs. Shaw. It felt like a secret between the two of them, particularly given her rejection and subsequent behavior. "Please convey my appreciation to Jenkins. This shirt is even better than the last."

"He'll be pleased to hear it. I know he's worked hard to achieve your satisfaction."

"It's too bad more of the staff don't share that sentiment," Bran muttered.

"Indeed." Hudson was well aware of the issues surrounding several members of the staff. Aside from Kerr, the upstairs maid, Foster, possessed a rigidity that drove Bran mad, and the cook continued to complain about the changes Bran requested. She also failed to implement his instructions, much to his and Evie's chagrin.

He kept thinking of Evie's comments yesterday.

"Hudson, I think it's time to make some changes with the staff."

Hudson's eyes widened briefly, but then he exhaled. "For a moment there, I thought you meant me. You don't mean me, do you?"

"Of course not. What kind of person would I be to drag you from Barbados only to terminate your employment? I'm afraid you're stuck with me."

"Excellent. Who's getting dumped?"

"Foster—I don't care for the way she treats Evie. And the cook, probably. No matter how many times I tell her not to serve Evie turtle soup, she continues to do so." And any other number of dishes, but that one was the most traumatic.

Hudson shook his head. "Ghastly."

"And then there's Kerr." Bran grimaced. "I'd hoped he would adjust to our routine, but his disdain is palpable, and frankly, he casts a gloom over the household."

Hudson opened his mouth to respond just as Kerr appeared in the doorway. Bran worried he'd maybe overheard what he'd just said, but it was impossible to tell by looking at him. He wore the same scornful expression that always pinched his face.

"Mrs. Shaw is here," Kerr said haughtily, stepping aside as she moved past him into the office.

She stopped short at seeing Hudson and blinked. "I didn't mean to interrupt."

"And this is why I would prefer not to show people to your office," Kerr announced with a great deal of frost. "As *normal* people would expect," he muttered before taking himself off.

Hudson coughed delicately. "Pleased to make your acquaintance, Mrs. Shaw." He gave Bran a look that said the situation was probably a disaster and then quickly fled. The coward.

Bran's cravat had never felt tighter. He rotated his neck, turning his head from side to side. "Good afternoon. I don't, ah, suppose you overheard what we were discussing?" If she had, then Kerr had.

Her gaze was sympathetic. "I'm afraid so." She sat down in the chair she'd used last time, her reticule in her lap. "But it sounds as if it needed to be said, if not in that fashion, perhaps."

Bran went behind his desk and flung himself down in his chair, stretching his legs out in front of him. "That was not my intent, of course. But yes, it's overdue. You heard what Evie said yesterday when she compared him to Abbott. I can put up with his obnoxiousness, but when it comes to my daughter, I won't tolerate that sort of behavior. And if she's noticing it… Well, it's time for him to go."

"You plan to officially dismiss him, then?"

"Yes. Along with Foster. She's the upstairs maid."

"I recall her name from the last time I was here. I didn't like her attitude about Evie's cut finger."

It was good to hear that he wasn't alone in thinking Foster was lacking. Lacking? She was practically insubordinate. Like the cook, who was *definitely* insubordinate.

"The cook is also a problem."

"Her dishes aren't very good?" she asked. "Or is it just that she doesn't make marzipan with Evie?" She smiled at the last, and he knew she was joking.

"Well, I *would* like a cook who could do that. I'm afraid your sister has set an expectation I can scarcely achieve, particularly in my current predicament. I can't even get the cook to make the food I want or in the manner I want it."

Mrs. Shaw winced. "That *isn't* good. You've spoken to her?"

"Repeatedly."

"Then yes, it may be time to let her go as well." Her gaze turned sympathetic. "I'm so sorry. You'll be happier in the end, however."

Of that he was certain. He was also rather certain that this conversation was incredibly easy and comfortable and somewhat banished his feelings of disquiet from yesterday.

He studied her a moment, noting that she'd forgone her typical drab clothing. She'd done the same yesterday. "You look lovely today. That gown is quite fetching."

Her cheeks colored, and she tipped her head down. "Thank you." The awkward air from yesterday invaded the room, and he regretted commenting on her appearance.

But she had to know he found her attractive? He'd kissed her, for heaven's sake. She'd also turned down his marriage proposal, so perhaps awkward was the best he could hope for. He considered bringing it up, just to smooth out any discomfort. But then he thought of what she'd told him before she'd run off—that she couldn't have children. He did want more of them, and if she was barren, she couldn't be his countess. His disappointment was as strong today as it was at the ball.

He decided to plod forward as if it had never happened since it seemed she was keen to do the same. "Shall we review the candidates before they arrive?"

She nodded, clutching her reticule tightly. "Yes, please."

A few hours later, Bran freed his throat from the

confines of his cravat. He'd tossed his coat aside as soon as they'd finished the last interview, but he'd managed to keep the rest of his clothes on until after Mrs. Shaw had gone. It had been no small feat. All in the name of avoiding that awkwardness they were both doing a good job of ignoring. Or pretending to ignore.

"Papa?" Evie came into the office, her gaze darting about the room. "Is Mrs. Shaw still here?"

"No, sweetling. She left after we finished interviewing potential governesses."

She sat down on the chair Mrs. Shaw had used. "Is one of them going to be my new governess?"

Bran suppressed a groan of frustration. "No." He hadn't cared for any of them, and neither had Mrs. Shaw. Which meant he had to conduct more interviews. Plus the ones he would need to conduct for the numerous gaps in his staff he was about to encounter. Bran dropped his head toward his desk and massaged his suddenly throbbing temple.

"Why don't you just hire Mrs. Shaw?"

He snapped his gaze to Evie's. "She isn't a governess."

"No, but why can't she be? I like her ever so much, and I think she likes me. I'm certain she could teach me how to be a lady." Evie swung her feet as if to provide a visual reminder for *why* she needed a governess.

Bran frowned. She was still so young. He wanted her to swing her feet. "I'm not sure you need a governess right now."

"But Papa, Becky is going to have one. I shall need one too."

"That's no reason to have one. Becky also has a little brother. Are you going to ask for one of those too?"

"No, but maybe a little sister. Becky says her mama is

having another baby." Her eyes narrowed. "She says it better be a sister."

Bran stifled a laugh. As if they could choose. He thought of Mrs. Shaw and instantly sobered. She couldn't even *choose* to have a child, apparently. He felt bad for her. Observing her with her niece and nephew, and with Evie, she seemed naturally inclined toward children.

Then maybe she'd actually like to be a governess, his brain suggested.

Evie jumped off the chair and came around the desk to where he sat. "Please, Papa?" She blinked at him, and her mouth formed a small pout. "Please ask Mrs. Shaw?"

An image of her bustling about his house, offering opinions about his staff and arranging marzipan lessons for his daughter, burst into his head. He leaned back in his chair and let the fantasy take hold. Having her near would test their attraction. He'd almost certainly want to kiss her again. Which would be bad. He might be somewhat ignorant about being an earl, but he was fairly confident one did not kiss one's governess.

He focused on his daughter's pleading face. "Evie, I really don't think she'd be interested in being a governess. She doesn't need employment. Her sister is a duchess."

"But maybe she'd *want* to. Can't you just ask?"

He could… "What if she said no? Would you accept that?"

She raised her chin a notch. "I would. I'm quite grown up, Papa."

He chuckled at that and drew her onto his lap. "Not so fast, sweetling." He pressed a kiss to her cheek and blew air against her soft skin, making a rather impolite sound. She loved that.

Evie giggled. "Papa! Does that mean you will?"

"Yes." How could he refuse his very heart? Or her logic—indeed, what did it hurt to ask? "But I'll remind you not to get your hopes up. Promise?"

She rested her hand over her heart. "I *promise.*"

"Very well." Now Bran just had to work on not getting *his* hopes up.

Chapter Seven

"ANY NEWS FROM Lucy or Aquilla?" Nora asked their guest, the Duchess of Clare, who was simply "Ivy" to them.

Ivy set her teacup down on the table. "Nothing yet. They both write to me nearly every day." She let out a brief laugh. "Indeed their correspondence has increased along with their bellies."

Nora nodded knowingly. "Because they have to sit more than normal—at least that's how I felt. And at this stage, it's especially frustrating because they likely have spurts of energy."

Ivy rested a hand on her round midsection. "Yes, I'm beginning to feel that way too."

As usual, Jo felt disjointed from the conversation, having no experience to add anything of value. She ate another cake and mused that it was the only way her belly would ever grow. Ugh, what a depressing thought. She turned her mind to all the bad things that could happen, up to and including her own death in childbirth. It was a merciless tactic, but the only one she had to combat the disappointment and depression.

"It's much different from last time," Ivy said quietly.

Jo snapped to attention, not certain she'd heard her correctly. She glanced over at Nora, who smiled warmly at her friend.

"Are you nervous at all?" Nora asked.

Ivy nodded, taking a moment to answer. "I try not to think about it too much. As I said, things were so different. I never had enough to eat, and I was ill." She looked over at Jo. "I don't mind sharing my secret with you, but very few people know. I had a child about ten years ago. She was born early and didn't survive. At the time, I was living in a workhouse." She stroked her belly, and Jo wondered if she even realized.

"I'm so sorry for your loss," Jo said, thinking that if she were to miraculously become pregnant and then lose the child, she might very well not recover. And yet it was always a possibility.

"I've convinced myself over the years that it was for the best—for everyone. The life she would've had to endure as a bastard with a mother in a workhouse..." Her voice broke, and she looked away. "My apologies. I cry at the slightest provocation these days." She let out a tremulous laugh as she pressed her fingertips to the corners of her eyes.

"But you didn't stay in the workhouse," Jo said, stating the obvious but hoping that Ivy might tell her what had happened. Hers seemed an example of a complete change of fortune.

Ivy shook her head. "I moved to another one after that and found a benefactress who recognized that I had education and poise. She helped me to find work as a companion. I changed my name and left that life behind."

Jo blinked, pondering how marvelous that must have been in her circumstance. "And you enjoyed being a companion?"

"I did, very much. I would still be happily working for Lady Dunn if not for West." Her lips curved up. "I did try to dissuade him, but he was most persistent."

Jo still wanted more information so she decided to speak candidly and hope that her sister wouldn't comment. "I've been considering employment—as a companion or a governess."

Ivy pivoted toward her. "Indeed? The most important thing is finding the right employer. I was fortunate to work for women who were generous enough to allow me time to devote to my personal interests. They treated me as a person, not a servant. After my experience and the kindness of my benefactress, I felt it was my duty to dedicate my energy to supporting workhouses where I could. My employers supported those endeavors."

"You were quite fortunate. However did you manage that?"

"It wasn't easy, and I did turn down several offers of employment." She exhaled, her spine straightening. "I'd decided that I was going to live my life as I chose."

That was a luxury Jo actually possessed. She didn't *have* to take employment, so she could be selective.

"It's too bad that Lady Dunn isn't still looking for a companion. I think she's quite happy with Sarah. I believe she has a friend who is looking. If you'd like me to inquire, I'd be happy to do so."

"I keep trying to encourage Jo to marry again," Nora said, offering Jo a nervous smile, as if she knew she was being an annoying older sister. "I know she'd like to have a family of her own."

"Well, marriage isn't for everyone," Ivy said, and Jo suppressed the urge to give her sister a childish smirk. "I never planned to marry, and I daresay West is one in a million. He had to be to win me over." Ivy winked at Jo.

Nora picked up her teacup. "Who's to say Jo won't find her own West or Titus?" She peered at Jo over the rim of her cup as she took a sip.

"Who's to say I won't find an employment situation like Ivy had?" Jo asked with a touch of irritation. "Anyway, I tried marriage, and I didn't care for it."

Ivy gave her a knowing glance. "I'm sorry to hear it. It's difficult not to cast all men in the vein of our first experiences. The father of my first child promised to marry me and didn't. You can perhaps deduce why I'd sworn never to trust another man."

Easily. Jo knew that not all men were like Matthias. In fact, most of them weren't. But how could she know she wouldn't get one of the few who were? Or who were potentially even worse.

"Yet you did," Nora said. "What made you change your mind?"

Jo couldn't tell if Nora genuinely wanted to know or if she was trying to demonstrate a point to Jo. It had to be the former, of course, but if it achieved the latter, Nora wouldn't quibble.

"It really was just West." Ivy's smile was soft and secretive. "He insisted I was missing something, and that if I had the courage to try, I just might find it. He was right. I never imagined I'd find happiness like this. I'd resolved that it was for other people, and it was up to me to create my own contentment, which I did being a companion." She looked at Jo. "As I said, I'd be happy in that role still if that's where I was today."

But she'd been tempted with something more. Jo thought of Knighton's proposal. That hadn't been tempting. It had been frightening. And heart wrenching. But even if she could bear children, she didn't know him well enough to accept his proposal.

She doubted very much he was anything like Matthias, but how could she know that, really? Until she stepped into his bedroom, she couldn't. The thought of opening herself up to another man in that way… She wasn't sure she could do it. Kissing Knighton the other night had been a grievous mistake.

Ivy departed a short while later, and Nora moved to sit beside Jo on the settee. "I'm sorry for meddling."

"Thank you."

"I'm just not sure you'll be happy as a companion or a governess. But, that's not my decision to make. I hope you know you'll always have a home here."

The irritation Jo had felt earlier was replaced with regret. When Nora had needed a home, Jo hadn't been able to give her one. "That means so much to me. Especially since I didn't do the same for you."

Shame welled in Jo's chest, but what could she have done differently? Matthias never would have let Nora come to stay with them—not with her scandalous past. When Jo thought of the scandal Matthias could have caused, well, she wanted to tell him what a hypocrite he was.

Nora clasped Jo's hand. "I don't blame you for that *at all.* I know Matthias didn't care for me."

Jo let out an acerbic laugh. "It went a bit beyond that. For a vicar, he wasn't particularly Christian."

"I hope someday you'll confide in me. If you want to." Nora hugged her briefly before standing. "I'm going to look in on the children."

Jo sat for a minute, her mind turning to what Ivy had said about taking employment. Perhaps she could just talk to Lady Dunn's friend—

Her thought was interrupted by the arrival of Abbott. "Lord Knighton is here to see you, Mrs. Shaw."

Jo rose. What could he want? Evie wasn't here. "Me, you say?"

Abbott gave a single nod. "Just so. Shall I show him

up, or are you indisposed?"

"Show him up, please." Perhaps he just wanted to review yesterday's interviews. Although, she couldn't think what more there was to discuss. They'd agreed that none of them were right. As it happened, however, Nora had conducted her interviews yesterday and today, and before Ivy had arrived, had suggested another candidate.

Knighton entered the drawing room a moment later, looking effortlessly handsome. He was also wearing gloves. She hid a smile.

He bowed. "Good afternoon, Mrs. Shaw. I hope I'm not calling at an inopportune time."

"Not at all. Would you care to sit?" She gestured toward the seating area she'd just stood from. "I'm afraid we still have the remnants of a tea tray, but I can have a fresh one brought up, if you like."

"That won't be necessary, thank you." He walked to her, moving with an easy grace that was somehow animalistic, she realized. Almost like a cat. "I wanted to talk with you about the governess position."

Jo sat back down on the settee and almost instantly regretted it because he lowered himself right next to her. "I have good news on that front, actually," she said, edging slightly away from him. "My sister had a difficult time choosing a governess. Apparently, two of her candidates were quite good. She was pleased to hear that she could recommend one of them to you since your candidates were not as successful. Would you like me to arrange for an interview?"

"I don't need to conduct further interviews. I've found whom I want to hire."

Jo straightened. "Is that so? Did you interview someone new today?"

He shook his head. "No. I want you."

Those three simple words sent a shiver down her neck. "I beg your pardon?"

"I want you." His dark eyes bored into her with singular intent. The room seemed suddenly warm. "As Evie's governess."

Ah yes, that clarification meant everything. She exhaled, realizing she'd held her breath. "I'm…surprised." She was many other things too, but thought that description would suffice.

"Evie begged me, I admit, but once I started thinking about it, I had to agree that it's a spectacular idea. You know Evie, and I think you like her—"

"Immensely." Jo didn't want him to doubt that.

His lips quirked into a half smile. "Good. She definitely likes you. I can't think of anyone better. You're intelligent, well-connected—and that seems important, not that I particularly give a damn—and you were most helpful yesterday with my…household issues. Furthermore, you seem up to the challenge of our foibles. I don't think our bare feet or food particularity will concern you."

She clasped her hands in her lap. "I'm really not sure I want to take employment. I'm still trying to find my way."

He rested his arm along the back of the settee, bringing his hand within touching distance of her shoulder if she only leaned back an inch. "You'd enjoy every freedom you do now. You may come and go as you wish, and I'll provide you with a large bedchamber in the main living quarters. I understand governesses often sleep in the servants' area, but not you."

Ivy's comments floated through her mind. *"They treated me as a person, not a servant."* What Knighton was offering was surely the best position she could imagine.

He continued his verbal assault. And it truly was an assault as she became less and less able to defend against why this wouldn't work. "Mostly I want to provide a stable, happy environment for Evie. Coming to England has been a huge change for her, and so far, Mrs. Poole has exceeded my expectations. Which is good given the problems we've had with other members of the staff. With you, I know what to expect and so does she."

How could she argue with him when he laid it out like that? Moreover, how could she say no to Evie? The girl had lost her mother and her home. If having Jo as her governess would ease her stress, Jo simply couldn't refuse.

And yet, there were…issues.

She tried to think of how to articulate her fears. All the while, he stared at her expectantly, making her feel warm, which wasn't to say unpleasant. On the contrary, sitting this close to him reminded her of his hands and his mouth on her, and goodness, the heat flashing through her was becoming a problem.

"Don't you think things might be awkward?" When he didn't respond, she dug for more. "After what happened at the ball."

His eyes flickered with awareness. "Yes, the ball. Things needn't be awkward. We're friends, aren't we?"

Friends who'd kissed each other and who'd proposed marriage and who'd rejected said proposal. "I think so, yes. But there can't be…" She coughed, then lifted her chin, unwilling to be brought down by any sense of embarrassment. "I was clear the other night about any romantic future."

His brow arched slightly, causing her to relax. "Yes,

quite."

"Good."

"Is that a yes?"

It wasn't a no. But she had so many reservations! She also felt just the tiniest bit excited. To have a purpose every day and to spend time with a precious child was precisely what she needed. What she *wanted.*

"I suppose we could try it," she said tentatively while emotion barreled through her chest. The moment of excitement had been replaced by a shaft of dread. He planned to marry again. What then? She'd watch him take a countess and just sit idly by? Of course she would. She'd had her chance, and she'd rejected him. That didn't change the fact that she *was* attracted to him. Even while fear of what would happen if she acted on that attraction would undoubtedly prevent her from doing just that.

"What if things don't work out?" she asked. "I wouldn't want to disappoint Evie."

He nodded once. "I understand. I wouldn't want that either."

"It would have to be a temporary arrangement until we were sure." The war inside her head wasn't going to reach a conclusion. She needed time to weigh everything. "I'm going to have to think about it."

"That still isn't a no. Which means I can harbor hope." He stood. "I can't ask for more than that."

She rose alongside him. "I'll let you know when I've made my decision."

He bowed again and quickly departed, leaving her to feel as if her life had just turned upside down. Again.

IT HADN'T EVEN been a full day since Bran had offered the governess position to Mrs. Shaw, but with each passing hour, he grew more anxious that she would say no. It was an odd yet familiar sensation, the feeling that things were beyond his control. He'd felt that way for much of his life until going to Barbados, where he'd been beholden to no one. But now, being back here, the old anxiety had returned.

Well, not the *old* anxiety. This was something new, he had to admit. He wanted Mrs. Shaw to accept the position—for so many reasons.

"Papa, Papa!" Evie shrieked as she came tearing into his office, her bare feet skidding across the floor. Tears streamed down her cheeks, and there was blood on her lip.

Bran shot out of his chair and rushed to gather her into his arms. "What is it, sweetling?" He held her up against his hip thinking he rarely carried her this way anymore.

"I lost my tooth." She curled her lower lip down revealing a new, larger void in the center of her teeth. "Foster says I'm going to have bad luck forever!" She started crying anew, thick rivulets streaking down her face.

He held her close to his chest as the maid came to the threshold and peered into the office, her lips pursed and her gaze narrowed. "I said no such thing. I said she *could* have bad luck if the tooth wasn't properly disposed of."

What the devil was she talking about? Bran stroked Evie's back as she clung to his neck. "Why on earth are you scaring my child?"

"I'm not scaring her."

"Clearly you *are*. Even if that is not your intent. Have

you no sense?"

Foster's eyes narrowed further. "I could ask the same of you since you saw no reason to do the right thing with the first tooth."

Evie wailed even louder, her body quivering. "She said that if we don't burn the tooth, bad things will happen to me, and we *can't* burn the first tooth I lost."

Bran glared at the maid, his patience gone. "Your employment here is terminated as of this moment. Pack your things and leave by the end of the day. And do not ask for a reference."

Foster's face drained of color. She steadied herself on the doorframe as Kerr appeared just behind her.

"My lord," he said sharply. "You can't just turn her out. That is not how things are done."

"Yes, I'm aware I don't do things to your satisfaction, Kerr. How could I not be?" He didn't bother keeping the acid from his tone. "However, I will not be dictated to when it comes to my daughter!" His voice rose until he shouted the last.

Evie hugged him even tighter and buried her face in the crook of his neck. Her hot tears soaked his shirt.

"Kerr, you are also dismissed. Immediately." Bran glowered at both the butler and the maid—rather, the *former* butler and the *former* maid—until they turned about and left.

Evie lifted her head, and Bran turned with her before setting her gently on the chair near the fireplace. "What am I to do, Papa?" She held out her hand, which he realized had been clutching her tiny bloody tooth. "I only have this tooth to burn—or whatever it is. Foster didn't say what we needed to do, only that it was vitally important." Her words were unsteady, her face blotchy. Bran wanted to drag Foster back in here so he could yell at her again.

Evie had lost her first tooth on the voyage from Barbados. He'd no idea what had become of it. "We'll just have to do our best with this tooth," he said. "I bet Mrs. Poole will know. We'll ask her when she returns." It was her afternoon off.

Fresh tears spilled from Evie's eyes. "Papa, I'm nervous. Can't we find someone to help?"

Nervous. That was a word he didn't like to hear from Evie. She didn't suffer from the same frustrations he'd felt as a child—the behavior that had earned him the nickname "Bran the Defiant"—but when she was very agitated, as she was now, she became inconsolable. She'd begun to signal these episodes by saying she was "nervous."

He scrambled for a solution, and the words Evie had uttered a moment ago rose in his mind: *vitally important.* That phrase reminded him of Mrs. Shaw.

But of course. It was too simple. "How about we go to the Kendals'? I bet the Duchess or Mrs. Shaw could help us."

Evie's tears slowed, and she wiped the back of her free hand over her cheeks. "Yes, Papa. Let's go at once."

"Just as soon as we're properly dressed." He tickled her toes, eliciting a soft giggle that sounded like music to him.

After placing Hudson in charge of the household, which caused a few raised eyebrows but thankfully no outbursts such as the ones demonstrated by Foster and Kerr, who were busy packing their things, Bran drove Evie to the Kendals' town house in his phaeton.

They were disappointed at the door, however, when Abbott informed them that the family was out.

Crestfallen, Evie asked if that included Mrs. Shaw.

"Actually, it does not," Abbot answered with a twinkle in his eye. "Would you like me to see if she is available?"

"Oh yes, please." Evie bounced with barely suppressed energy.

Abbott ushered them inside. "Wait here in the hall."

As it happened, Mrs. Shaw was just descending the staircase. Her gaze fell on them. "Good afternoon, my lord, Evie." She smiled. "I'm afraid Becky and the others are at the park."

Bran stepped forward, his hand resting against the back of Evie's neck. He could feel the slight tremor that coursed through her. "That's all right, I'm certain you can help."

Evie ran to Mrs. Shaw with her hand extended. "I've lost my tooth, and Foster said we have to burn it with a special ceremony or something, and we don't know what that is. Mrs. Poole is off this afternoon. And my first tooth wasn't burned at all. I lost it on the ship, and now I don't know where it is. Foster said I would have bad luck, especially since it was my first milk tooth."

Bran walked up beside them at the base of the stairs and saw that Evie's lip was trembling and that tears had gathered in her eyes. He caressed the back of her neck once more and said soothingly, "Foster is full of stuff. Mrs. Shaw will help us." He looked at Mrs. Shaw expectantly, hoping she actually *could* help them. His muscles grew taut as he awaited her response.

Mrs. Shaw squatted down to Evie's level. "Yes, Foster is full of stuff. Let me see." She looked at Evie's mouth.

Evie lowered her lip again to show her the new gap.

"Impressive." Mrs. Shaw gingerly picked up the

tooth from Evie's hand. "The first thing we must do is rub the tooth with salt."

"But what about my first tooth?" Evie whined, her forehead creased with worry. "Foster said I would have terrible bad luck for ever and ever because I didn't burn it."

Mrs. Shaw frowned. "Foster is misinformed and ought not speak of things she clearly doesn't understand. Burning a tooth is important here in England, but you didn't lose your tooth in England, did you? The rules do not apply to that tooth."

Hope leapt into Evie's gaze while gratitude and wonder stole over Bran's soul. "They don't?" Evie asked.

Mrs. Shaw firmly shook her head. "Absolutely not. Everyone knows this. Well, everyone who isn't Foster, apparently."

The corners of Evie's mouth crept into a small smile. "Papa dismissed her."

Mrs. Shaw's gaze found his. "Good for your papa," she said softly, and Bran felt another tremor deep within himself. "Come, let's go to the kitchen. I wager Cook will be delighted to help us."

Of course she would, Bran thought. She made marzipan with children. He ought to ask if she had a sister since he was about to be in the market for a cook. Now that he'd dismissed Kerr and Foster, he was keen to be rid of her too.

Mrs. Shaw took Evie by the hand and led them down to the kitchen. The cook, a tall, slender woman with dark hair and bright gray eyes greeted them with a smile.

"Well, if it isn't Lady Evie." Her voice carried a slight Irish lilt. "What brings you here today? It's not time for marzipan yet."

"No," said Mrs. Shaw. "We're here on another errand. Lady Evie has lost a milk tooth, and we need to salt it."

The cook's eyes shone, and she grinned widely, revealing a mouth full of rather crooked teeth. "Do you know what song you're going to sing?" she asked Evie.

Evie glanced at Bran, her brow furrowed again, before she looked to Mrs. Shaw. "You didn't say anything about singing."

"Not yet, I haven't." She dragged a short stool over near the fireplace and gestured for Evie to come join her. "Sit, and I'll explain everything."

Evie sat, her head tipped up as she waited, rapt, for instructions. Bran went to stand beside her, also eager for what was to come next.

Mrs. Shaw laid the tooth flat in her open palm. "First, I'll rub salt on it, and while I do that, you must sing a song. Any song will do. Do you have a favorite?"

Evie glanced at her father. "I learned a few songs on our ship, but Papa probably wouldn't like it if I sang them."

Bran knew precisely what songs she was referring to. "No, that wouldn't be appropriate." He coughed. "How about 'Baa Baa Black Sheep'?"

Evie nodded, turning her attention to Mrs. Shaw, who looked as though she was trying not to laugh. "Very good," she said.

The cook carried the salt cellar to Mrs. Shaw. "Your mother's supposed to rub the salt on, but since you don't have a mother, perhaps your father ought to do it." She glanced from Evie to Bran to Mrs. Shaw.

"No, no," Bran said quickly. "I've no idea what to do. I'll leave it to Mrs. Shaw."

Her brown-green eyes flashed with something. She swallowed as her lids fluttered close for a moment. "While you sing, I'll rub the salt on. When you're finished with the song, we'll take the tooth to the fire and throw it in."

"Is that all?" Evie asked.

Mrs. Shaw nodded. "That's all."

Evie's frame relaxed, her shoulders dipping. "That doesn't sound terrible. I assumed it would be terrible since Foster was so cross."

Mrs. Shaw looked toward Bran and murmured, "I'm glad she's gone."

"No more than I," he whispered.

Mrs. Shaw spooned some salt onto her palm and looked at Evie. "Are you ready?"

Evie started singing, the soft notes of "Baa Baa Black Sheep" filling the kitchen. The cook's assistant and the scullery maid stopped their work to listen, and Mrs. Shaw covered the tooth with salt and rubbed the ivory surface with her thumb and forefinger.

When Evie finished, Mrs. Shaw smiled. "Time for the fire, then." She took Evie's hand again and led her to the fire. Bran followed them, somewhat entranced by the whole scenario.

Mrs. Shaw squatted down beside her. "I didn't have a mother either, so my sister is the one who did this for me. And she added something special. When we threw the tooth into the fire, I made a wish. Would you like to do that?"

Evie's eyes were wide as she listened. "Yes," she breathed, sounding as if she were in awe. Bran had to admit he was too.

"We'll do it together," Mrs. Shaw said. "Put your hand around mine, and I'll count to three." Evie wrapped her fingers around Mrs. Shaw's as she said, "One, two, three."

They flung the tooth into the fire.

Mrs. Shaw turned to Evie. "Did you make your wish?"

"I did." Her gaze locked on to Mrs. Shaw's. "Are you going to be my governess? Papa said you were thinking about it."

Bran was standing to the side. Mrs. Shaw didn't turn her head to look at him, but he caught the subtle twitch of her shoulder. He briefly closed his eyes, wishing Evie hadn't said anything. He didn't want to scare Mrs. Shaw away.

"I *was* thinking about it, but I've decided to say yes."

Bran's pulse quickened.

Evie's face bloomed into a wide grin. "Then my wish already came true."

So had Bran's.

Chapter Eight

THREE DAYS LATER, after church, Jo arrived at Lord Knighton's home. Her home now. Nervousness tripped through her along with a dollop of excitement. Nora, Titus, and Becky had come along to deliver her.

The footman opened the door of the coach, and Nora inclined her head toward Jo with an encouraging smile. "You go first. We'll follow in a moment."

Jo stepped out into the gently falling rain and looked up at the stone façade. It was one of the larger townhomes she'd been in, with nearly as many rooms as the Kendals'. Or so she thought. She supposed she'd have a full tour shortly.

She made her way up the small flight of steps, and the door came open. A footman, garbed in smart livery, stood with his hand on the latch. "Good afternoon, Mrs. Shaw."

"Good afternoon." She wished she knew the man's name but vowed to learn it, along with everyone else's. She swept her gaze around the hall and saw that the earl and Evie were standing next to each other, clearly awaiting her arrival.

"Welcome," Lord Knighton said.

Evie dipped a very nice curtsey. "We're glad you're here." She looked and sounded as if she'd rehearsed that. The Evie that Jo had come to know would've bounded over to her the minute she walked through the door.

Jo crooked her finger at Evie and dropped down to

look the girl in the eye.

Evie moved to stand in front of her. "Did I do something wrong?"

"Not at all. I only wanted to tell you that even though I'll be your governess, I'm still Jo. We needn't become formal." Jo winked at her, and Evie grinned.

She wrapped her arms around Jo's neck, surprising her with a fierce hug. "I'm ever so glad you're here. Things are much better since Foster and Kerr and the cook left. Except for the toast. The toast has been quite burned."

Jo straightened and looked over at the earl. He turned his neck, and she thought his cravat must be irritating him. "I need to hire a replacement," he said. "The assistant left with her, so one of the scullery maids is attempting to prepare meals." He frowned. "I'm sorry you're arriving in the midst of a bit of upheaval."

"As it happens, I know how to make toast without burning it."

"That's true," Nora said from the open doorway behind her. "I taught her myself."

Jo turned as the footman welcomed Nora and her family inside.

Evie ran over to Becky. "Let's go upstairs. Mrs. Poole helped me set up a table to draw. I have pencils and paper and books with pictures we can copy."

The girls dashed up the stairs while Nora called after them, "Not too long, girls. We're only staying a short while."

Lord Knighton turned to the duke. "Kendal, how would you like to sample some of my private stock of rum? This is different from what I sent you, a smaller batch."

Titus rubbed his hands together. "You've been holding out."

"I only serve it to people brave enough to visit me." He gestured for Titus to follow him toward his office.

"Can we talk for a few minutes?" Nora asked, looking about.

The footman inclined his head to a doorway off the right side of the hall. "The sitting room is just through there."

Nora and Jo turned and went inside. The chamber was bright and cheerful, decorated in hues of yellow and pale green. The furniture was relatively new and in seemingly splendid condition. Jo recalled Knighton asking her about refurbishment and deduced that he couldn't have meant this room.

Nora walked to a large painting situated in the center of the wall opposite the windows. "Is this his mother?"

Jo joined her and studied the image. The woman was young with dark eyes that looked very much like Knighton's. With her towering, powdered hair and ivory complexion, she looked regal and serene. "She looks like a female Untouchable."

Nora let out a gasp. "I was going to say the same thing!"

They grinned at each other and laughed, reminding Jo of days gone by. "I'm going to miss seeing you every day. That was nice after so many years apart."

Nora sidled closer until their arms touched as they continued to look at the portrait. "Yes, it was. I'm still not entirely happy with your decision." She turned toward Jo. "But it's your decision, not mine."

They'd discussed this at length over the past few days. Nora had repeatedly assured her that she could return to them at any time, no matter where they were.

All their homes were open to Jo, under any circumstances. Jo loved her sister so much. She just wanted Nora to be happy for her.

Jo pivoted to face her sister. "I'm looking forward to tomorrow in a way I haven't in a very long time."

Nora clasped Jo's hand. "That is all I could hope for."

A short time later, Nora and her family took their leave. Knighton joined Jo in the sitting room. She stood near the window watching the coach pull away, then turned to face him where he stood just over the threshold.

"Would you like to see your bedchamber?" he asked.

She nodded, glad that whatever awkwardness that may have lingered between them after their encounter in the garden at the ball had finally dissipated. "This is a lovely room."

He glanced around, his brow drawn. "You think so? I've always loathed it. It's my mother's favorite room."

Jo gestured toward the portrait. "Is that her?"

"Yes, she sat for that when I was five. I remember it distinctly because I interrupted one of her appointments, and she was furious." He spoke of her in a cool, dispassionate tone.

She was curious about his apparent dislike of his mother but didn't wish to query him about it. Not today. Instead, she focused on the room. "What don't you like about this chamber? It's very bright. The colors remind me of a summer day. I'd think it might remind you of the tropics."

Knighton moved farther into the room. "I could see where you might come to that conclusion; however, it reminds me of my mother, not Barbados."

"Is this at the top of your list of things requiring

refurbishment?"

"No, that would be my bedroom. It's dark and depressing. I want bright and…sunny." He looked at her with interest, his head tipped to the side. "Like Barbados."

"I see." For some reason, the mention of his bedroom summoned that odd sensation. She realized it wasn't awkwardness but expectation. As if something were about to happen, or *could* happen if things were different.

Which they weren't.

"Speaking of my mother, she's coming for a visit tomorrow to meet Evie."

Jo was surprised they hadn't met yet. He and Evie had been in England for several weeks. "You haven't seen her at all?"

He shook his head. "No, she's been in Durham with her sister. I admit I didn't immediately write to tell her I'd arrived." There was no regret in his statement.

"I'm sorry you don't care for her." Jo hadn't meant to say anything, but apparently couldn't help herself. "My apologies. It really isn't any of my concern."

"You're part of the household now. I think it *is* your concern. I hope you realize that I don't see you as a typical governess. I should very much like your input on a variety of things, starting with helping me to find a cook. Can you really make toast?"

She smiled at the eagerness in his question. "Yes, I really can."

His gaze darted up for a brief moment. "Thank God. That's the only thing Evie will eat for breakfast, and our temporary cook burns it beyond recognition. Evie won't touch it. She doesn't like food that's black in any way."

Jo recalled his comment that she was particular about food. The instance with the biscuits and whether they were plain flashed in Jo's mind. Evie had been anxious about tasting one and had only done so cautiously.

"Well, I shall be delighted to make her toast in the morning. Shall we take the tour?"

"Indeed." He pivoted and started to put out his arm before letting it rest at his side, perhaps realizing she was the governess, not someone who should take his arm.

She walked to his side, and he led her from the room. Over the next half hour, he showed her every chamber. There was something about each that he disdained, and she quickly came to understand how much he disliked his family. It was heartbreaking, really, and she longed to know the particulars, but wouldn't ask.

When they arrived at the nursery, Mrs. Poole and Evie were playing with her dolls. Evie showed Jo around the room with great enthusiasm, including the corner where they would do lessons. Jo knew that Evie was already a good reader, and was eager to see what else she could do.

Evie pulled a map from a shelf and unfolded it, laying the parchment flat across the table in the corner. "I thought we could use this for our lessons."

Jo peered at the well-worn paper featuring the world. Judging from the tattered edges and deep creases from the folds, it was evident that Evie looked at this often. "I'm certain we can."

Glancing at her father, Evie said, "Papa gave it to me so that I could see where he was from. It seemed so far away, like another world." She pointed to a small island. "This is Barbados, where I'm from. Now it's very far away." Her voice turned sad.

"On the map, yes, but it's in your heart, isn't it? And that's very close. In fact, that's part of you."

Evie placed her hand on her chest and looked up at Jo. "Yes." She smiled. "Are we going to start lessons today?"

Knighton cleared his throat. "No, we're going to give Mrs. Shaw some time to acclimate. Tomorrow will be soon enough. I need to show her to her chamber now."

"Will I see you at dinner?" Evie asked Jo.

Jo wasn't certain if a governess ate dinner with the family but suspected not.

"Of course," Knighton answered. He looked over at Jo and gave an infinitesimal nod. It seemed she wouldn't be a typical governess at all.

"I hope it's something edible," Evie said with a grumble as she returned to her dolls.

"Yes, me too," Knighton murmured. "I'll find us a cook this week, Evie."

They departed then, and the earl led Jo downstairs to where the bedchambers were located. "Evie doesn't sleep in the nursery," he said. "When we arrived, she didn't want to be far away from me, so her chamber is just down from mine." He pointed to the right. "This way"—he turned left—"is my chamber and yours."

Her chamber was near his? Oh dear, that seemed…problematic. But why should it? They'd agreed they were friends and that what had happened at the ball was in the past. She had no reason to believe anything similar would happen, even if her stomach fluttered when he was close. As he was now.

"That is my chamber." He indicated a door across the corridor. She wanted to peek inside, to see if it was as dark as he said. She had no reason to doubt him but merely wanted to see for herself. Perhaps she could offer suggestions on how to brighten it up.

Oh, that was nonsense! She couldn't refurbish his bedchamber, even if she *was* an atypical governess. Surely that was beyond the realm of propriety. His future countess would help him with that. Her stomach knotted at the thought of a future countess. How would it be to live here with them? Would she still be an atypical governess then?

"And here is your chamber." He went to the door opposite his and opened it.

Jo stepped inside and wondered what he'd dislike about this chamber. A four-poster bed stood against one wall, and there was a hearth with a chair angled in front of it, a desk in front of the windows that overlooked the street below, and a tall armoire in one corner.

"I just realized that you may perhaps require a maid," he said.

She turned. "You really don't understand the role of a governess, do you?"

He looked utterly nonplussed. "I understand very little about any of this earl business. Please enlighten me." He folded his arms over his chest.

"To start—and you know this much—my room should likely be upstairs near the nursery."

"But it's not going to be. I refuse to change my mind on that. What else?" His dark gaze seemed to dare her to find something.

"I probably ought not take meals with you, and definitely not when you have company—such as your mother tomorrow."

A look of horror flashed in his gaze. "Oh, she won't be staying for any meals. And I want you to eat with us.

So does Evie. I'm not altering that either. What else?"

"I don't need a maid." She hadn't had a personal maid at the vicarage. They'd had a housekeeper and one maid who'd served as a ladies' maid whenever Jo needed one.

"Ever?"

"Not dedicated to me. When you hire a replacement for Foster"—he'd told her about the open positions in his staff during their tour— "you could retain someone who could act as an occasional ladies' maid." Wait, she was a governess. They didn't have ladies' maids! "Never mind. Governesses don't have maids."

"Nevertheless, you shall have one. Or rather, *access* to one."

She wanted to protest but somehow realized it would be ignored.

"What about this chamber? Is everything to your satisfaction?"

Jo went to the armoire and opened it. Her clothes were already inside. She closed the door and went to the desk. It was supplied with parchment, quill, and ink. "Yes, thank you." She looked over at him, the bed separating them. "What about you? What is the thing you don't like about this room?"

He unfolded his arms. "Nothing. I've scarcely been in this room—it was used for guests." He glanced around. "In fact, this may be my favorite room in the house."

"I have an idea. I presume you brought some things with you from Barbados? Things that were maybe in your house there?"

"Yes, they're still packed in crates."

"Unpack them as soon as possible and place at least one thing from Barbados in each room. That way, you'll have something everywhere to remind you of home."

His gaze softened when she'd said "home." He was homesick, she realized. And Evie likely was too. Jo would work on finding a way to try to make England feel like home to them.

He walked around the bed to stand in front of her. Close enough that her belly fluttered with awareness again. "That's an excellent idea," he said. "Thank you." He eyed her for a moment. "I'm very glad you agreed to become our governess. And I say 'our' because I think you'll be teaching me as much as you'll be instructing Evie. I've much to learn about my new role, and for the first time, I don't feel completely overwhelmed by it."

The flutters in her belly grew and spread, sending a pleasant heat to the far reaches of her body and all points in between. "I'm glad."

His lip ticked up into a half smile. "I'll leave you to it, then." He turned and walked toward the door.

"My lord?" she called, halting him in his tracks.

He pivoted. "If I can't convince you to call me Bran, you could at least refer to me as Knighton."

She inclined her head. "I wanted to thank you for this opportunity. As well as remind you that this is a trial. If for any reason either of us—or Evie, for that matter—feels as though it isn't working out, we must terminate the arrangement at the earliest possible opportunity."

His brow furrowed, and for a moment, she feared he might argue. "All right. However, I feel comfortable in assuring you that neither Evie nor I will feel that way."

He said that now, but expectations were a tenuous thing. Jo nodded, and he left, closing the door behind him.

Her shoulders sagged as if the energy had exited the room along with him. No, she wasn't going to be a typical governess at all.

Chapter Nine

BREAKFAST THE FOLLOWING morning was a smashing success, and Bran couldn't have been more relieved. Evie had declared Mrs. Shaw the best toast maker in the world and now swore she wouldn't eat anyone else's. Bran had told Mrs. Shaw that Evie wasn't joking. Mrs. Shaw had responded that she was up to the challenge.

He hoped she meant for the long term, but respected her desire to take things slowly. It was a smart strategy—for all of them—but he recognized the inherent self-preservation. He would likely do the same thing.

Bran sat on the floor and opened the crate that had just been delivered to his office. His insides melted as soon as he saw the contents—their life in Barbados. Why had he waited so long to open this? Perhaps he hadn't been ready. Leaving had been painful, and these were just a reminder of that agony.

They also brought joy. Memory after memory assailed him as he looked at the shells in the jar that Evie had collected on the beach. They used to take walks together, at first with her mother, and then just the two of them after she'd died. Every time Evie found a shell, she clutched it in her hand until they arrived home, and then she'd drop it into the jar, which had sat on Bran's desk. Well, it would go right on this desk too. He pulled the jar from the crate and twisted his body to set it on the corner where he could look at it every time he sat there.

Turning back to the crate, he eyed a book and couldn't recall why it would be in this box. He picked it up and opened the cover. A pressed flower, dulled from age but still vivid in its color, smiled up at him. He remembered now—there were dozens of them in this book. He wondered if he could somehow frame them and hang them in every room of the house. Yes, that was precisely what he would do.

"My lord?" Bucket, the footman who most often performed the duties of butler since Kerr's dismissal, came to the doorway. "Lady Knighton has arrived. She's in the sitting room."

Every muscle in Bran's body tensed. "Thank you, Bucket. Don't forget—I don't want tea or anything else. Even if she asked for it," he added as he stood from the floor.

Bucket stifled a smile. "She did, in fact."

Bran liked that Bucket saw humor in the situation. "I suppose I should don my coat." He'd brought it downstairs in anticipation of his mother's arrival but hadn't put it on yet.

Crossing to the chair near the fireplace where the coat was draped across the back, Bucket picked it up and held it for Bran to slip into. The footman brushed at Bran's shoulders before Bran turned to face him.

"You could be a valet, Bucket."

"Perhaps someday. Or a butler." He shrugged. "Kerr always told me I've much to learn."

"I'm sure he did. I'm not sure anyone is up to Kerr's expectations," Bran said with more than a touch of sarcasm.

Bucket didn't hide his smile this time. "You may be right."

"Will you notify Mrs. Shaw that Lady Knighton is here so that she may bring Lady Evie to the sitting room?"

"At once." Bucket turned crisply and departed.

With great reluctance, Bran made his way to the sitting room. At the threshold, he paused. His mother stood with her back to him, her pale blonde hair unmarred with white, at least as far as he could tell from this distance. He doubted he'd get close enough to see. She was angled toward the now-bare space on the wall where her portrait had been.

Perhaps sensing his presence, she turned. She was still beautiful, her skin pale and only slightly wrinkled, her eyes dark and commanding, her stature poised and regal. "Knighton." She shook her head. "How odd that sounds on my tongue when I look at you." Her gaze took stock, raking him from his head to his feet. "You look well, if a bit…wild. You need to trim your hair. And probably a new valet since he allows you to be seen like that." Her criticism was as familiar as it was grating.

"My valet is exemplary, thank you." He inclined his head toward the void on the wall. "I thought you'd like to have your portrait. I've no need of it."

Her eyes hardened, and he instinctively flinched. That was the look she wore just before she took him to task or beat him with whatever implement she could find. But just as soon as it happened, the moment was gone. She seemed to relax, and the air in the room loosened. Bran exhaled.

"I do like that portrait, but it ought to stay in one of the houses. Perhaps it would be best to take it to Knight's Hall. I presume you'll go there in the summer?"

He gave a single nod. He'd like to go there immediately, thinking he'd prefer it to London, but he had too many obligations here. He was still trying to find his way in the House of Lords, though Kendal had been most helpful.

She circuited the room. "You look like your father, except the eyes, of course."

Yes, he had her eyes. Damn them.

"I never would've imagined it, but you're taller than either of your brothers and more broad shouldered. They took after my side of the family, I suppose." Her father and brothers had slighter builds—and thinner hair. But Bran had no idea how his brothers had aged, nor did he care.

She sat down on the settee and stared at him. "Aren't you going to sit?"

He supposed he must. He went to a chair that was situated near the hearth—about as far from her as he could manage—and lowered himself slowly. His entire body was on alert just as he'd been as a child. He'd never known what would set her off, only that it was almost always him. His disdain of clothing, his particularity about food, his hatred of being touched.

"You're as aloof as ever," she said.

Particularly with you. "And you're as critical as ever. I am not your child anymore."

Her eyes flashed with that coldness again. "You will always be my child."

Unfortunately. "Yet I am now the earl, and I would demand a measure of respect."

Her eyes widened briefly, and she inclined her head. "Spoken like a true earl." Was that pride in her voice? Bran took no pleasure in it. "I'm glad to see it," she said. "Will you be looking for a countess?"

He didn't want to share his plans with her. He didn't want to share anything with her. He had no intention of reestablishing a relationship of any substance. "Yes."

"Excellent. There are several lovely young women who've come out this year and last. Lady Philippa Latham would be a grand match, but the rumor is that she'll wed the Earl of Saxton. Ah well, he is the heir to a dukedom, so I suppose you can't compete with that."

This was the mother he knew—blaming him for things that he couldn't control. Except in his youth, she'd insisted that he could control what he wore or ate. She'd never understood the near pain it had caused him. Sometimes donning clothing had been akin to a thousand pins poking into his skin. Or what he imagined that to be anyway.

"Nor do I wish to," Bran said. "I'm not in any hurry to marry. Furthermore, I do not want or need your advice or assistance."

"You must beget an heir. At least I hope you can. Eight grandchildren and not one of them is a boy." The contempt in her voice was clear. "I managed two spares, and sadly, they were needed."

Did she miss his brothers? He'd thought she would've been practically prostrate with grief, but she'd never been terribly demonstrative. In fact, one of the things that bothered her most about Bran's "defiance" was his open and deplorable show of emotion.

"Believe me, I wish I hadn't been needed." Then he could be back in Barbados, and he wouldn't have had to tear Evie away.

The muscles in his mother's jaw clenched. "Yes, well, here you are. We all do our duty."

"Tell that to my daughter. She's left the only home she's ever known and now finds herself in a strange place."

Her eyes flashed with offense. "England isn't strange. It's her home. She simply requires care to help her adjust."

Bran narrowed his eyes at her for a moment. "You assume I haven't thought of that. She has a nurse and a governess. Both are quite accomplished."

"Wherever did you find them?" She asked as if he wouldn't know where to look. And he supposed he hadn't if not for the help and support of the Kendals, and most importantly, Mrs. Shaw herself.

As if conjured by his thoughts, she arrived at the sitting room door with Evie. Both of them looked rather charming—their gowns were the same color. Had they planned that?

Evie eyed her grandmother with a blend of curiosity and caution.

Bran's mother reacted to the direction of his gaze, pivoting on the settee so that she faced away from him and toward the doorway. "My goodness, is this Lady Evangeline?" The question held a wonder that Bran had never heard from his mother. It made him unsettled.

Evie took three steps toward her and performed a beautiful curtsey. "Good afternoon, Grandmother."

"Come and sit with me, dearest." She patted the settee next to her, and Bran had to bite his tongue lest he tell Evie to sit somewhere else instead. "Is that your governess?" She flicked a half-interested glance at Mrs. Shaw.

"Yes," Evie said, smoothing the skirt of her dress down over her knees after she perched on the edge of the settee. "Mrs. Shaw is the sister of the Duchess of Kendal. She's a splendid governess."

Bran's mother's eyes darted to his with surprise. "Indeed?" She looked toward Mrs. Shaw, who remained at the threshold, her expression serene. "Are you going to join us, Mrs. Shaw?"

Bran blinked at his mother. Had she just invited the governess to sit with them? Bran would've wagered everything he owned against such an occurrence.

Mrs. Shaw's brows elevated slightly as she looked to Bran. He understood her question and inclined his head in response. She moved slowly into the room and took the chair to his right, across a low table from the settee with Evie and her grandmother.

Bran watched as his mother smiled dotingly at his daughter. He'd never, ever seen an expression like that on her face. "How do you like London?" she asked Evie.

"It's a bit dreary compared to home," Evie answered.

"Now then, *England* is your home," she said disapprovingly. There was the mother he knew and despised.

"I suppose it is now." Evie's tone was sullen, and she kicked her legs a few times. She stopped abruptly, and Bran attributed that to the glance she darted toward Mrs. Shaw. Bran looked in her direction and saw that she was watching Evie with encouragement. Her presence was somehow helping this moment, and Bran wouldn't forget it.

"Come now, dearest," his mother said, making Bran cringe with the use of an endearment. He tried to think of what she'd called him and realized she hadn't called him anything nice or pleasant. He'd just been sardonically referred to as "Bran the Defiant."

"I know England must be very different, but you'll come to love it more than you did that other island.

Ours is far bigger, you know. And we have large, remarkable cities and of course many more people like us."

"What do you mean, 'like us'?" Evie asked.

Yes, Bran wanted to know the answer to that too.

"I mean more educated and refined people. Your father is an earl now. You understand how important that is, that he has very specific duties to his country, people, and the crown." She flicked a glance toward Bran, as if asking if he understood that as well. Of course he did. It was like an albatross around his neck.

Evie looked at Bran and gave him a small smile. "Yes, but he's still my papa."

Bran's mother addressed Mrs. Shaw. "What do you plan to teach Lady Evangeline?"

"All manner of things. I've only just begun my employment. I'm still ascertaining what she knows."

The dowager countess pursed her lips. "She's only five. What can she possibly know?" Her aghast tone made Bran's teeth grate.

"I'll be six next month, and I can read," Evie said, somewhat defensively which only exacerbated Bran's irritation. How dare his mother make Evie feel bad—Bran wouldn't tolerate it. "And I know my numbers up to one thousand."

"She's already completing mathematical equations," Mrs. Shaw added.

Bran's mother looked at Evie and…smiled? "How wonderful. What a bright girl you are."

Bran was shocked to see her approval. He distinctly recalled her saying that his younger sister needn't learn anything from books, that her most important accomplishments were to be beautiful and accommodating. That his sister had adored books from a very young age had been a problem, and so she'd learned to hide them.

"She reminds me a bit of Gwen," Bran said, thinking that he ought to arrange to see his sister. "Do she and her husband ever come to London?" She'd married last year, and they lived somewhere in the north of England.

"They haven't yet. I just saw them last month, and they're quite well."

Bran wouldn't take her word for it. He and Gwen didn't correspond often, but she'd written to him when she'd become betrothed, and she hadn't sounded all that enthusiastic. But then what did he know? She was ten years his junior, and as a result they'd never been very close.

His mother turned her attention back to Mrs. Shaw. "How did you come to be a governess? Your sister is the Forbidden Duchess, is she not?"

Bran flinched at the nickname. He recalled the conversation he'd had with Kendal and the others at Brooks's. But to hear his mother say the name in front of the duke's sister-in-law seemed rude. Then again, Bran could fit everything he knew about Society's rules into his pocket.

Mrs. Shaw, to her credit, didn't react. Her composure and expression remained serenely intact. "Yes, she is. I'm widowed, and I wished for an occupation of some kind."

"I see." His mother pursed her lips and gave Mrs. Shaw a condescending glance that flayed Bran's nerves.

He wouldn't stand for any sort of disparagement about Mrs. Shaw from his mother. "We're quite fortunate to have her, aren't we, Evie?"

Evie's eyes glowed, and her face took on the most

animation it had since her arrival. "Oh yes. She's such fun." She smoothed her hands over her skirt again. "She also teaches me many things."

"Well, that's good, then. Now, Lady Evie," his mother said, "as the daughter of an earl, you must learn to comport yourself with poise and confidence. You must be well-spoken but not overly talkative. I'm sure your governess will ensure these things." She sent another patronizing look toward Mrs. Shaw. "Nevertheless, I shall be here to oversee your upbringing as well."

Bran froze. He didn't want her meddling in their lives. He hadn't given much thought to it but rather hoped she'd go back to Durham. Where *had* she been living since her husband had died? It didn't really matter, nor did Bran care.

"Aren't you returning to Durham?" he asked tightly.

"No, I'll stay in London for the Season. I've rented a small town house." She smiled at Evie. "Now I can visit often."

Bran abruptly stood. If he didn't move, he worried he might say or do something he shouldn't, such as cast off his cravat. He paced to the windows and back again, noting that Mrs. Shaw was watching him.

She rose from her chair and looked at her charge. "Come, Evie. I think we've stayed long enough. It was a pleasure to meet you, Lady Knighton."

"And you, Mrs. Shaw. I do hope you'll keep me apprised of Evie's progress. I'll be sure to send along anything I think would be helpful in her tutelage."

Mrs. Shaw blinked, and Bran suspected her smile wasn't entirely genuine. "That is most kind of you. I shall look forward to it."

"Goodbye, Grandmother," Evie said as she slipped

from the settee.

"Goodbye, dearest."

Bran gripped the back of his chair as Mrs. Shaw and Evie left. They were scarcely gone before he turned on his mother. "You will not participate in Evie's upbringing. I'll allow you to visit *when invited* and nothing more."

His mother stood, her gaze frosting. "Without the influence of a mother, she needs me."

"No, she doesn't. I'd rather she were raised by wolves." He stepped around the chair and speared her with an intense stare, allowing all the rage from his childhood to wash over him. "You forfeited the right to be a mother every time you called me worthless, every time you struck me, and every time you looked at me with disappointment and loathing. As you pointed out, I will always be your child. I should think that would've counted for something, but with you, it didn't. As a parent myself, I feel a connection to my child—to love and cherish and protect her. I never felt any of those things from you. I won't allow you to poison my daughter."

She stared at him a long moment. "Poison?" she asked softly. "I don't think I poisoned you at all. Just look at the man you've become. Your father would be so proud."

His father, but not her. And he wasn't even sure he believed that. "I think it's time you go. I'll inform you when you may visit again."

She nodded, and he was surprised that she didn't argue or berate him. He was also glad.

After she left, he made his way to his office, feeling a bit dazed by the entire encounter. He stripped off his cravat and tossed it onto a chair along with his coat. He unbuttoned his waistcoat but didn't remove it.

His mother was everything he remembered while managing to be something different at the same time. Was she simply a better grandmother than mother? He shook his head, unsure if he'd ever be able to puzzle it out.

"Lord Knighton?" Mrs. Shaw's voice intruded into his thoughts.

He'd moved behind his desk and looked toward the door where she stood. Again, he wanted to ask her to call him Bran but knew she would say it wasn't seemly. His eye caught his discarded clothing, and he remembered that he didn't care. "I'd like you to call me Bran."

Her eyes widened, and she gave her head a small shake. "I couldn't."

"You *could*. Knighton still seems so foreign to me. Could you please try?"

"I'll try, but I make no promises."

"Fair enough. Come in." He gestured for her to sit in the chair that wasn't draped in his garments. "Sorry, I'm afraid I had to disrobe."

"I see that. I'm growing used to it. Or trying to, anyway." She dropped into the chair.

"If you'd like to go about without your corset, I wouldn't object."

Her eyes widened again, but the reaction in their depths was different. This wasn't surprise, but perhaps shock with a dash of…titillation? He suffered his own reaction—desire. He thought of her without her corset. Or her chemise. Or any of her clothing. He abruptly sat down, lest she notice the hardening of his cock.

"I came to talk about your mother." She ignored his last comment, and he decided that was for the best. It was bad enough that half his brain was currently fantasizing about her, nude and spectacular.

"My mother," he repeated in an effort to coax his *entire* brain to focus on what it ought.

"Evie was nervous to meet her."

"I know. And how did she feel after?" Bran mentally chastised himself for not immediately going up to see his daughter. He'd been too wrapped up in his own response.

"Better, but… She doesn't know what to make of the relationship between you. She asked me if you liked her. Haven't you discussed any of this with her?"

Hell. "I hadn't thought it was necessary." Because they'd been in Barbados. But now they were here, and his mother apparently wanted to be an active part of their lives. He wanted to throw something. "It is, of course."

"I think so. I'm happy to help in any way that I can."

To do that, she'd have to understand. "Will it come as any surprise to you to hear she was as cold a mother as you can imagine? I was a difficult child, by all accounts, and my brothers were perfect. We looked different—they were beautiful and golden-haired—and we acted different. They were charming, and I was…defiant."

"But you *are* handsome." She immediately blushed and looked down at her hands.

His cock, which had begun to diminish, grew once more. "Thank you."

"What do you mean defiant?" she asked.

"I refused to wear clothing or eat what I was served and any number of other things. I didn't try to be naughty or difficult. I just was. My mother showed no compassion, no care. She punished me for every shortcoming and ensured that I knew I wasn't as good as my brothers. She constantly told me that it was fortunate I was the third son and would never be called upon to be the earl."

While he'd spoken, she'd raised her hand to cover her mouth, which had opened wider with each horror he'd revealed. She finally lowered her hand to her lap. "I'm so sorry. Of course you don't want her participating in Evie's care."

"I do not. I informed her that she would be allowed to visit once a month, upon my invitation. Some months I may not feel inclined."

She nodded slowly. "I don't know what to say. I'd thought losing my mother was the worst that could happen to a child, but I think I was wrong."

Yes, he thought it was perhaps better to have lost a loving parent than to have suffered one's abuse. "Do you remember her?"

She shook her head, and there was a deep sadness in her gaze. "Not really. I was five when she passed."

"Evie already doesn't remember hers." He glanced toward the open crate on the floor. "Those are our things from Barbados. There's a miniature of Louisa in there. I should put it in Evie's chamber."

"That's a lovely idea. I wish I had one of my mother."

"Have you no image of her?"

"My father has one. He'd always intended to have it copied for Nora and me, but he never managed to do so."

Bran nodded. "You're not close to him?"

Her shoulders arced in a slight shrug. "Not particularly. Nora says he was different before Mama died, but I don't remember."

He supposed that made sense, especially if he'd loved his wife. Bran wondered if he seemed different after Louisa's death. He didn't *feel* different. But then he wasn't sure the love he'd felt for her had been the kind that altered one's soul. He knew what that felt like because it was how he'd describe his love for Evie.

Mrs. Shaw looked at the crate. "You took my advice."

"It was excellent, yes. Thank you." She'd been here only a day, but already he felt her presence quite profoundly.

"I'm glad." She studied him briefly, then stood. He didn't want her to leave yet. "I think you should talk to Evie about your mother—don't tell her the specifics, but she should understand why you think it's best for her to have a limited relationship with her grandmother."

Bran scrubbed a hand along his jaw. He wasn't sure how to do that, but she was right that he needed to. "I'll do that." He stood and walked around his desk to where she was standing. "I can't thank you enough for agreeing to be Evie's governess. You've already made such a wonderful impression on the household—on us."

Pink bloomed in her cheeks. She was incredibly lovely. He remembered the pillowy softness of her lips beneath his and the fervent grasp of her hands on his back and neck. The temperature in the room elevated, and he was glad he'd shirked his coat.

"That's…good." She pulled her gaze from his and turned toward the door. "I need to get back upstairs." She quickly fled, leaving Bran to realize he had a very big problem. Yes, they were friends. And yes, they could make this arrangement work. But he still wanted her. And if he was reading her correctly, she wanted him too.

Chapter Ten

"SO THE PRINCES were buried there?" Evie pointed at the White Tower.

"They were, but then they were moved." Becky scanned the guidebook in her hand. "I can't believe they were murdered."

Evie shivered. "Let's read the part about the Jewel Office again."

Jo looked over at the White Tower and tried to imagine the two boys but decided she didn't want to. She'd much rather enjoy this pleasant spring day with Knighton, Evie, and Becky.

They'd made plans to come to the Tower of London and had invited Nora and Titus and their children. Titus had been unable to attend, and Nora had decided that this excursion might be a little too much for Christopher yet. Consequently, Knighton had offered to just bring Becky along. The girls were having a marvelous time, and Jo, as the governess, was delighted to see them reading the guidebook Knighton had purchased for sixpence as soon as they'd arrived.

The girls walked a few feet in front of them, and Knighton noted, "What a dreadful story to include in the guidebook. Don't they realize children might read it?"

"It's history," Jo said, though she agreed with his assessment that it was a bit ghastly. "It's important for children to learn history, even when it's ugly."

"I suppose that's true. I recall learning all sorts of

things about various battles."

The girls had moved a little farther ahead but still well within sight. Becky turned her head to look at them. A moment later, Evie did the same.

"They look like they're plotting something," Knighton said.

Perhaps, but they were five-year-old girls. What could they possibly be up to? "Nonsense, they're just having fun. I'm glad they have each other."

"I am too. Becky's made this transition far more bearable for Evie." He shot her a warm glance. "As have you."

Jo didn't think she'd done all that much. "I appreciate the sentiment, but I've scarcely done anything."

He paused and looked at her intently. "You shouldn't do that."

She stopped. "Do what?"

"Diminish your talent or your gifts. You're an exceptional woman."

She blushed and turned from him to start walking again. He kept doing that—making her blush. He said things to her and looked at her in ways that evoked a heady response. Matthias had never, ever made her feel like that.

He had, however, made her feel worthless, as if she were a grave disappointment. She supposed that was why she balked from praise. "I don't know what to say to that."

"That's just it. You don't have to say anything. Accept who you are."

She thought she had, but it did seem that she was trying to sort out who she was. She was the vicar's widow and the duchess's sister. But who was Jo? Right now she was a governess, and it was the most comfortable she'd felt. With the exception of the way Knighton provoked her. The other day in his office after his mother had left, there'd been several moments when she'd been drawn to him, both from the things he'd revealed about his childhood and from the way he'd looked at her. Then she'd gone and called him handsome, voicing the thought that had vaulted into her head when he'd compared himself to his brothers. She'd immediately wanted to defend the notion that he wasn't attractive, and she'd done so without thinking of the consequences.

She glanced over at him. "I'll…try."

"Good," he said, looking appeased. "Need I remind you of the critical role you played in hiring the cook yesterday?"

"All I did was ask her to demonstrate something so we could be assured of her skill." She realized she was doing it again. She *had* contributed something valuable. "It was a rather good idea, wasn't it?'

He smiled at her. "*Yes.* It was brilliant. Not only were we able to test her cooking, we also learned how she worked in the kitchen with the other staff. They liked her immediately."

This was true. The poor scullery maid who'd been cooking—or trying to, anyway—had practically cried with relief when she realized she wouldn't have to do it anymore. "I've been thinking about Tilly," Jo said. "She isn't very happy in the kitchen, and she mentioned to me that she'd been hoping to train to be a maid. You could move her into the open position upstairs and find someone else to assist Mrs. Fletcher."

"See why you're so invaluable?" he asked. "You've just given me an idea. Rather than interview candidates for the butler, I think I'll promote Bucket. He's demonstrated an excellent fortitude and willingness to learn. He's also ambitious."

"He sounds well suited. That means you'll only need a new footman and whatever assistance Mrs. Fletcher requires in the kitchen."

"So it seems. I wonder if Mrs. Fletcher knows of people to hire. I'll speak with her later. Thank you for your assistance with these issues." He paused to look at her. "I'm not at all sure what we would do without you."

She was about to demur but caught herself. "You're welcome."

The girls had stopped up ahead and were speaking with a boy who was perhaps a few years older than them. Jo and Knighton caught up and overheard their conversation.

"That's where they chopped off people's heads," the boy said.

"Like Henry the Eighth's wives," Becky breathed, her eyes round.

"One woman was struck eleven times before she died!" the boy declared, eliciting gasps from both girls.

"Thomas!" A woman came striding toward them. "There you are. You mustn't wander off." Her gaze caught Jo's. "Good afternoon."

"Mama, this is where they beheaded all the political prisoners," Thomas said.

"Not all of them," Jo said. "This is where the more private executions took place, particularly those of women. Most were public and occurred on Tower Hill."

"Can we go see that too?" the boy asked his mother.

The woman glanced at Jo again. "Uh, we'll see."

"It's not too far." Jo gestured to the northwest. "It's just beyond the tower that way."

The woman smiled. "Thank you. Perhaps we'll see your family there later." Her gaze flicked from Jo to Knighton to the girls.

She thought they were a family.

Jo's chest tightened. That was the identity she wanted—and the one she couldn't have. But right now, in this moment, she could pretend…

The girls waved goodbye to Thomas as he and his mother walked to join the rest of their family, a man with two smaller children in tow.

"Do you want to go to Tower Hill?" Knighton asked the girls.

"I don't know," Evie said. "But I want to see the jewels. Can we go there now?"

"Yes, the jewels!" Becky crowed.

Knighton gestured forward with his arm. "Lead on."

The girls spun about with their guidebook and plotted a path past the church to the Jewel Office. Knighton paid the shilling admission fee for each of them, and they went inside, where it was quite crowded.

"This is a popular exhibit," he said, as they were forced closer together by the number of people crammed into the space.

"Yes," Jo murmured, all too aware of his proximity and fresh clean scent that reminded her of sunshine and summer. She imagined all of Barbados must smell like him.

They made their way to the first exhibit, and Jo worked to keep her eye on the girls. "Don't get too far ahead," she cautioned them.

"Yes, Jo," Evie answered.

Jo imagined what it would be like if she'd called her Mama as that boy had done outside. Had Knighton heard what the woman had said about them being a family? He had to have, yet he hadn't said anything.

Just stop with all this nonsense. They are not your family.

No, they weren't, but she was, as Knighton had said, an important part of their household. At least for now. She'd take that and cherish it for as long as it lasted.

Knighton stood just behind her—close enough that she could feel his presence against her back. And then he touched her, a slight push as he leaned into her. "My apologies," he murmured near her ear. "It *is* crowded."

Jo's body burned where he'd touched her. She ached to press back but wouldn't dare.

This was not good. The awkwardness she'd feared had progressed to an agitation. Within the household, they'd become familiar—sharing information and working in tandem to solve problems, such as with the staff—and they slept across the hall from each other. That alone was enough to send Jo into a state of hyperawareness that sometimes made it difficult to find sleep. She'd never experienced a pull toward her husband. Being with him had been a duty and a chore. Knighton was altogether different, as evidenced by the kisses they'd shared at the ball. They'd left her wanting more, which frightened her. She had to believe intimacy was far more appealing than what she'd experienced, and yet she was too afraid to find out.

Not that it mattered. It wasn't as if he were knocking on her door, seeking her out.

They moved on to the next exhibit, the girls chattering excitedly. Jo loved watching their enthusiasm. "They're really enjoying themselves," she said to Knighton as they followed behind.

"Yes. Are you?" he asked as they stopped at the next exhibit.

"I am." She turned to face him and at that moment was jostled from behind so that she was pushed into him. She caught his shoulders as his arms came around her waist. She sucked in a breath, too aware of her breasts grazing his chest and the intensity of his gaze.

"I've got you," he said.

She ought to step away from him, but she could still feel people behind her, forcing her too close. Then she noticed that both girls were staring up at them with avid curiosity.

Jo withdrew her hands from him as if she'd been burned and backed away, bumping into whoever was behind her. She forced a laugh. "Too crowded. Let's hurry through the exhibit."

She flicked a glance toward the girls, who seemed to blink in unison before pivoting toward the next display.

Knighton slipped a finger between his cravat and his neck. "Yes, let's."

Was he all right? She realized he looked a bit flushed, perhaps from the crowd.

For the rest of the tour through the Jewel Office, she was careful to keep the girls between her and Knighton. He kept fidgeting with his cravat, and beads of sweat had gathered at his temple.

When they were finally outside again, the girls walked ahead, once again poring over the guidebook.

She walked beside Knighton. "Your clothes are bothering you."

He inhaled. "Yes, but it's more than that. The jostle of people inside… I find it intolerable."

"It was quite close." She looked at him intently. "Were you uncomfortable?"

"Vastly. I hate other people touching me."

She knew he couldn't mean everyone. "What do you mean? Evie hugs you, and it doesn't seem to cause you discomfort."

His features relaxed, and she realized just how tense he'd been. "No. Evie doesn't cause me discomfort. But when I come into contact with almost anyone else, I feel as though I want to crawl out of my skin."

That sounded awful. And he'd said "almost anyone." Where did she fall in that spectrum? They'd touched more than once inside, including a rather intimate moment, not to mention the kisses they'd shared at the ball.

He seemed to follow the path of her thoughts. He paused, his gaze boring into hers. "I don't mind you touching me. In fact, I rather like it."

The heat she'd felt in the exhibit gathered between them and expanded into something palpable. It wasn't awkwardness or even agitation between them any longer—it was something far more primitive. And she had no idea what to do about it.

"DO TELL ME how your visit with your mother went last week," Lady Dunn said as she set her teacup down. "I see her portrait is no longer there." She inclined her head toward the bare spot on the sitting room wall.

Bran uncrossed his legs. "It went as well as could be expected, I suppose. I've set specific limitations regarding our interaction, so I don't believe she'll be a nuisance. Must we speak of her?"

Lady Dunn chuckled. "Of course not. But beware, my boy, she's always a nuisance, even if you don't see her."

That was probably true, and he ought to ask what damage his mother could do, but decided he didn't want to know. So long as he didn't have to spend time with her, he would be well.

"What did Evie think of her?" Lady Dunn flashed him an apologetic glance. "I'm still talking about her. Never mind."

"It's fine. You care about Evie, and I can't quarrel with that. My mother was pleasant, but she didn't bring marzipan."

Lady Dunn laughed. "Well, neither did I today, but I did bring Evie some ribbons. Will she be coming down, I hope?"

"Yes, with her governess."

"Excellent. It's Mrs. Shaw, is that correct? I've met her before. I'm surprised she decided to take a position as a governess. She's a widow and the sister of a duchess. One would think she could marry quite well."

Yes, she could. But Bran knew she didn't want to—at least not to him. "I'm not certain she wishes to marry again."

"Fascinating." Lady Dunn gave her head a shake. "Some women prefer their independence. I can't find fault with that since I am one of those women. I also knew I'd never find another man I loved as much as my husband. So I didn't bother. Perhaps it's the same for her."

Bran hadn't considered that. She'd mentioned that she couldn't bear children, but maybe it was more than that. Or maybe it wasn't that at all. Maybe that was an excuse she'd used to avoid telling him the real reason—that she still loved her husband. Did that even make sense? Why wouldn't she tell him the truth? He suddenly wanted to know and vowed to find out.

Mrs. Shaw and Evie appeared at that moment, stepping into the drawing room. Evie went straight for Lady Dunn, who held her arms out for a hug.

"Lady Dunn," Evie cried as she squeezed her. "Did you bring more marzipan?"

"I did not," the viscountess said with a touch of regret. "I hope you aren't cross. I did bring you some ribbons." She opened a bag and showed her the bright colors.

"I love them!" Evie turned her head toward Mrs. Shaw, who stood just inside the room. "Look, Jo!"

Mrs. Shaw stepped forward and examined the ribbons. "Lovely." She dipped a curtsey to Lady Dunn. "My lady, it's nice to see you again."

"And you." Lady Dunn gave her attention to Evie once more. "You must call me Lady D. What do you think?"

Evie nodded. "It's all right that you didn't bring marzipan. I learned to make it at my friend's house." Her eyes widened with mischief, and she smiled. "I'll be right back!" She dashed from the room, and the three of them turned their heads to watch her go.

"Ah, to be able to move like that," Lady Dunn said wistfully. "Sit, Mrs. Shaw. Tell me, how do you like being a governess?"

Mrs. Shaw took a chair near Bran's. "I enjoy it immensely. Evie is a delightful child."

"Yes, you couldn't ask for a better charge, I think. And I imagine you're proving quite helpful to Knighton as he navigates London." Lady Dunn cocked her head to the side. "Although, you're relatively new to town yourself, aren't you?"

"Yes. I've only been here a matter of weeks really. In

fact, I think Knighton and I might have arrived around the same time." She glanced toward him, and it was as if they had a shared history. Of course they didn't, but they were building one.

"She has been most helpful, however," Bran pointed out. "As you know, I've had trouble with the staff, and Mrs. Shaw has been instrumental in smoothing things out."

Lady Dunn gave Mrs. Shaw an approving look. "Have you, then? How wonderful." She tipped her gaze back to Bran. "I did notice you have a new butler. He's quite young. Are you certain he's up to the task?"

"Yes. He stepped in to help with things after I dismissed Kerr, and it occurred to me that he could do the job quite well."

With a cluck of her tongue, Lady Dunn smiled again. "Just like you to resist convention and do what you please."

"That does seem to be working for him," Mrs. Shaw said.

Bran turned his head toward her, surprised by her comment. It wasn't defensive, per se, but she'd leapt to his aid. More and more he felt as though they operated like a team. This was dangerous territory.

Evie ran back into the room and unfurled her hand in front of Lady Dunn. There on her palm was the marzipan turtle she made at the Kendals'. "This is what I made. We have turtles like this on Barbados. Would you like to have it?"

Lady Dunn gingerly picked it up and brought it close to her face to study. "My goodness, this is quite dear. You really want to give it to me?" Her gaze was tinged with emotion as she looked at Evie.

Evie nodded. "That way you have something to

remind you of me, just like I have something to remind me of you."

"My dear girl, this is the most precious thing. But I daresay I don't need an object. You are far too difficult to forget." She set the turtle on her lap. "I'll treasure it, thank you."

Pride welled in Bran's chest. He'd often wondered if he'd be able to raise Evie by himself, especially given his quirks. But she seemed to be doing all right, which he supposed meant he was doing all right too.

They chatted for a while longer about Barbados, and Bran told his godmother about the pressed flowers he'd found and how he wanted to have them framed.

"I know just the place where you can have that done," Lady Dunn said. "I'll write down the address."

"I'd appreciate that," Bran said.

Mrs. Shaw stood. "It's time for us to return to our lessons, Evie."

Evie had sat next to Lady Dunn and now reluctantly pushed to her feet. "If we must. See you next time, Lady D."

"Next time, sweet Evie." Lady Dunn gave her another hug and then Mrs. Shaw took her back up to the nursery.

"Such a wonderful girl," Lady Dunn said. "And Mrs. Shaw seems invaluable."

He recalled using just that word the other day at the Tower of London. "Incredibly, yes. We're very lucky."

Lady Dunn watched him a moment. "It occurs to me that she could be a potential countess. I sensed a certain…connection between the two of you. Have you considered it?"

Hell. He'd more than considered it. He'd bloody well asked her. And she'd rightfully refused. She'd been correct in her assessment—they'd barely known each other, and he'd rushed to ask her. But now they'd been acquainted several weeks, the last of which she'd spent in his household. He saw her multiple times a day, and their bedchambers were across the hall. As of yet, he hadn't encountered her coming or going, but that was only a matter of time. What would happen then? He was more than attracted to her; he wanted her. He thought of her often, particularly when he went to bed at night and imagined her so close and yet so far away.

"Ah, yes. I've considered it."

Lady Dunn's expression flickered with surprise. "Indeed? Is there a reason you wouldn't pursue it?"

Because he'd already been rejected? He might consider trying again, since they knew each other better, and he was certain they held each other in mutual esteem. But there was the matter of her not being able to give him more children. And that, unfortunately, made it a moot issue.

"There are…complications. I don't believe it's possible."

Lady Dunn's eyes narrowed, and she waved a hand. "Stuff and nonsense. Anything is possible if you try."

Bran didn't believe that. As a child, his mother had railed at him about his idiosyncrasies, telling him that if he only *tried*, he'd be able to get through the day wearing everything he ought. "That's something you tell children to motivate them."

"It's also something you do if you're tenacious. Have I misjudged you?"

Tenacious. Did he want Mrs. Shaw that badly?

Yes.

Perhaps he should try again.

"I'll consider it some more."

"Good. Do let me know how it goes."

Lady Dunn left a short time later, leaving Bran to wonder just how he was going to make his next move.

Chapter Eleven

JO SET THE book aside on her nightstand. She wasn't particularly tired, but she wasn't enjoying the story either. It was supposed to be a romance, but the characters seemed lacking somehow. Probably because she kept comparing one of them in particular to Knighton.

Bran.

He'd urged her to call him that, but she couldn't. At least not out loud. In her mind, she could think of him as Bran. Just as she thought of him in his preferred state of dress—a loose shirt that exposed his neck and pantaloons or breeches that hugged the athletic slope of his hip and backside. It was an incredibly distracting image, particularly when she was supposed to be focused on other matters. Such as teaching his daughter.

She rolled onto her side but didn't turn down the lamp. In years gone by, she'd wait, nervously, to see if her husband would come to her. He never warned her, just entered her chamber whenever he saw fit. If she had the lamp lit, he invariably turned it down, preferring total darkness when he came to her bed.

How she'd hated those nights.

Stop thinking of him.

She turned her mind back to Bran and instead recalled the feel of his chest beneath her fingertips the other day at the Tower. There'd been a moment when she'd thought he might kiss her again. Which was foolish since they'd been in the middle of a crowded exhibition.

Still, she imagined the sensation—his lips covering hers, their bodies pressed together.

A rap on the door jolted her to a sitting position. No one had ever come to her chamber at this hour. Her first inkling was that it had to be Evie.

Jo climbed out of bed and wrapped a robe around her night rail before padding across the chamber on bare feet.

She opened the door, and her pulse immediately sped. "Knighton."

He stood just over the threshold, garbed in his usual ensemble, but without any stockings or shoes. His feet were as bare as hers. "Good evening. I hope I'm not disturbing you."

"No. Is everything all right?"

His hair was a bit tousled, as if he'd stood outside in a breeze. She saw him on the prow of the ship that had brought him here, his hair wild and his eyes narrowed against the sun. A shiver danced along her spine.

"Yes. Might I come in? I've something to discuss with you."

Alarm overtook the haze of desire that had stolen through her at the sight of him. Was he here to dismiss her? Calling on her at this hour and in her bedchamber seemed…odd. But then she'd well established that Bran was unusual. In fact, she liked that about him.

She peered past him into the corridor. "It's a bit unseemly."

His brow furrowed. "No one knows I'm here. Anyway, so much of what I do is unseemly, why should this be different?"

A bubble of laughter formed in her chest, which

helped her to relax. After all, she had nothing to fear from him. "Come in." She opened the door wider, and he stepped inside. Closing the portal behind him, she moved past him. "What did you wish to discuss?"

He moved closer until he stood about a foot from her. It was well within the proximity that triggered the fluttering in her belly. In fact, over the past several days, she'd only to be in the same room with him to experience a pull toward him that bordered on magnetism. This was *completely* different from when Matthias had come to her room.

His dark gaze settled on hers. "You."

Her flesh tingled with awareness as it had that night at the ball and again at the Tower. When she'd been certain of his intent—that he wanted her. "Me?" The word came out like a mouse's squeak.

"More specifically, your inability to have children. Are you certain of that fact?"

She deflated, feeling suddenly worthless again. Maybe this *was* like Matthias all over again. "Quite."

He tipped his head to the side, regarding her with skepticism. "Indeed? How can you be certain?"

"I was married for eight years. My husband came to my bed…often." In the early years. But the frequency of his visits had diminished. He'd been eager to get her with child, desperate even. And when she'd failed, he'd grown angry and bitter, blaming her both for a lack of skill and ability. As a woman, if she couldn't please him nor give him a child, what point did she have?

Pain shot through her as his taunts and abuse rolled through her brain. She'd pushed them aside for so long.

"That doesn't necessarily mean anything," Bran said, drawing her back to the present, away from the self-loathing. "Perhaps you merely need to try with someone else."

She blinked at him, uncertain she'd heard him correctly. "What are you suggesting?"

"That you invite me into your bed."

Jo took a step backward even while her body thrummed with want. Her brain, however, railed against the idea. She was an abject failure when it came to womanhood. Surely her husband's proclivities and her lack of conception proved that.

"No."

He winced—a very quick tightening of the muscles around his eyes—and if she'd blinked she would've missed it. "Is it that you're still committed to your husband's memory?"

A dark laugh escaped her. She'd done a very good job of hiding the failure that was her marriage. So much so that people kept wondering if she was still in love with Matthias. She'd *never* loved him. She'd hoped to, but he'd crushed that on their wedding night. "Definitely not."

Knighton's brows had climbed at her reaction and now his gaze flickered with approval. "I see," he murmured. He moved forward, narrowing the gap between them to what it had been. "So why refuse me? I want you—very much, if truth be told, and I suspect you want me too."

She did. Also very much. Hell and damnation, this was a terrible tangle. "I can't. I'm not… You wouldn't enjoy it."

His eyes widened briefly before he blinked. Then he stared at her, his lips parting. "I beg your pardon?"

Oh, this was too humiliating. "You need to leave."

He closed the distance between them and took her

hand. He was warm where she was ice cold. "I would too enjoy it."

She tossed his words back at him. "How can you be certain?"

He raked his gaze over her, lingering on her breasts before skimming the rest of her body and then coming back up to rest on her face. "Because I am."

"Well, I am not." She tried to pull her hand free, but he tugged her against him until their chests met. She gasped, and he wrapped his arm around her waist, holding her captive to him.

"You're trembling," he said softly, rubbing his thumb along the back of her hand. "Why are you afraid?"

"I'm not afraid."

"You're lying. Tell me. Have you any reason not to trust me?"

She didn't. "It's too…horrifying."

"Let me understand. You were married eight years, and you think I wouldn't enjoy bedding you. That leads me to think your *idiot* husband said he didn't enjoy bedding you. There was clearly something wrong with him."

Nothing he said could've been more perfect. Jo let out another laugh, this one loud and sharp. She quickly covered her mouth with her free hand.

Bran's brow arched. "I'm right, then. See, the problem was him, not you. You are lovely and beautiful, and you make my teeth ache with need."

His words enflamed her, tempting her to do exactly as he suggested and invite him into her bed. But there had to be a million reasons she shouldn't. Unfortunately—or perhaps fortunately—she couldn't think of one.

For some reason, she told him the truth. "Matthias

could barely reach completion. He said it was my fault, that a real woman would satisfy him. It turned out he preferred the company of men—I caught him a few years ago with his lover. He said that was my fault too, that my lack of skill and inability to give him a child had driven him to find solace elsewhere."

"It's a very good thing he's dead." Bran uttered the words with such chilling menace that Jo shivered. "Everything he ever said to you is a lie."

God, how she loved his chivalrous defense. It only made her want him more. "But what if it isn't?"

"It doesn't seem to be enough for me to tell you that I know. So let me show you." He let go of her hand and brought his fingertips to her face. He lightly traced her lips with the pad of his thumb and caressed along her jaw. "I'll ask you again: will you invite me to your bed?"

She should say no, but she was past the point of should and ought. She wanted to believe what he said but knew she needed to experience it for herself.

She slipped her arms around his waist and pressed her body into his. "Yes."

"Oh, good."

He lowered his mouth to hers, his hand cupping her face as he kissed her. Softly at first, then more deeply as his tongue delved past her lips and explored her mouth. Thoughts and memories of Matthias drifted away under the onslaught of Bran's seduction. She gave herself over completely to him.

His hand moved to the back of her head, clasping her to him as he speared into her mouth. The kiss blossomed into something she'd never experienced—it was hot and wet and filled with desperation. She dug her fingers into his lower back.

He steered her sideways and pivoted her until she felt the bed against her backside. He lifted her and set her on the edge, parting her legs so he could stand between them. Her night rail didn't allow her thighs to completely open, but it was enough that he stood flush with the bed.

Sliding his lips along hers, he moved the kiss to her cheek and jaw, trailing heat to her earlobe and then down along her neck. All this was new territory, her flesh tingling with desire and her core throbbing with need. Not once had she felt this…this *lust.* Maybe there wasn't something wrong with her after all.

But just because she felt this way didn't mean he did.

Except he seemed rather engaged. His hand came up and cupped her breast through her night clothes. Her nipple pulled taut and hard beneath his touch, and she gasped.

He slipped her robe from her shoulders, and it fell down her arms. She pulled them free, and the garment pooled on the bed around her. The neckline of her night rail was rather large, and he tugged it to the side so that he could push her breast up over the edge.

He pulled his head back and looked down at her, his thumb and finger working her nipple into a tight bud. "You're magnificent," he whispered, the words dark and harsh, but oh so arousing.

His hand left her, and she gripped his waist again. "Don't stop."

Peering down at her, he arched a brow. "You like that?"

She nodded, her throat dry with need.

He fingered the edge of her night rail. "I only wanted to take this off. Is that all right?"

She nodded again as he reached for the hem.

"You're going to have to lift up."

Raising her backside, she helped him tug the garment up to her waist. Then he whisked it over her head and tossed it aside.

"Beautiful," he murmured, putting both of his hands on her. He cupped her, his palms massaging her flesh, sending shards of stark need straight to that core between her legs. "So round and perfect. I have to taste."

What?

Before she could fully process what he'd said, his mouth was on her breast, wet and searing. She let out a low cry full of surprise and wonder and craving. She squeezed her eyes shut as if she had to shut down at least one of her senses so that she could survive the barrage.

His movements were light at first, his lips and tongue gently working her flesh. Then he took more of her into his mouth, his hand holding the globe captive to his attention. He pulled back and blew on her before suckling her once more. Instinctively, she thrust her hand into his hair and held him to her. He repeated the actions, blowing and sucking, all while his other hand worked the other breast.

The pulsing between her legs amplified, and her breaths came hard and fast.

"See? You're spectacular."

His words managed to permeate her thick haze of lust. "Are you…enjoying yourself?" she asked, sounding breathless.

"Immensely. I can't get enough of you." As if to punctuate his statement, he moved his mouth to her other breast and took her deep into his mouth, licking and sucking and lightly grazing his teeth along her flesh.

"*Bran.*"

He pulled back, and she opened her eyes. He stared at her, a half smile curving his lips. "You called me Bran. I hope that means that I may call you Joanna. Mrs. Shaw seems rather formal in this instance."

She nodded. "But not outside this room."

"As you command." He took her hand and pressed it to the front of his pantaloons. "Can you see for yourself that I'm enjoying this?"

His cock was rock-hard. She'd been well acquainted with Matthias's, though she didn't think it had ever felt this…substantial. Getting him to full arousal had required a great deal of effort with her hands and mouth, and she'd loathed every minute of it.

She'd expected to flinch upon feeling Bran, but this was already so different from every one of her other experiences. "You're big."

He chuckled. "I'll take that as a compliment."

Since he'd put her hand there, she had to assume he wanted her to do something. "Do you want to show it to me?"

"In a bit," he said. "I've more fun to have—I'm *quite* enjoying myself. Are you?"

She nodded, feeling shy. The throbbing between her legs had lessened a bit since he'd stopped touching her.

"You don't seem entirely convinced. I'll take it personally if you don't enjoy the hell out of this." He lightly pushed her back. "Lie back."

As she reclined over the mattress, his hands came around her breasts once more, stroking and cupping them and reigniting her need. His hands moved down her stomach, tracing over the plane, making her shiver, until they settled on her hips. He guided her legs apart, and again embarrassment washed over her.

She wouldn't ask him to stop, however. Not now. Probably not ever.

"Don't you wish to turn out the light?" She sounded small and tremulous, nervous.

He didn't stop his movements. "Why would I do that? Then I wouldn't be able to appreciate your beauty. I want to see every inch of you." He ran his thumb along the crease between her legs. "*Every* inch."

His fingers played with her flesh, teasing and stroking. Any sense of embarrassment fled and was replaced with sheer pleasure and an overwhelming sense of longing. Matthias had barely touched her there, just to find his way inside. It had been enough for her to realize that something could feel good. Maybe. She wasn't sure. She'd tried touching herself and had felt a mild satisfaction a few times, but this sensation, this incredible arousal, was unlike anything she'd ever known.

Then his finger slipped inside her. She closed her eyes and spread her thighs as wide as they would go, shameless in her need to feel him.

"I think you *are* enjoying this," he said, sliding his finger in and out of her wet sheath.

She wanted to move, but Matthias had always told her to lie still. Bran used his other hand to touch the top of her sex, and she couldn't help her response. She bucked up off the bed, crying out.

"Oh yes, you most definitely are enjoying yourself." He leaned over her—she could feel him against her sensitized breasts. "And lest you think I'm not, rest assured that I am." He kissed her, his tongue meeting hers in long, sweeping movements that echoed what he was doing between her legs.

Suddenly, he was gone from her mouth, and she felt wetness against her sex. Her eyes flew open, and she brought her head up to see what he was doing. His head was buried between her legs, his mouth and tongue kissing her there the way he'd done to her mouth.

Oh, this was too much. She fell back against the bed and closed her eyes once more. He took his mouth away, and she whimpered. His finger stroked into her once more as he worked her flesh. Then his mouth was there again, and she was awash in a building need. It was like a storm gathering, the dark clouds heavy with moisture and tumult. She was those clouds, ready to burst, and yet she wasn't sure she could.

"Come for me." His husky words rained over her, and she moaned as her muscles began to clench. His fingers pumped harder into her at the same time his mouth suckled that sensitive spot at the top of her sex, and her body simply flowed away from her. Like a ship setting sail that she was powerless to stop.

Deep, mournful cries filled the room, and she'd no idea where they came from. Contractions racked her core as lights flickered behind her eyelids. Pleasure arced through her.

She'd no idea how long she spun through the darkness, but eventually, she came back to herself. Her body was limp and exhausted, but utterly sated. Now she knew. The knowledge stole her breath and pushed emotion into her throat.

"Are you all right?" he asked softly.

She opened her eyes slowly and managed to focus on the canopy. She tipped her head to the side and saw him watching her. He seemed genuinely concerned, his gaze warm and sincere.

"I think so. I've never experienced...*that.*"

"Sex with your husband wasn't like this." It wasn't really a question but a statement. And one coated in disdain at that.

"No. He didn't do the things you did."

"Not ever?" Bran shook his head. "Your husband was a fool."

She considered whether to tell him the truth, but that would be to admit the ultimate shame. "He said it was my fault he didn't want me. He said I ruined him...for women." She turned her head away from him and reached for her robe. She felt his hand cover hers.

"Don't." He pulled her up to a sitting position and kissed her. His lips tangled with hers in a sweet dance, and she was surprised to feel desire ignite within her once more. He ended the kiss and looked into her eyes. "It wasn't your fault. He was who he was, and if he didn't like women, that wasn't your fault." He stroked his knuckles along her jawline. "I am desperate to sink into your beautiful sex, but maybe not tonight."

His words seared into her—the first part. She clutched his shoulders. "Yes, tonight. After that, I want to feel the rest. Please."

His lips curved into a purely male and rather predatory smile. "If you insist."

"I do."

He tugged his shirt off and dropped it to the floor.

She stared at the hard planes of his chest. He was broad and muscular, with small red-brown nipples and a light dusting of brown hair between them. "I've never seen a man's chest before." She flicked a glance toward his face. "My husband never removed his shirt. So I've nothing to compare you to. However, I feel certain other men must be wanting next to you."

"You are a boon to my pride." He clasped her hand and pressed it to his chest, laying the palm flat.

She simply felt him for a moment, relishing his heat and hardness. Then she moved it up to trace the hollow of his throat and over along his collarbone, then down to one of those dashing little nipples. "Does this feel the same for you?" She tweaked it lightly. "When you touched me there—" Her breasts felt full and heavy, and heat sparked through her core.

"You liked it."

"Yes." She sounded breathless and eager.

"It's not quite the same, but yes, I like it. I like everything and anything you would want to do to me."

Her mind flashed to the things Matthias had required her to do. She'd performed them out of duty, but for the first time, she saw the allure of touching a man's cock. Not just any man, Bran.

She arched a brow at him and scooted forward to the edge of the bed where he stood. "Anything?" She reached for the buttons on his pantaloons and worked them free.

"Joanna. What are you doing?"

"Exploring. You've done much to dispel my anxiety and my fears. This is part of that. May I?" She hesitated before slipping her hand into his smallclothes. Only he wasn't wearing any beneath his pantaloons. This didn't surprise her given his dislike of most clothing.

He pushed at the garment and wiggled his hips until they fell down his legs, then he kicked them aside. "How's that?"

She stared at his sex, the length curved up from a nest of dark curls. A bead of moisture perched on the tip. She curled her hand around him and stroked his flesh. She went slowly, taking her time to feel every inch of him.

He reached out and caressed her breast, his touch rekindling her arousal and fueling her hand to move faster. She briefly cupped the heavy sacs at the base before bringing her hand up and sliding it back down then repeating the action several times.

His breathing became louder and his fingers pulled and massaged her nipple, distracting her, but in the most delicious manner. She ran her thumb over this tip, finding the moisture. More took its place, and she used her hand to stroke it over his flesh. He moaned.

"*Joanna*."

"You could call me Jo. If you like."

He kissed her in response, his mouth open and wet, claiming hers with a ferocity that drove her to the brink of madness. But a wonderful, delirious madness that she couldn't wait to feel again.

He tugged at her nipple, drawing her to gasp into his mouth. Then he rolled it between his thumb and forefinger before pulling again. Sensation dove through her, making her dizzy with need.

He turned her and pushed her back onto the bed, following her onto the mattress. His hand moved down over her belly and found her sex once more. He tore his mouth from hers. "Are you wet for me?" He pressed his finger into her. "Oh yes. You are an amazing woman, Jo. I will thrash any man who dares say otherwise."

Everything he said increased her urgency. She wanted him inside her now. She wanted that ultimate completion, that unattainable pleasure she'd never dreamed she'd find. "Bran. I need you. Now."

"You are perfect." He kissed her again, hard and deep, his tongue tangling with hers as he moved his body over hers.

She clasped his back, her fingers digging into his flesh as he positioned his cock at her sheath. He worked his way inside, slowly. *Agonizingly* slow.

Opening her thighs and bringing her legs up, she moved her hands down and gripped his backside, pulling him into her with one swift stroke. He filled her so completely and she instantly felt a stab of pleasure. It lessened as he pulled back but then came back tenfold when he surged forward again.

She closed her eyes and cast her head back, moaning. "Yes. Oh my, yes."

He eased back, and she squeezed his flesh, urging him to come back, to move faster.

She opened her eyes and looked up at him. He was watching her, the muscles of his face strained.

"Can I move?" she asked tentatively.

"God, yes. Please do." He drove into her again, and this time, she rose to meet him, arching her hips off the bed.

He groaned and finally moved faster. He claimed her mouth once more as his movements became frenzied, his hips snapping into her thighs.

With each thrust, another stone in her wall crumbled to the ground. Until at last, she broke free. Ecstasy crashed over her, and she cried out, clutching at him as the only anchor in a world that had turned upside down.

He kept moving as wave after wave of pleasure washed over her. Then he tensed, and he shouted. Something incomprehensible and wild. This was *nothing* like anything she'd ever experienced. She was profoundly grateful to him for this gift.

He fell against her but quickly moved to the side so

that he was only partially on top of her. He cupped the side of her face, turning her head toward him, and kissed her. It was quick but delightfully thorough, reminding her of how wonderful she felt.

He rolled completely to his side, and she tucked her head beneath his chin, listening to his heartbeat slow. She closed her eyes and inhaled his fresh, sunny scent. There was something else now too, a musk that spiced the air around them. She nuzzled against his chest, happier and more satisfied than she could remember being.

They lay like that for a while before he pressed a kiss to her forehead. "I should return to my chamber. And you'll want to clean up, probably."

She didn't want him to leave but knew he must. "Yes."

He left the bed and walked around to pull on his pantaloons. As he buttoned the fall, she found her night rail and pulled it on over her head. She'd tidy after he left.

"I took no precautions, so if you *are* with child, I will marry you."

He didn't ask. He expected. Everyone always expected things of her.

But none of that mattered because she wouldn't be with child. "I appreciate your concern, but as I told you, I cannot conceive."

He swept up his shirt and took a step toward her, his sapphire eyes blazing in the lamplight. "I am not convinced, especially after what I learned of your marriage. Take heart, Jo." He leaned in and kissed her. "Good night."

And then he was gone. Jo stared into the empty chamber. Tonight had opened up a world she didn't believe existed. After nearly a decade in the dark, she felt as though the sun had come out and bathed her in warmth and light.

Then he'd mentioned a child, and a dream she'd long ago buried had flashed through her mind. But that was foolish—she knew it wasn't possible. Damn him for summoning even a hint of hope.

As much as it pained her, she almost wished she'd remained in the dark.

Chapter Twelve

BRAN WOKE UP feeling refreshed but also a bit unsettled. Which was odd since he'd enjoyed the best sex of his life the night before. To think that Jo's husband had said she wasn't a real woman… If the man wasn't already dead, Bran would take him out and beat him.

And yet Jo's revelations had made him feel strange. They'd reminded him a bit of his own marriage. It had been far different, of course, but they'd had problems in the bedroom. They'd maintained separate beds because Bran didn't like to feel someone next to him. It stemmed, he knew, from his childhood when he'd loathed being touched by anyone. His brothers had made a game of it, going out of their way to bump into him or find some reason to touch him. It had just been another way for them to torture him.

When he'd gotten older, maybe twelve, he began to learn to suffer through it. He didn't want to give them the satisfaction anymore of frustrating him. He thought he'd conquered that problem, but when he'd married Louisa, he realized he hadn't. She hadn't been too upset about having separate bedrooms, but when it came to sex, she was invariably disappointed when he left her immediately after.

That he'd stayed with Jo last night, even for a short time, had surprised him.

Hudson came to assist him with his preparations for the day, and after Bran was bathed, he started his massage. "You're quite relaxed this morning, my lord. Your shoulders are particularly loose. If I didn't know better, I'd say you were with a woman last night."

They'd noticed years ago that having sex seemed to improve Bran's tension and anxiety. He saw no reason to lie to Hudson. The valet was Bran's closest confidant, and Bran knew anything he told him would be kept inviolate. "I was. I must say, I do feel remarkable today. I'm not even dreading a cravat."

"Well, that's inspiring," Hudson said. "Since you didn't leave the house, I assume it was Mrs. Shaw?"

"Why not the new cook?" She was a few years older than Bran with a rather plain face but a charming, effusive demeanor.

Hudson laughed. He moved down Bran's right arm. "I've watched you with the governess. I haven't seen you look at a woman like that in a long time. Maybe ever."

Bran tipped his head to peer up at him. "What about my wife?"

"It was different. Don't ask me how, it just is. Perhaps because Mrs. Shaw is the governess. She's *forbidden*, and that makes her more attractive."

Bran supposed that was possible, but whatever the reason, he couldn't argue with Hudson's assessment—this was different. Jo was different.

He recalled her sense of wonder and the absolute joy she'd taken from their coupling. She'd truly thought she was to blame for her disaster of a marriage. And make no mistake, it sounded like an utter disaster. Because of her blackguard husband.

Hudson had moved to his left arm. "You're tensing up. What's the matter?"

"Just thinking of something I shouldn't." He

couldn't focus on Jo's husband—it would drive him insane. He had to think it would be even worse for her. She'd lived with him, with his cruelty, for eight years. That left a mark. It had to. He knew from experience. It wasn't until he'd gotten away to Barbados that he'd realized the damage his family had done. On his own, he'd learned to accept who he was and forge his own path without their expectations or demands.

Jo deserved to feel the same freedom and to find the ability to bury the past.

Hudson finished with his massage. "Are you ready to finish dressing? You did say you weren't dreading a cravat."

Bran didn't have to leave the house for a while yet—later he was meeting with Kendal, who'd pledged to help him find his way in the House of Lords. His secretary would be here shortly, but Bran didn't bother with formality with Dixon. "I haven't completely lost my edge," he said wryly. "I'll don the rest before I leave for my appointment."

Hudson inclined his head as Bran stood and left the dressing room. As he walked out of his chamber, he stared at the door to Jo's room. Was she there? No, she'd likely be upstairs with Evie.

He wanted to speak with her but didn't want to interrupt their routine. There'd be time later. He went downstairs, and Bucket met him at the stairs. "Good morning, my lord. A letter arrived for you, and I placed it on your desk."

"Thank you, Bucket. My secretary will be here shortly. Please show him to my office."

Bucket nodded. "Of course."

Bran strode to his office and saw the letter on his desk. He recognized the flourish on the K of his name.

It was from his mother. He didn't really want to open it but supposed he must. Whenever one of her letters would reach him in Barbados, he could ignore it and simply say it had been lost. That happened to correspondence all the time. He also used it as an excuse to write to his parents infrequently. He hadn't bothered writing to his brothers. However, in retrospect, perhaps he should've written to Gwen more often.

Sitting behind the desk, he opened the missive and laid it flat on the desktop.

Knighton,

It's still so strange to address you as such, but I'm getting used to it. I must say you surprised me. Perhaps traveling across the world was precisely what you needed. I should like to know what events you'll be attending in the near future so that I may present you to my friends.

None? Bran supposed he ought to go to something, but reasoned that if Kendal could avoid such nonsense, so could he.

And it wasn't just that his mother would be there, though that was a large part of it. He really didn't care to see her. That she was treating him with deference and even a bit of respect was strange. He didn't know what to do with that.

I look forward to visiting again soon and spending time with my granddaughter. Please advise me when I am invited. I understand your reticence where I'm concerned, but let us not focus on the past. I've missed watching you grow into a man, and I don't wish to miss Evangeline's maturation.

Was this some sort of backward attempt at an apology? He stared at the words on the page, wondering what he could expect from her. He realized he'd thought she'd treat him the same as she always had, but of course it was different now. He was a grown man, the earl. Could he allow a different relationship with her? Did he even want to?

I hope you'll let me know if I can be of assistance to you in any way. I have many skills that could be useful, particularly until you take a new countess. I am and shall forever remain,

Your Mother

Tension coiled through his muscles, and he realized he'd need another massage, probably before he went to meet Kendal. He had no idea how to respond to his mother, so he wouldn't. He wasn't ready for her to visit again either.

He sat back in his chair and stared at the ceiling. What the devil had happened to his life? He missed the sun, the smell of ginger lilies, the feel of the warm sand on his bare feet.

And yet England wasn't as terrible as he'd feared. His household was shaping up, Evie had found a dear friend, his mother was no longer treating him as an aberration, and he'd met Jo.

He liked her very much. And as he'd anticipated, he especially liked bedding her. He hoped she felt the same way and anticipated speaking with her. He rose, intending to find her, damn the routine.

Except Dixon arrived at that moment so he sat back down. There'd be time to speak with her later. And time for his anticipation to grow.

AFTER SUCCESSFULLY AVOIDING Bran for the first half of the day, Jo was glad for the excuse of taking Evie to see Becky in order to avoid him in the afternoon. As it happened, he'd gone out as well, so her plan hadn't even been necessary.

And now, as she sat with Nora in her sister's drawing room, she wondered why she'd bothered at all. Last night had been amazing—never mind the damper he'd thrown on her euphoria at the end—and she ought not feel embarrassed around him.

Perhaps embarrassed wasn't the right word. Her greatest fear was that if they were together, everyone would know what had transpired, as if the evidence of their sin would be written on their foreheads for the world to see.

Sin? Was that how she saw it? She'd listened to Matthias for far too long. He'd told her that sex was a necessary sin—provided they did it to beget a child. And when that didn't happen, what was the point of it? She'd begun to think that it had all been a ruse to cover his own shame.

After Bran had left her, she'd lain awake for some time thinking of what had transpired. He'd completely rewritten everything she knew about intimacy and sex—about herself. She *wasn't* less than a woman, and sexual acts *weren't* horrible. They were, with the right person, quite spectacular.

"You keep doing that," Nora said, eyeing her

carefully.

"What?"

"Smiling to yourself. Is there something I should know?"

Written on her forehead, indeed. Jo leaned forward and plucked a biscuit from the tray. "No." She took a large bite to prevent herself from saying anything further. A part of her wanted to tell Nora what had happened. They'd always shared things. In fact, the only things Jo hadn't told her had been to do with Matthias and their marriage. And it wasn't that she'd been keeping secrets. No, she'd been struggling to survive the guilt and shame of it all.

Nora's eyes narrowed in that older-sister way that seemed to peel away a younger sibling's artifice. "You used to tell me things. I fear the closeness we once shared is a thing of the past."

Oh, she was good. Jo swallowed too quickly and coughed.

Nora's gaze shaded with concern. "Are you all right?"

Jo took a sip of lukewarm tea and nodded. "Yes. I'm fine. I'm better than fine, actually. I don't know that I've been this fine in quite some time."

Nora's eyes widened. "Is that so?"

Jo glanced around the room but knew they were alone. "Something happened with Br—Lord Knighton."

"Were you about to call him by his Christian name?" Nora shook her head. "Never mind. I think I can perhaps guess. I always suspected that the two of you had sneaked off during the Harcourt ball, but every time I tried to broach the subject, you diverted the conversation."

Jo shrugged. "I wasn't ready to say anything." She'd also thought it a one-time occurrence. Could the same be said of last night? He'd given her the impression that he'd like to do it again, and she had no intention of turning him away.

"I hope you won't think this a terrible question, but is that why you went to become his governess, so the two of you could have an affair?"

She couldn't be serious. Jo's jaw dropped, but she quickly snapped it closed. "No." At least not as far as she knew. Was it possible Bran had manipulated the situation to his advantage, that he'd hired her in order to seduce her?

That was absurd. Evie had practically begged for her to be hired. But if that had only served Bran's desires, so much the better. Jo felt a bit queasy.

"That was a terrible question to ask," Nora said.

"Yes, it was," Jo responded quietly. She folded her hands in her lap. "After the marriage I endured, I think I deserve a smattering of happiness."

Nora stood up from her chair and joined Jo on the settee, sitting close beside her. She smiled encouragingly. "Of course you do. I wish you'd tell me what happened with Matthias. I sense you were far more miserable than you've ever let on, and I feel terrible about it."

You should, a tiny voice at the back of Jo's mind said. She hushed that voice. And then she braced herself to finally tell her sister the truth—or at least a portion of it.

"I lay with Bran last night because he's unbearably attractive, and he makes me feel like a desirable woman. Matthias never made me feel like that. He made it clear he disliked sex because I wasn't very good at it, that I was utterly lacking."

With each word she'd uttered, another shade of color had leached from Nora's face until she was nearly white. It took her a moment to respond, but when she did, there were tears in her eyes. "Jo, I had no idea."

"Of course you didn't. I never wanted you to know that I was unhappy. Nor did I want to dwell on it—and I still don't."

Nora blinked. "I understand completely. I wish I'd known."

"What would you have done?" Jo asked. "Nothing. Anyway, it's in the past now, and as I said, I don't wish to dwell on it."

Taking a deep breath, Nora smiled brightly. "Your strength and courage is an inspiration." She gave Jo a sly look. "Things with Knighton are different from with Matthias, I take it?"

"I had no idea what I was missing."

Nora giggled. "It's quite lovely, isn't it?"

Jo grinned. "I might use other words beyond lovely. Such as astonishing. Or incredible."

"And this has been going on awhile?" Nora asked.

"No, just last night, but I expect it will happen again." She *hoped* it would happen again.

Nora's expression dimmed. "I would be remiss if I didn't caution you. What are your plans? Will he marry you?"

"He did offer—at the Harcourt ball, actually."

Nora gaped. "You *were* keeping secrets."

Jo laughed softly. "No, I simply didn't see any reason to tell you something that was of no consequence. We barely knew each other then. Anyway, I can't marry him. He needs a countess who can provide him with an heir."

"So this truly is just an affair, then? What will happen when he does take a countess? Will you stop being Evie's governess?"

These questions were why she'd been hesitant to tell Nora. Or anyone for that matter. They were valid and reasonable, and she ought to consider them. She *had* considered them. It made her feel ill.

"I'm not thinking about that right now. I'm fully committed to Evie—I adore her."

"Of course. I just don't want to see you hurt. You've been through enough." Nora winced and shook her head. "Which is precisely why you deserve this. Just…be careful." She reached out and squeezed Jo's hand, then her eyes narrowed. "And if Knighton hurts you, he'll have me to answer to."

For the rest of the day, Jo couldn't help but think of what Nora had asked her. Had Bran hired her in the hopes that they would have a liaison? She knew that Evie had wanted her too, but Jo couldn't shake the idea that she'd somehow been manipulated. Maybe that was because no decision had ever been truly hers.

She should ask him, but her doubt got the better of her and she left dinner early, claiming a headache. He'd seemed disappointed but also kind.

He hadn't lured her into seduction. But even if he had, did she really mind?

Chapter Thirteen

BRAN COULDN'T DENY that he was frustrated. And not in a sexual way. All right, perhaps in a sexual way too. Could he help it if Jo had awakened a stirring desire within him? He'd thought of little else the past day and a half, and given her behavior, he wasn't sure she'd thought of him at all.

She'd done a fair job of avoiding him all day yesterday and again today, and she'd brushed him off last night with some excuse about a headache. He had to assume he'd done something wrong, but he'd no idea what.

This had happened periodically with Louisa. She'd become cross with him and wouldn't lie with him until he'd apologized. Sometimes he'd discovered what he'd done—said something off-hand that she'd taken poorly or been ignorant of something he shouldn't have been—and others, he'd no idea. Nevertheless, he'd learned that apologizing went a long way to curing a woman's gripes.

He'd try that today with Jo.

Evie came bounding down the stairs with Jo following at a more sedate pace. "Ready for our picnic, Papa?"

He swept her up into his arms and spun her around, making her squeal. "I am, sweetling." He set her down and looked at Jo, who watched them with a half smile. "Let me just grab our picnic basket, and we'll be on our way."

Bran picked up the basket that the cook had prepared for their outing, and Bucket opened the door for them. Bran waited for his daughter and Jo to precede him. He noticed that as soon as they were outside, Evie took Jo's hand. It was a simple gesture, but it warmed his heart to see Evie so comfortable and happy here.

They paused at the bottom of the stairs, allowing him to catch up. Then Evie took Bran's hand too.

Bran recalled walking along the beach in Barbados like this. Except the woman on the other side of Evie had been her mother. He doubted Evie remembered that.

"What have you been doing today?" Bran asked.

"This and that," Evie said. "We measured distances on my map. Did you know that Barbados is over four thousand miles away? Of course you did. You know everything."

Bran laughed. "I do not, but I appreciate your confidence."

"What don't you know?" Evie asked as they made their way toward Green Park.

"So many things, most of them to do with women," Bran said, still thinking of Jo and what he'd done to upset her, if anything.

Evie scrunched her face up and looked at him. "What do you mean?"

He realized he'd said the wrong thing. Again. "Er, nothing. I don't know much about making my way in London society. I get all these invitations, and I've no idea what to do with them."

"You should accept some probably," Evie said. "Right, Jo?"

Bran was curious to hear her opinion.

"Probably. Meeting new people might be nice."

Evie cocked her head to the side and swung her arms, forcing Bran to swing his too, not that he minded. "Hmmm, I'm not sure," she said. "Papa doesn't really like to meet people. He likes to be at home. With me." She grinned up at him.

"That's true. But Mrs. Shaw has a point. I'm an earl now, and I should form some connections at least."

"Becky told me that balls are spectacular with beautiful music, a million candles, and everyone is in their finest. She says her mama wears the prettiest ball gowns." Evie turned her head to Jo. "Do you go to balls?"

"I have. Once, anyway." She flicked a glance toward Bran, and he knew she was thinking the same as him—that the best part of that ball hadn't been music or candles and certainly not clothing. "Governesses don't really go to balls," Jo said.

Evie frowned. "That doesn't seem fair. Why can't you have fun?"

"Let me see if I can explain," Jo said. "It's a bit complicated. There is a hierarchy to London Society, and certain groups aren't invited to Society events such as balls."

"What's hierarchy?"

"A sort of ranking. Such as with peers. A duke is the highest rank, then marquess, then earl, then viscount, and so on. We'll study Debrett's later. *Much* later."

"Becky told me her father is more important than mine. I told her that wasn't true, but I guess it is?" Evie looked at Jo and then Bran.

"I don't think importance has anything to do with it," Jo said.

Bran snorted. "It's all chance. In most cases, some

forefather was given a title that's passed down from father to son. It's entirely possible that someone who's a duke or an earl doesn't really deserve to be." Or want to be, as was Bran's case.

"So most peers haven't really earned their position," Evie deduced, showing a keen intelligence that made Bran's pride swell.

"That's one way of looking at it," Bran said. He hadn't earned his, and he was certain everyone would agree with that fact.

"Well, that's rather silly, isn't it? Ranking people based on their family and allowing that to decide who can go to a ball." Evie stuck her tongue out and trilled her lips to make a rather rude sound he'd taught her a few years ago. He glanced at Jo to see her reaction. She stifled a smile, and Bran did the same.

They'd arrived at the park and paused at the entrance. "Where shall we go?" Jo asked, looking down at Evie.

Evie turned her head this way and that as if she were getting her bearings. At last she pointed to the Queen's Basin. "Over by the water, I think."

As they made their way toward the reservoir, they passed another family, the mother and father holding the hand of a small boy who walked between them. Well, he didn't walk so much as float since he was little enough that they picked him up from the ground every few steps. He giggled every time he took flight, and again Bran recalled similar times with Evie and Louisa. He hadn't really missed his wife in the last couple of years, and especially not since they'd traveled to London. A wave of nostalgia hit, surprising him with its force. He missed his former life, his *home*, and everything that encompassed.

When they reached the water, Bran set the basket down. Jo came to open it at the same time he did, and their hands brushed.

She jerked away, her eyes flickering with a myriad emotions—so fast that he couldn't discern them all. Or any of them really. "I was just going to spread the blanket."

He took a step back. "Please."

She glanced at him before turning her attention to the basket and went about setting up the picnic.

Evie had strolled to the fence surrounding the reservoir, and Bran joined her. "Papa, can we go to the ocean? I miss the ocean."

"Yes. I don't think it's terribly far. I would like that too."

"But it won't be like home. Barbados, I mean." Evie's voice held a note of resignation. She was coming to terms with the fact that they didn't live there anymore. This both relieved Bran and made him sad at the same time.

"No, it won't be the same." Nothing was the same. He looked over to where Jo laid out their picnic. It also wasn't all bad either. "You like it here at least a little bit, don't you?"

Evie turned to him and glanced up at the sky. "I'm glad it's sunny today. I miss seeing its happy face." She took his hand again. "Don't worry about me, Papa. I'm fine. I want to make sure *you're* happy. Come on, let's go eat. Cook said she packed little salmon sandwiches!"

Fish was one of the few things Evie adored, and their new cook had made sure to make it available to her at every meal.

They returned to the blanket, where Jo had everything neatly and appetizingly organized. There was something very natural and comfortable about the entire thing—walking to the park hand in hand, having Jo set up the meal, and now the three of them sitting down together to eat. He could picture them as a family quite easily. The impediment, whether she could give him a son, loomed at the back of his mind. Then came Evie's proclamation that titles were silly. Or at least the inheritance of them. It was all so arbitrary, he realized. They had so little control over things, and that frustrated him.

While they ate, Evie told stories about Barbados, regaling Jo with tales of her pets, including her horse, all of which they'd left behind. Why hadn't he gotten her a new one? Or a cat or a dog? He was an idiot.

"Do you ride well?" Jo asked her.

Evie nodded after finishing the last of her sandwich. "Yes. Papa started teaching me when I was three."

Jo glanced at him in mild alarm. "Goodness, that seems so young."

Bran shrugged. "Things were different there." He looked at Evie. "It occurs to me that you need a new horse. I'll look into it. Would you like that?"

She nodded, smiling widely. "Ever so much, thank you!"

"Evie!" A girl's squeal carried across the reservoir.

Evie squinted in that direction and then jumped to her feet. "It's Becky!"

Becky was with a woman but quickly darted away from her to run around the reservoir. Evie dashed from the blanket to meet her.

Bran smiled as he watched them.

"You're an exceptional father," Jo said quietly.

Bran turned his head and saw that she was watching him intently. "I try. She makes it very easy."

The girls came to the blanket, their arms linked. "Papa," Evie said. "Becky has invited me to come to her house for the afternoon. May I go?"

"I'm not certain it will be all right with the duchess." Bran looked over at Jo in silent question.

"Mama would say it's fine," Becky said, turning to Jo. "Wouldn't she, Aunt Jo?"

"I'm sure she would," Jo agreed.

"Do you have plans for the afternoon?" Bran asked.

"Nothing that can't be postponed," Jo said, turning to Becky. "I can come fetch you later."

Becky's governess finally caught up to them at the blanket. "Good afternoon."

"Good afternoon," Bran said. "The girls have hatched a plan to spend the afternoon together. Can you think of a reason Evie can't return home with you?"

The governess was quiet a moment before shaking her head. "I cannot. I'd planned to work on sewing this afternoon." She smiled at Evie. "Would you like to join us in that endeavor, Lady Evie?"

Becky looked at her friend eagerly. "We're going to make dresses for the puppets Father brought home the other day."

"Oh, that sounds marvelous!" Evie turned to Bran with pleading eyes. "Please, Papa?"

It sounded as though it would be all right with everyone, and he couldn't ignore the fact that it would leave him alone with Jo. "Yes, you may go. Jo will fetch you later. I have to meet with my secretary." He planned to talk with him about procuring a horse.

The girls danced in delight and a few minutes later headed back the way they'd come with the governess.

Jo began to repack the basket.

"Are you in a hurry to return home?" Bran asked.

"You said you have an appointment."

"I didn't say it was immediately."

She kept her gaze averted and busied herself quite thoroughly with her task.

"Jo."

She tipped her head toward him.

"Sit with me. Please."

It took her a minute before she finally sat down next to the basket. Her shoulders were stiff, her back arrow straight.

He scooted closer to her so that only a matter of inches separated them. From here he could just catch her scent. It tantalized him almost as much as her simple proximity. Her long lashes fluttered against her cheeks as she blinked toward the basin. Her lips were slightly parted. He imagined taking her in his arms and kissing her, pressing her back against the blanket, the sun warming them from above. He suddenly had an image of doing the same thing, but back on Barbados, on the beach, with the warm surf stealing over their bodies. His cock grew stiff, and he forced himself back to *this* moment.

"You've been avoiding me. Did I do something wrong? Do you regret the other night?" He held his breath, almost afraid of her answer.

She flashed him a tentative glance. "I… It's nothing."

He moved a bit closer until they were nearly touching, his hip and her knee. "It's never nothing where you're concerned."

She swung her head toward his and pierced him with an inquisitive, almost accusatory stare. "When you asked me to be your governess, what were your intentions?"

He blinked, unsettled at her dark tone. "For you to be Evie's governess. I'm not sure I understand your question."

She pressed her lips together, and he sensed she was dissatisfied with his answer. But of course she was. He had no idea what she was talking about. Unless…*hell.* He sorted it out just as she said it: "Did you hire me so that you could seduce me?"

"Of course not." Except that he *had* hoped to at least kiss her again. "I did not hire you for that sole purpose. However, I am also not sorry that things between us…progressed."

"So you considered the possibility?"

"I would be lying if I said I wasn't hopeful—if you recall, I proposed marriage to you."

"Which I firmly declined," she said sternly. "And would still decline."

He began to grow irritated. Yes, she'd made her rejection of him quite clear. "Because of that, I didn't think anything would happen. But I stand by what I said: I don't regret it." He peered at her closely. "Is there some other reason you declined my proposal?"

"I don't need one. I should think the reason I provided for my refusal would be more than enough."

It would—he needed an heir, and she supposedly couldn't give him one. However, he now wondered if it was more than that. He knew she'd been unhappy in her marriage, that her husband had been the worst sort of ass. Perhaps she didn't see any point to marriage, especially if she couldn't have children.

His head was beginning to ache. Women were incredibly complicated. "Yes, your rejection was more than enough. I truly didn't expect to seduce you, nor did I plan to. I'm not a glutton for punishment."

Her features softened. "I never meant to injure you. My apologies."

"Would you like to return to the way things were?" He feared he knew the answer to that. It seemed that she *did* regret what had happened.

She leaned toward him, and his breath caught once more. "I do not."

His pulse picked up speed, and he stared at her mouth. "I see. Well that's good to know." If frustrating, given their current location. He wanted to take her into his arms. "I would kiss you now, if I could."

Her lips parted, and her chest rose and fell more rapidly as her breathing quickened. "I would like that. Tell me."

What was she asking? What he would do? "I'd come closer and press you back onto the blanket. Then I'd put my mouth on yours, and I'd slide my tongue inside."

"I'd meet you. And I'd strip your cravat away." She gave him a sultry look that told him she knew just how much he would like that.

Her words fired his lust. His cock began to throb. "I would lift your skirts—"

"Knighton!" A loud feminine voice interrupted their mutual verbal seduction. Bran turned his head and saw Lady Dunn and a younger woman, her companion, he thought, coming toward them.

Bran swore silently. He needed to get up. And demonstrate his full arousal to all and sundry. He glanced toward Jo, who looked suddenly anxious. He took her hand and helped her stand. "If you could just position yourself slightly in front of me, that would be helpful." He dipped his gaze down toward his groin, and her eyes widened.

She nodded infinitesimally and clasped his hand while he stood. Then he pulled her to her feet.

"Good afternoon, Lady Dunn," Bran said.

"Good afternoon, how delightful to see you here." She transferred her gaze to Jo. "And you, Mrs. Shaw. Is Lady Evie somewhere about?" She looked around.

"No, we encountered Lady Rebecca, and she went home with her," Bran said. "Mrs. Shaw and I were just about to pack up the remainder of our picnic."

"How charming." Lady Dunn gave him a knowing stare sparkling with approval. "Will I see you at the Andover ball this evening?"

He couldn't be sure but thought it was probably one of the many invitations he'd ignored. "Ah, I wasn't planning on it."

Lady Dunn clucked her tongue. "My dear boy, you must get out more. You needn't stay for a long while, just show your face. And allow me to introduce you to some people—it will make me so happy." She looked at him expectantly, her gaze hopeful.

He wanted to refuse but couldn't. "I'll find you there."

She grinned. "Excellent. I'm so glad we ran into you this afternoon. See you tonight." She turned to Jo. "Good afternoon, Mrs. Shaw."

"Good afternoon, Lady Dunn." Jo waited until Lady Dunn and her companion had turned about before bending down to pick up the blanket and quickly folding it before stashing it in the basket. She handed it to Bran. "Would you mind taking this back to the house? I'm going to walk straight to Nora's."

Disappointment that he wouldn't get to spend the

walk with her dampened his mood, but he took the basket. "Of course. I'll see you later."

She blinked, as if confused by that statement. "You have a ball to attend. I expect you'll return rather late, and I will likely be asleep."

Hell and damnation, why had he agreed to go to the damn thing? To please his godmother. "I'll endeavor to return at a reasonable hour."

She shrugged. "If you're so inclined. See you at dinner." She turned, and he watched her circuit the reservoir.

What had happened? She'd flirted with him—no, *teased* him—before Lady Dunn's untimely arrival, and now it was as if she were coated in frost. Well, he'd warm her up later.

He could scarcely wait.

SLEEP CONTINUED TO evade Jo as she flipped to her back once more and stared at the canopy overhead. She was jealous. Jealous of all the people at the stupid Andover ball tonight who got to spend time with Bran. Of all the women he'd dance with.

Do you really think he'll dance?

She rose up on her elbow and punched her pillow with a grunt. He might not dance, but he was still moving about in a world she had cut herself off from when she'd agreed to become his governess. It wasn't lost on her that Lady Dunn hadn't asked if *she* was attending the ball tonight.

Which had led Jo to wonder if she could. She'd considered asking Nora when she'd gone over there to fetch Evie but had ultimately decided against it. Nora would've asked if she was having second thoughts about being a governess. And she wasn't. No, she was having second thoughts about what she was doing with Bran.

She settled back against the pillow and exhaled. She'd meant it when she'd told him she didn't regret lying with him the other night. And she'd thoroughly enjoyed their banter before Lady Dunn had interrupted them. She envisioned another magical night before them. Instead, he was at a ball. Without her.

She threw off the covers and stood from the bed, sliding her feet into a pair of slippers. Pulling on her robe and tying the sash, she made her way from the room. Maybe a book would help her fall asleep.

She crept down the stairs and made her way to Bran's office. It was dark and cold without him in it. It wasn't *completely* dark—embers from the fire burned low in the grate. She set her candlestick on his desk, and her eye caught the jar of shells. Evie had told her that she'd collected them in Barbados every time she and her father had walked along the beach. It sounded idyllic. She'd thought of it today as they'd walked hand in hand to the park. It was impossible not to imagine them as a family, not when she felt like they were, or at least could be very easily.

If it weren't for her problem.

And that was the issue. Every day Evie and Bran stole a little more of her heart, and when the time eventually—and unavoidably—came for him to take a wife, everything would change.

She turned from the shells, her chest pulling. The crate of things he'd brought from Barbados was pushed up against the bookshelves, the lid propped beside it. Several items had made their ways into various rooms, including a miniature of his wife, which now hung in Evie's room.

Louisa Crowther had been very beautiful, with shining golden hair and a soft smile. Jo could see the resemblance between her and Evie and wondered if Bran was reminded of her every time he looked at his daughter. Had his marriage been a happy one? She simultaneously wanted to know and yet didn't. It would be easier to think her death hadn't adversely affected him in the way that Matthias's hadn't upset Jo.

She knelt next to the crate and picked up a coin, wondering if it had been mistakenly dropped inside or if it was a memento of some kind. It was rather worn, the edges dull and smooth. She set it back into the crate and her knuckles grazed an object wrapped in paper.

Carefully, she uncovered the item. It was a small golden box with a rope dancer. Jo gasped softly at its exquisite beauty.

"That's a music box."

Jo swung her head toward the doorway. Bran stood there, his cravat and coat missing and his waistcoat unbuttoned. She was growing used to seeing him thus, but he never failed to make her think of an untamed animal. He was an aberration, a gentleman who refused to adhere to Society's rules and requirements, and he made no apologies. All that just made him more attractive to her.

She blushed at being caught prying through his things. "I was curious. I didn't mean to intrude."

He stepped over the threshold. "I don't mind. I went upstairs to your chamber as soon as I arrived home, but you weren't there."

She set the music box back in the crate and stood. "I came for a book, and then I saw the crate."

He went to it and leaned down to look through it for a moment. "Did you find a small key with the box?"

"No. It was wrapped in paper, and that was the only thing inside."

He straightened. "The key has been missing for some time. I'd hoped it had magically appeared. The box was a gift to Louisa from her parents when we married." He bent to retrieve it. Holding the box in one hand, he lifted the glass top. He pointed to a hole in the intricate design of the rope dancer. "See here?" At her nod, he continued. "The key is inserted here. After you turn it a few times, the music plays, and the dancer jumps up and down on the rope. It's an automaton."

She wished she could see it. "How clever."

"Quite. If only I could find the key, but I'm sure I can find a shop here in London that can fabricate another."

"I'm sure you could, yes."

He put the glass lid back down and set it on one of the bookshelves. "Then I'll give it to Evie. She used to listen to it constantly when she was very young. I think she may have been the one to lose the key. I wonder if she even remembers it."

"It would be a nice thing for her to have since it belonged to her mother." Jo had a handkerchief her mother had made and nothing else. "Do you miss her?" She hadn't meant to ask, but the question had simply leapt from her mouth.

He stared at his desk for a moment, his brow creasing. "Not really. I wish she hadn't died, especially for Evie's sake."

"Were you happy?" Jo asked softly.

He turned his gaze toward hers. "Happier than you were, I imagine. She was a kind and lovely woman."

The jealousy Jo felt earlier burned through her again, which was petty. She oughtn't be jealous of a dead woman. Just as she oughtn't be jealous of him going to a ball.

But she was. When she thought of him, dazzling and unbearably handsome beneath a thousand candles, her heart ached. "How was the ball?" The question sounded brittle to her ears.

He stepped toward her, and she turned to fully face him, her back nearly touching the bookshelves. "Boring."

"In what way?"

"In every way." He advanced on her, closing the distance between them. "I detest such nonsense."

She pressed her back against the shelves. "Then why did you go?"

"To please my godmother." He brought his chest flush with hers.

She could feel his warmth through the meager layers of their clothing. "Is that right?"

"Mmm." He lowered his head and pressed hot kisses along her neck.

She arched her head back as far as it would go before the bookcase stopped her. Fire and need ignited in her belly and spread through her limbs before coiling in her core. "Did you dance?"

"Twice."

Another shaft of jealousy sliced through her. "I'm…surprised."

His tongue licked along her jaw. "I am too." He straightened, his mouth a bare inch from hers. "Are you upset that I went to the ball?"

"No." She answered too quickly and saw the doubt in his gaze.

His eyes darkened as he untied the sash at her waist. He pushed the garment open and then pulled his shirt over his head, leaving just her night rail between them. "Rest assured, I would much rather have been here with you. Doing this." He kissed her, his tongue capturing hers in feverish want.

She clasped his shoulders and held him tightly, her body quivering with desire. He kissed her deeply, his body pressing into hers so that she could feel the hardness of his cock. Need sparked between her legs, and she rotated her hips against his. He met her movements, thrusting into her.

She needed more.

He cupped her breast through the night rail, his fingers finding her nipple. The fabric was thin and seemed to only intensify the sensation as it rubbed against her desperate flesh. His mouth left hers and trailed down her neck to the top of her breasts. He pushed her nipple up and caught it with his tongue, drawing lush, wet circles over the fabric before grazing her with his teeth.

She gasped as stark lust shot through her. This was even more intense than the other night. She wanted him so badly. Here. Now.

He seemed to understand as he found the hem of her night rail and lifted it to her waist. His hand came between her legs, stroking her as she widened her stance to open her thighs.

And then he was gone. She whimpered. But he was back momentarily after dragging the chair toward them. He pushed it to the bookshelf, on her right.

He reached for her right leg, grasping her behind the knee and lifting. "Put your foot on the chair."

She did as he said, and immediately knew why he'd

done it when his hand moved between her thighs once more. This opened her more fully, gave him better access. And oh, did he make good use of it.

She curled her hand around his neck, gripping him with harsh need as his finger entered her. He stroked in and out, teasing her arousal. She needed his mouth again.

Cupping his neck, she pulled him toward her and kissed him. He groaned into her mouth. His fingers worked faster, his thumb pushing on that sensitive spot that made her want to cry out.

He tugged his mouth from hers. "I can't wait." His breathing was ragged and wild.

She pulled at his hair. "I don't want you to."

He withdrew his hand from her, and she felt him undoing his fall between them. He shoved her night rail up once more and pushed her foot farther over on the chair, opening her wider. Then his cock nudged her opening. She was desperate to have him inside her.

She dug her fingers into his back as he entered her in one quick, filling thrust. She moaned, and he kissed her again, bringing heat and ecstasy.

He began to move, but she felt wobbly. He seemed to sense this as he lifted her by the waist. He broke the kiss. "Wrap your legs around me."

Again, she followed his command, and again he filled her, this time causing a cascade of light behind her eyelids as she squeezed them shut. Pleasure swept through her, lifting her high on wave after wave of rapture. She held on to him tightly as he drove relentlessly into her eager body.

He moaned as he took her mouth again, his tongue mimicking the movements of his cock. Each thrust sent her farther over the edge until uncontrollable spasms racked her body. He gripped her waist and buried himself deep. She felt his release as he shuddered.

He kept moving, a bit more slowly, but still filling her and prolonging her pleasure. After a minute, he withdrew, easing her legs from him. She found her footing before he let her go. She opened her eyes and saw him sprawl in the chair, his eyes closed, his head cast back, and his chest pulsing as he caught his breath.

Her gaze drifted to the still-open door, and panic filled her. Her night rail hung crooked around her waist. She smoothed it down and drew her robe closed, tying the sash tightly around her. "We can't let that happen again."

His eyes flew open. "Why?"

She hurriedly closed the door. "Anyone could've walked in." Her gaze dipped to his open fall and his spent cock.

He swore quietly and fastened the buttons. "If only you weren't so damned desirable. I'll try to restrain myself unless we're in your chamber. Or mine." He looked up at her, his eyes still dark with pleasure.

Want tore through her, but her earlier misgivings rose to the front of her mind. "Maybe we shouldn't do it at all. If someone were to find out. Or Evie—"

He jumped up and pulled her into him, his hands clasping her waist. "They won't. We'll be more careful. *I'll* be more careful."

It was so much more than that. This was a temporary thing. But she couldn't seem to form the words to push him away, as she surely must.

He caressed her face and kissed her softly. "Don't worry yourself. It will be all right. I promise." He smiled. "There is no reason we should deny ourselves this gift. This joy."

Her throat suddenly burned. It was a gift. And a joy she'd never known. It would end someday—sooner or later—but for now it was enough. It had to be. She wasn't willing to let him go.

Chapter Fourteen

"WHERE ARE WE going, Papa?" Evie peered up at Bran as he guided her across the street toward Hyde Park.

"I told you it's a surprise."

"It looks like we're going to the park. But why?"

"It's a *surprise*."

Bran grinned as they entered the park, barely able to contain his excitement. It was early—barely midmorning—but there were a handful of people milling about. He strode toward where he'd instructed the groom to wait. Ah, there he was.

Evie tugged on his hand. "Papa, you're going too fast."

"My apologies." He'd quickened his gait when he'd seen the groom—and the surprise.

As they drew near, Evie sucked in a breath. "Papa, that's Miller." The groom. "And that's a *horse* with a child-sized saddle."

Bran tipped his head to the side. "I think you may be right. Shall we investigate?"

"That's my surprise!" She pulled her hand from his and started to run, stopping herself almost immediately. Knowing better than to race straight for an animal, she adopted a more sedate pace and approached the horse.

Bran caught up and squatted down beside her. "This is Artemis. Would you like to meet her?"

Evie nodded. She slowly approached the beast and held her hand to the horse's nose. "It's nice to meet you, Artemis. I'm Evie. Shall we be friends?" Artemis nuzzled her hand, and Evie giggled. "She likes me, Papa."

"Of course she does." He joined her and stroked Artemis's muzzle. "Would you like to ride her?"

"Now?"

Bran smiled. "Of course. That's why we're here. If I'd just wanted to introduce you, I'd have simply done that at the mews."

"Oh yes, Papa. Will you help me up?"

He lifted her into his arms and set her onto the back of Artemis. Evie perched on the saddle then swung one leg to the other side so that she was situated astride. She tucked her dress under her legs as she always did at home. Rather, in Barbados. Someday he'd stop thinking that. Wouldn't he? "Now, walk for a few minutes to learn each other. And then nothing over a trot."

"Yes, Papa." Evie picked up the reins. "Come on, then, Artemis." She guided the horse into a gentle walk.

Bran walked abreast of them along the path.

"Oh, she's magnificent, Papa. Thank you!"

Bran's heart swelled. It wasn't home but it was the closest he'd felt yet.

Evie threw him a glance. "I'm going to trot over to that tree, all right?"

He nodded, stopping as he watched her take off, expertly guiding the animal. She had an excellent seat.

"I say, is that your child?"

Bran turned at the query and vaguely recognized the man. "Have we met?"

The man's lips tipped up, but it wasn't really a smile. "Yes, at Brooks's. I'm Talbot. Friend of your brothers."

That's right. Annoying chap. "Yes, that's my

daughter."

"This isn't an appropriate time to have her riding in the park. In fact, I'm not sure there is an appropriate time. She's terribly young. Should she even be on a horse?"

Bran's muscles tensed, and his ire rose. He focused on Evie, who'd turned and was now riding back toward them.

"Good heavens, is she riding *astride*?"

Evie waved at them, then performed an expert turn to ride back to the tree. She went a bit faster than a trot, but she was so brilliant, he didn't care.

"Ghastly!" Talbot declared.

Outraged, Bran spun about. "Did you just refer to my daughter as ghastly?"

"Not her, but her activity. Perhaps you simply don't know better, since you've been in the middle of nowhere for—"

Bran advanced on the man with what he hoped was a menacing stare. "We were not in the middle of *nowhere*, and I know very well how to raise my own child. If I want to allow her to ride her horse astride in Hyde Park on a fair Wednesday morning, I shall."

Talbot's eyes widened, but he didn't retreat. "You can't talk to me like that."

"The hell I can't. You spoke ill of my daughter. Rather, her activity." He narrowed his eyes. "It's the same to me."

Talbot sputtered. "I was merely trying to help."

"I'd say you need to work on honing that skill. If not, you may end up insulting someone to your own detriment."

Now Talbot's eyes narrowed. "Are you threatening me? Careful, lest you find yourself without allies in this strange land."

"If you're referring to yourself, I didn't count you among them in the first place. Now, take yourself off before I lose my temper."

Talbot smirked. "You'll regret this interaction." He turned on his heel and stalked off.

Bran glared after him. "Doubtful."

He walked back to where he'd been just as Evie arrived, now at a walk.

"Who was that?" she asked.

"No one important." He held his hands up and helped her dismount. "You went above a trot."

"I'm sorry, I couldn't help it. She's so wonderful, Papa." Her brow furrowed as he set her on the ground. "Are you upset?"

Upset? Not particularly, but definitely agitated. "Why would I be?"

Before he could straighten, she ran her hand over his forehead. "You have those lines when you're tense. Do you need a massage?"

On the ship, there were several days when Hudson had been ill from the motion of the sea. He'd been unable to perform his daily massage, which had made Bran, well, agitated. Or at least made him more likely to be agitated. Evie had noticed this—she was aware of Bran's morning massage routine—and had offered to fill in for Hudson. She didn't have the strength he had, but Bran found it didn't matter. Just having someone press on certain points, his shoulders, his elbows, his wrists, helped.

Without waiting for him to respond, she took his hand and ran her fingertips over his wrist, squeezing and pressing. He straightened his spine and willed the stress from his body as she worked.

She moved up to his elbow and repeated the treatment. “I can’t reach your shoulders.”

“That’s all right.” He offered her his other arm.

“Yes, everything will be all right, Papa.”

He peered down at her, wondering if all children were as intuitive as her. “I hope so. Are you happy here, Evie?”

“I think so. Most days. Today is a very good day.” She glanced toward Artemis, who was back in the care of the groom. “I have Becky and Jo. They make things better.” She pressed her lips together as she massaged his arm up to his elbow. “Do you have anyone that makes things better?”

Bran’s heart twisted. He didn’t want her worrying about his happiness. That was his job. “I have you.”

“I know. We’ll always have each other. You tell me that all the time.”

He did. “And that’s fine by me.”

“Someday, I’ll get married and live in my own house,” she said. “Who will you have then?”

He squatted down again, and she let go of his elbow. “Evie, my darling girl, that is a very long time from now. I don’t want you to worry about me. I have everything I want. Everything I *need.* Right here, with you.” He touched the tip of her nose with his forefinger and smiled.

Her eyes—they reminded him so much of the sea around Barbados—narrowed slightly. “I’m still going to take care of you. Someone has to.”

He laughed at the seriousness of her tone. “I am the luckiest of men.” He swung her up into his arms again, lifting her high above his head, making her squeal. “Do you want to ride Artemis back to the mews? Walking only.”

"Yes, please!"

He set her back on the saddle, and the groom led her from the park. Bran walked alongside, his brain churning her words.

Someday, I'll get married and live in my own house. Who will you have then?

He immediately thought of Jo. The last week had been incredible, truly the best days since he'd arrived in London. Just this morning, Hudson had commented that he'd never seen Bran so relaxed. Their massage time had become quite short over the past few days, he realized.

But there was no future with Jo—according to her. He nurtured a hope that she might be mistaken about her fertility, that where her lousy former husband had failed, Bran would be victorious.

And if he wasn't? He still needed to find a countess. However, the more time he spent with Jo, the less he was interested in doing so. What sort of earl did that make him?

He wasn't sure, beyond the sort that allowed his daughter to ride astride in Hyde Park and cause a stir. Bran looked around as they left the park. Had anyone else seen Evie riding? If so, had they arrived at the same conclusion, that Bran was a horrible parent?

A surge of homesickness assailed him. He looked at Evie to gain his bearings once more. Yes, they would always have each other. Thank God for that.

JO ARRIVED AT Lady Satterfield's tea in the company of her sister. The countess was known for hosting social events in the late afternoon at which she served tea and cakes. People came to gossip and be seen. Jo had attended a couple of them since arriving in town and had accepted Nora's invitation to join her today. They were the first to arrive.

Lady Satterfield smiled widely as they entered the drawing room. "Good afternoon, dears! I'm so glad you've come." She hugged Nora. "You are positively radiant, as usual. Pregnancy quite agrees with you." She turned to Jo. "And I must say you have a look about you—a merry twinkle in your eye, I think. Becoming a governess must agree with *you*."

"Yes." Or maybe it was the nights she spent in bed with her employer. She struggled not to blush at the thought of her wanton behavior. And she didn't dare look toward Nora who would likely give her a knowing smile. Jo had seen her the other day and had confirmed that their liaison was ongoing.

"Tell me, how is Lord Knighton adjusting to London?" Lady Satterfield asked. He seems to attend about as many Society events as my stepson."

Nora let out a short laugh. "Not quite as few. Titus, as you know, hasn't been to a ball since yours at the start of the Season."

"He doesn't seem to care much for those sorts of things," Jo said.

"Ah well, we'll have to think of another way to get him out and about." Her brows briefly rose, and she smiled at Nora. "I've just the thing. Isn't it time for you to convince Kendal to host another dinner party?"

"Yes, I think so." Nora looked at Jo. "Do you think Knighton would come to that?"

Jo wasn't certain but knew that he liked Titus. "Probably."

"Excellent," Lady Satterfield said. "This will be such

fun." The countess's gaze gravitated to the doorway. "Excuse me, guests are arriving."

Over the next half an hour, several guests arrived and gravitated around the room in a few clusters. Jo sat among a grouping of several other women, including Nora, when another arrival joined them. It was Bran's mother.

Her gaze found Jo's. "Good afternoon, Mrs. Shaw. How surprising to see you here."

Jo wasn't certain if she meant any insult but decided not to take it that way. "Good afternoon, Lady Knighton. This is my sister, the Duchess of Kendal." She gestured to Nora, who sat in the chair beside her.

"I'm pleased to make your acquaintance. My daughter and your granddaughter have become the best of friends."

"How fortuitous," Lady Knighton said with a bright smile. "I'd say Lady Evangeline is making the transition to her father's new position rather well if she's befriended the daughter of a duke." She laughed gently before perching on a settee angled to the side of Jo's chair.

One of the women in the group addressed the lady beside her. "I heard Lord Talbot saw Lord Knighton in the park yesterday." She glanced around the circle, her gaze resting for just a moment on Lady Knighton.

Another woman, with dark brown hair and a nose that turned up at the end, walked up behind the one who'd just spoken. "Lord Knighton, you say? Yes, I heard he allowed his daughter to ride *astride* at Hyde Park yesterday morning. Can you imagine?"

Nearly everyone in the group—with the exception of Nora, Lady Knighton, and, of course, Jo—shook their heads in disapproval.

The woman continued, "And when Talbot—his wife is my dear friend—tried to offer advice on the matter, Knighton practically called him out! It was horrendous. Talbot was mightily offended."

More condemning looks were exchanged along with a few sounds of disapproval.

"Well, he's new to all this," another woman chimed in. "He just needs some guidance. A proper English wife will rein him in."

Jo stole a look at his mother. The muscles in her face were drawn tight, and she stared at the woman who'd just spoken. Then she let out a sparkling laugh that was as counterfeit as any Jo had ever heard. "He always was Bran the Defiant. That's what we called him when he was a boy. Getting into scrapes and making trouble." She waved her hand. "I think he likes the attention."

Jo masked her horror. Bran would never parade Evie around the park for attention.

The woman with the dark brown hair who'd joined the group blinked, and a bit of color crept into her cheeks as she looked at Lady Knighton. "Are you the earl's mother?"

Lady Knighton's answering smile was superior. "I am."

The blush staining the woman's cheeks deepened. "My apologies, I meant no offense."

Everyone stared at Lady Knighton. "I'm sure you didn't."

The air was so thick with tension that you could practically see it. Jo darted a speaking glance at Nora, who rushed to say, "I've heard him called the Duke of Defiance. Isn't that dashing?"

The first woman—the one who'd brought up Talbot seeing Bran in the park—clapped her hands together.

"Oh, he has a nickname! Like your husband."

Nora clenched her jaw. "Yes, like my husband." She threw Jo an apologetic look, realizing too late that perhaps that hadn't been the right thing to say.

Another woman nodded. "The Duke of Defiance… It *does* sound dashing. And perhaps a bit dangerous."

"There's already a Duke of Danger," someone else pointed out. She turned to Bran's mother. "I'm Lady Wolcott. My younger sister is on the Marriage Mart. Will Knighton be going to Almack's?"

"I'm certain he will at some point. Finding a countess is chief among his priorities since returning to England. He is, as you can imagine, quite busy acclimating to his new title." Lady Knighton craned her neck and seemed to preen beneath the suddenly sycophantic stares of the rest of the women.

Jo leaned over to whisper in Nora's ear. "What is it about an available Untouchable that turns perfectly well-mannered women into vultures?"

Nora brought her hand to her mouth to hide a smile. "I don't know, but it always does."

"How splendid to hear that he's searching for a wife," one of the older women in the group said. "I've two daughters, one of whom is a widow. She could transform him—and his daughter—in no time."

He didn't need transformation! Irritation burned Jo's throat as she sought to keep her mouth closed.

Lady Knighton nodded, her features serene but her gaze cool. "Yes, whomever he marries will need to become a mother immediately, if she isn't already. My granddaughter is lovely, but she does need a feminine hand."

She *had* a feminine hand—Jo's.

Jo couldn't stand another moment. She vaulted to

her feet and left the group. Nora came on her heels, and they retreated to the windows away from eavesdropping ears. Still, Nora spoke softly.

"Are you going to speak to him about allowing Evie to ride astride in the park? He can't do that."

"Yes." But she suspected he wouldn't care. If he didn't see a problem with removing his clothing in front of a woman he barely knew, which he'd done with Jo at just their second meeting, he likely didn't give a fig what anyone thought about Evie riding however she wanted to.

What would he think of the gossip, however? Especially when it came to his daughter? Furthermore, what would he think of his mother adding fuel to the fire?

"I didn't help matters," Nora said, as if reading her thoughts. "I was just trying to put him in a more positive light."

"I know, and I understand." She just hoped Bran would. She considered not saying anything, but didn't want him to hear rumors from someone else, though she'd no idea who that would be.

Nora moved to talk with another guest, leaving Jo to contemplate the other part of the conversation—when they'd discussed his marital prospects. Her stomach churned with nausea when she thought of him taking a wife and of that wife becoming Evie's mother.

She wanted those things.

Yes, *she* wanted them. Too bad she couldn't have them.

Chapter Fifteen

BRAN SUPERVISED THE hanging of the framed flowers around the house. They'd been delivered yesterday, and he was thrilled to see them on the walls. Evie had decided where to put each one, including the four that were now forming a square pattern where his mother's portrait had hung in the sitting room.

Thinking of her dampened his mood, but since she was due to arrive any moment, it was bound to happen.

The day before, Jo had attended a tea at Lady Satterfield's. People had gossiped about Evie riding in the park, which had absolutely infuriated him, and then his mother had made comments about him being a difficult child.

Jo had vacillated on whether to tell him—she didn't wish him to be upset. He'd been glad she had, but maybe it would've been better not to have known. Since then he'd been a bundle of tension. Hudson had performed numerous massages, and Bran had taken dinner in his chamber last night completely nude. In front of a fire because it was bloody cold in England, even in April.

He'd gone to Jo's chamber later, and she'd warmed him quite thoroughly.

When he'd awakened this morning, he'd sent a note to his mother summoning her for an appointment this afternoon. He meant to tell her to keep her mouth shut where he was concerned. And if she didn't, well, he had no compunction about cutting her out of his—and

Evie's—life.

A few minutes later, he heard the door and knew she'd arrived. Bucket showed her into the sitting room.

"Knighton," she said, "I was so pleased to get your invitation." Her gaze fell on the newly hung flowers. "Those are lovely." She went to look more closely. "Are these from your island?"

"Barbados, yes."

"Exquisite. Did you bring any plants with you?"

He hadn't but had been thinking today, looking at all the flowers, that he should have. "No."

"Pity. There's a marvelous conservatory at Knight's Hall, if you remember. And nothing in it really."

Hell, he'd completely forgotten. He'd done his best to block many of his memories.

"Perhaps you could have some sent over."

He stared at her, somewhat shocked that she'd made a suggestion he actually *liked*.

She turned from the wall and strode toward him. "I've brought something for you." She pulled an envelope from her reticule. "It's a letter from your father. I'd like you to read it."

Now? He took it from her hand. "I'll read it later."

She sat down in a chair and stared at him expectantly. "I'd like you to read it now."

"If it's so bloody important, why did you wait to give it to me? In fact, why am I just receiving it when he died over a year ago?"

"Because your father asked me to hold it for you and give it you after you arrived. It was too important to chance being lost." She looked away from him. "I didn't want to bring it the first time I saw you. I wasn't sure what to expect."

"You mean you had to *decide* whether you should give

it to me."

Color stained her cheeks, and she flashed him that icy stare. "Just read it."

His mind warred with itself. Curiosity about the contents fought with his reluctance to capitulate to what she wanted. In the end, curiosity won. He went to the windows and turned his back to her.

Opening the letter, he saw his mother's handwriting, not his father's. He turned his head to look at her. "You wrote this."

"He dictated it to me. He wasn't well enough to write."

So she already knew what it said. Perhaps that was why she wanted him to read it in front of her. He began to read.

Knighton,

That will be your name by the time you read this. You are now the earl, and with that title comes great honor and responsibility. I've no doubt you possess both traits and many more that will ensure you carry on the line with the utmost integrity.

I must apologize for so many things, but mostly for my treatment of you. I discounted your abilities when you were young. You were so defiant, so troubled. I truly didn't know how you would grow to adulthood, and so I think I gave up on you. You were also the third son, which is never an enviable position. In retrospect, your brothers were cruel—and even your mother, though she doesn't like me saying it and I had to threaten her to persuade her to write the words.

I see what you did in Barbados, the fortune you built, the life you created. You have far more fortitude and intelligence than your brothers. I was sad when they died, of course, but I am not sad that you will be the earl. I can think of no better person to carry on the mantle of duty and ensure our legacy for generations to come.

I love you, son. Be well.

Father

Bran read it a second time, then stared at the words until they blurred together. Blinking rapidly, he refolded the paper and turned toward his mother. "I'm surprised you gave this to me."

She stiffened. "I promised him that I would. I am a dutiful wife."

There was that word again—duty. For the first time, Bran felt more than a nagging responsibility. Perhaps he was meant to be the earl. And if he wasn't, it didn't matter. He *was* the earl.

His father was right that he'd built a grand life for himself on Barbados, and he'd done it from nothing. He'd already started to think of things he could do *for* Barbados now that he was the earl, such as working to free the slaves. Last year's rebellion had been terrifying and had made Bran take a stand against slavery. He was still in the minority, but perhaps he could use his position to change that.

"You're rather quiet," she said, interrupting his reverie. "But then you have a tendency to run toward sullen."

"I learned to hold my tongue around you. It was that or suffer the consequences." He took a few steps toward where she sat. "I'm still surprised you gave this to me. Or at least didn't amend it."

Her eyes flashed a chill once more. "Duty is the most important thing. Without it, what is our purpose, our worth? We could've been born anything—a hapless beggar on the street—but we weren't. *You* weren't." She spoke sternly, her voice carrying through the room. "You will be the earl, and you will be magnificent."

It wasn't exactly a rousing speech in the spirit of his father's endorsement, but it was almost certainly the best she could do. "I *am* the earl, magnificent or not."

She blinked at him, seeming a bit surprised. "Good. I hope that means you'll crop your hair and accept more invitations. You *must* get out more. I heard from many ladies yesterday with marriageable daughters. It's time you searched for a countess."

Jo rose in his mind, only to be overtaken by his father's words: *I can think of no better person to carry on the mantle of duty and ensure our legacy for generations to come.* If she couldn't give him an heir, how was he to ensure his family's legacy? His muscles bunched up, and his clothing grew tight.

"When you do go out, you need to act appropriately, as does Lady Evangeline. No more allowing her to gallop about the park *astride* a horse." She pursed her lips and scrunched up her nose, looking as if she'd just smelled bad fish.

He'd nearly forgotten why he'd invited her here in the first place. "I don't *need* to do anything. As you so aptly pointed out, I'm the earl. I can do whatever I damn well please."

She stood, staring him down with the frosty glare he recalled so well. "You've always been defiant. I suppose it's too much to expect you to change. I'd say you've earned your nickname."

His neck pricked. "What nickname?" He recalled the ridiculous names Kendal and his friends had told him.

"The Duke of Defiance. Apparently it's some sort of convention for categorizing eligible bachelors." She waved her hand. "Nonsense, but in this case accurate."

Who the hell had started calling him that? "Did you come up with that name?"

She looked affronted. "Of course not. I heard your governess's sister use it the first time, but by the end of the tea yesterday, I'd heard it from several people." She took a step toward him. "You see, you *must* make appearances. Your absence begets rumor."

"No, *you* start rumors. J—Mrs. Shaw said that you told everyone I was a difficult child. That doesn't exactly *help* me."

"I was trying to explain away your bad behavior in the park. Do not blame me for your mistakes."

Talking to her was like trying to sail in a hurricane. You could try, but you'd be much the worse for wear—if you made it through. "Get out."

She opened her mouth, but he cut her off. "Now. Before I ask Bucket to escort you." His lip curled, and for the first time, she shrank back.

Pursing her lips again, she spun around and stalked out.

Anger and frustration and deep-seated resentment boiled to the surface. He tossed the letter onto the settee and began to tear his clothes off. One by one, each piece landed in a heap on the floor until he stood in his smallclothes. He managed to stop before he'd completely stripped.

"Bran?"

Jo's familiar voice cut through the haze of disorientation and lingering rage. He spun toward her and closed the distance between them, tugging her into the room and then slamming the door shut.

"What did your sister call me yesterday?"

She blanched. "The Duke of Defiance."

"*Why?*" It was a question but he ground it out through his clenched teeth like a demand.

"She was trying to defuse the situation. People were gossiping about Evie riding in the park and you being rude to Talbot. Then your mother jumped in and told everyone you'd always been defiant. As you can imagine, that didn't really improve things. Nora sought to make you sound dashing and…desirable?"

He would maybe laugh at that absurd progression if it hadn't been about him. If it hadn't been about the one thing he despised being called. Because it was true, and he was powerless to stop it.

"Yes, I was difficult and *defiant.* Have you any idea how hard I tried not to be? How worthless I felt because I couldn't seem to help myself? All my problems were beyond my control. I wanted to be a good, dutiful son, but I just *couldn't.*"

Her eyes were wide as she listened. Then her gaze roved over him. "You're practically naked."

He said nothing, just glowered at her. But she didn't flinch. Instead, she came toward him. "What can I do?"

It was a curious thing, that as a general rule he didn't like to be touched, and yet Hudson's daily massage ensured that he didn't get too overwhelmed. He did, however, like to be touched by Jo. "Come here." He held out his hand. "Massage makes me feel better."

She took his hand between hers. "What do I do?"

"Apply a bit of pressure. Like this." He

demonstrated on her hand. "But a little more firmly, if you can."

She started along his fingers and worked up his hand to his wrist.

"Press here." He showed her the spot on the underside, and she followed his direction. "Now up to the elbow. And press here." He showed her that spot as well. She worked slowly and methodically. "The shoulder. It's better if I sit."

He went to the settee and sat down. "Come stand here." He gestured for her to move between his legs. "Put your palms on my shoulders and press down, then work your fingers in as hard as you can."

She pushed on him. "Like that?" He nodded, and she did it several more times before digging her fingers into his muscles. She massaged him for several minutes. He closed his eyes and immersed himself in the calming sensations.

Gradually, he became aware that his cock was hard as stone. At about that same moment, he heard a click. He opened his eyes and saw her walking back from the door. She'd locked it.

He closed his eyes again, wanting to lose himself once more in her touch. She massaged his other elbow and wrist, finishing with his hand. Then he felt her lips on his ear, her tongue tracing along the edge down to the lobe, where she suckled his flesh.

He inhaled sharply. Her mouth continued a path along his throat, then down to his collarbone. He felt her hand brush his thigh. Then her fingers stroked his cock through his undergarment. He pushed forward, seeking more of her touch.

She pulled at the waistband, and he lifted up so that she could pull his smallclothes down his hips and strip them away. He opened his eyes and saw that she was lifting her skirts. With one hand, she pushed him back against the settee. She put one knee next to his thigh and straddled him, setting her other knee on the opposite side.

Her eyes held his as she reached between them and stroked his length, pulling along his flesh—up and down and back again. Need gathered in his belly, his balls, everywhere. He arched into her hand, seeking more.

She lowered herself, and his tip found her wet heat. She guided him inside, slowly, torturously. Impatient, he thrust up, impaling her.

She sucked in a breath and clutched his shoulders, applying as much pressure as she had moments ago. But this was so much better.

Wiggling her backside, she settled on him, taking him as deep as he could go. Her lips took his in a searing kiss as she began to move. He gripped her hips and helped guide her up and down, sheathing and unsheathing his greedy cock.

She dug her fingers into his shoulders and tore her mouth from his. "Let me." She took his hands from her and pushed them up next to his shoulders. Staring into his eyes, she lifted herself almost completely off him before sliding back down. She did this several times, increasing her speed incrementally.

He feared he would die from the anticipation. The pleasure building inside him was a blessed torture. She brought him to the edge time and again before flinging him back from completion.

Then something shifted, and she gasped. Still, she kept her gaze locked with his, though her eyes narrowed. She began to move faster, her thighs slapping against his as she rode him fast and hard.

He rose off the settee, driving into her with fierce abandon. She kept his hands captive, and the sensation was incredibly erotic. He felt her muscles contract as her orgasm claimed her. She let him go and clasped his neck, gripping him tightly with her hands and her sex.

Blood pulsed to his cock, and his own orgasm came with a blinding white light. He grabbed her waist again, holding her while he thrust deep and let loose his seed.

She collapsed on him, her breathing ragged but so sensual. He could scarcely believe what she'd just done. In all the nights they'd lain together, she'd never taken command like that. He liked it.

He caressed her jaw and kissed her, his lips moving softly over hers. She kissed him back, her tongue teasing his before she gathered her skirts and pushed herself off him. He watched as she used her petticoat to dab between her legs, then let the garments fall. With the exception of her rosy cheeks and still elevated heart rate, she didn't look as if she'd just seduced him.

He, on the other hand, was sprawled nude and likely looked as if he'd been well and truly shagged. He couldn't help but smile.

She picked up his smallclothes and handed them to him. "You may want to dress." She picked up the letter, which had fallen to the floor amidst their exertions. "What's this?"

He pulled on his undergarment. "A letter from my father. You're welcome to read it."

She arched a brow in question before opening the parchment and scanning the missive.

Locating his breeches, he pulled them on while she read. He gathered the rest of his clothing, but merely piled it onto the settee.

She looked up from the letter. "He sounds like a proud father."

"He wasn't always. While he wasn't like my mother or brothers, he didn't put a stop to their cruelty. I never understood his complicity, but then I never understood why any of them despised me so."

"Your father didn't despise you."

"No, he gave up on me. Which is worse, really." He watched her face, afraid she would pity him. He didn't want that. "Still, I'm glad he wrote it."

She nodded once. "That he came to have such faith in you must be gratifying."

"Yes. And, surprisingly, a bit inspiring." He scratched at his jaw, feeling the slight growth of his beard. "I resented coming here, having to be the earl. I never expected it and sure as hell didn't want it. My brothers' death forcing me to come back here felt like their final taunt, as if they'd orchestrated the entire thing just to torture me from the grave."

"They didn't, of course, but if they had, you think they expected you to fail."

"Most certainly. But I've decided to succeed in spite of them. I find I'm quite eager all of a sudden. It feels…good."

She gave him back the letter. "I'm glad. Well, I need to get back upstairs."

The energy in the room had shifted during their conversation. The welcome languor of their postsex haze had dissipated far too quickly. But then he supposed that was to be expected given that it was the middle of the afternoon and they were in the sitting room.

She went to the door.

"Jo."

She turned, her hand on the latch.

"Thank you."

"You're welcome." Her gaze was enigmatic as she unlocked the door and left the room, closing it again behind her.

He frowned, thinking he ought to feel completely relaxed. Instead, a bead of discord had tunneled into his brain, unsettling him. He looked down at the letter in his hand, hearing that word—duty—like a relentless chime.

Doing his duty could mean a future without Jo. He wasn't sure he wanted to contemplate such a thing, but acknowledged that, as the earl, he might have to.

Chapter Sixteen

JO COUNTED THE days again, sure she'd made a mistake. When she came up with the same number, she tried a third time, and a fourth. Her menses were never this late. Maybe a day or two, but this was several days. Almost a week.

She stared into nothing while her mind tried to make sense of this. Nora had always tried to tell her that it was possible she wasn't barren, but Matthias had convinced her so completely. If she was with child…

Happiness exploded in her chest, forcing a strangled sound from her that was part sob and part exclamation of joy. She covered her mouth, her lips spreading in a smile.

Ever since she'd read the letter from Bran's father several days ago, a feeling of dread had lingered within her. She knew their time was temporary, but she had no idea when the dream would end.

And it was a dream. Days with Evie and often Bran, feeling like a family. Nights with Bran in which she felt more treasured than she ever imagined was possible. For the first time, her life was full and she was terrified it would vanish into nothing.

Now she had hope. Her first inclination was to tell someone—Nora, of course—but she was instantly afraid. What if this was nothing? What if there was no child, and her body was simply playing a cruel joke?

Surely fate wouldn't be that unkind to her. Didn't she deserve some happiness?

Her gaze settled on the clock sitting on the mantel in her room. Oh dear, she was late getting upstairs. Becky was likely already here.

A few minutes later, Jo entered in the nursery to find that Becky had indeed already arrived. She ran to hug Jo. "Aunt Jo! We're drawing, come see." She started to pull Jo toward the table where Evie was seated.

Jo laughed. "One moment, Becky."

Becky rolled her eyes but let go and returned to the table.

Jo turned to Mrs. Poole. "Sorry I'm late. I'm sure you're more than ready for a respite." This was the time of day when Mrs. Poole had luncheon.

"It's no bother. The girls are such a delight." Mrs. Poole nodded toward them, smiling. "See you in a bit."

She departed, and Jo joined the girls at the table. "What are you drawing?"

"My horse," Evie said without looking up from her paper.

Becky sighed. "You're so lucky to have a horse. Papa says he will teach me to ride this summer when we go to Lakemoor."

Evie looked at her friend now, her lips pouting. "That's so far away." She turned to Jo. "Do you know how far away that is?"

It was the Kendal seat in the Lake District. Several days' ride from London. "Yes, I've been there many times."

Evie frowned. "Whatever will I do without Becky?"

"Mayhap you can come with me."

Jo appreciated that the girls wanted to be together. They truly reminded her of the closeness between her and Nora when they were young. "I should think that Evie's father would want her to see their ancestral home. It's in Wales, just over the border." The girls' expressions settled into begrudging acceptance. "But perhaps we can arrange a visit."

Both girls practically bounced in their seats, instantly animated. "That would be wonderful," Becky said. "I've never been to Wales."

"And I've never been to the Lake District."

"Of course not, silly," Becky said. "You've never been anywhere in England."

"No, I haven't." Evie started drawing once more. "But Papa said he would take me to the ocean soon."

Bran had mentioned that to Jo a few nights ago, asking her where he should take Evie. Jo had only been to the ocean once and hadn't any helpful advice to offer.

Jo leaned toward her niece. "And what are you drawing?"

"My family. With the new baby. I want Mama to have another girl."

A family. Jo's heart squeezed. It was hard not to think that she might have a child growing inside her right now. How she prayed that were true. She pressed herself to focus on the girls, and not lose herself in what could be a fantasy. "She may have a boy."

Becky shook her head. "It's a girl's turn. First me, then Christopher, now another girl. It's only fair."

Jo missed the naïveté of youth. "Unfortunately, life doesn't work that way."

Becky looked up from her paper. "I'm still drawing a girl. If I wish hard enough, it will come true."

How Jo wanted things to be so easy!

"How come you don't have any children, Jo?" Evie asked, her attention still on her horse.

It was, in retrospect, surprising that they hadn't asked

her that before. Jo searched for the right way to answer that with five-year-old girls. "I just don't."

"Wouldn't you like them?" Evie asked, glancing at her.

"Yes, but as I said a moment ago, life isn't always fair, and wishing for something doesn't always make it come true."

Both girls stopped drawing and looked at her. "That's sad," Becky said, her brow furrowing.

Jo feared she was stealing a bit of their innocence. She reached out and touched Becky's hand. "But you mustn't stop praying for things—it does make a difference, I think." Or so she wanted to believe.

"Won't you marry again?" Becky asked. "Mayhap you'll have children then."

The hand that was still in Jo's lap gravitated to her stomach, her palm pressing against the flat plane. "Perhaps, but I'm quite content being a governess. It's very satisfying to be helpful to others, especially children."

"Yes, but you could be helpful to your own children if you got married," Evie said. "I think you should consider it." She exchanged a look with Becky, who nodded in agreement.

Jo couldn't help feeling amused by their advice. "Thank you, I shall."

And for the first time in nearly forever, she actually was. If Bran was still interested in making her his countess. He would be, wouldn't he? Hadn't he said that he'd marry her if she was with child?

She had an urge to tell him, but it quickly died in the face of her doubt and fear. She'd be patient. For a week at least. Yes, she could keep the secret for a week.

The girls continued drawing, and Jo went to tidy the

bookshelf.

"What are your favorite foods?" Evie asked, drawing Jo to look back toward the table.

"Let me see… I'm quite fond of pheasant and cod."

"I like cod," Evie said.

"And I love pheasant," Becky added.

Jo walked back to the table. "I think my favorite vegetables are carrots."

Evie looked up from her paper and made a face, her tongue darting out. "Yuck. I don't like vegetables."

"But you like fruit," Jo said. She'd discussed Evie's food preferences at length with Bran.

"Yes, but most of it isn't here or is hard to find. Just another reason Barbados is better."

"It isn't," Becky said firmly. This was the only thing the girls argued about.

Evie's eyes narrowed. "It is so. It's warmer. It's sunnier. It's prettier. And it smells better."

Jo couldn't dispute that London possessed interesting smells. "When you go to the country this summer, Evie, you'll see how lovely England can be."

She didn't look convinced. "We'll see."

Jo sought to divert the conversation. "My favorite sweet is trifle."

"I like rum cake," Evie said. "I haven't had it since I came here, but our new cook said she would try to make it for me." Her eyes glowed with excitement.

Becky continued drawing. "I like ices. Lemon is my favorite."

"I like those too," Jo said.

Evie cocked her head at Jo. "So you like pheasant and cod and carrots and trifle. Is that right?"

"Yes. I like many other things too, but those are my favorites." Jo wondered if there was a point to this conversation. Perhaps Evie was ready to sample some new things. "Would you like to try my favorite carrot recipe?" she asked Evie. "I can have Cook make it."

Evie winced. "Oh *no*. Thank you," she hastily added. She went back to drawing.

Jo spent the afternoon with the girls, giving them a sewing lesson, and then they made up silly songs until Nora arrived to fetch Becky.

The urge to tell Nora her suspicions was almost overwhelming, but Jo managed to not say anything. Once she was gone, Bran arrived home, and again the desire to share her secret bubbled inside her like an insistent pot of water. Instead, Jo pasted a smile on her face and tried her best to behave normally.

When Mrs. Poole took over command of Evie, Bran summoned Jo to his office.

She stepped inside as he was removing his waistcoat. He was entirely familiar to her now in nothing more than his shirt on his upper half. In fact, when he was fully dressed, it gave her a bit of a start. He was incredibly handsome no matter how he was garbed, but in truth, she preferred him wearing nothing at all.

Bran leaned back on the edge of his desk, his gaze sweeping over her. He never failed to look at her with a hunger that stirred her desire. "I wanted to speak with you about decorating. Specifically, my bedchamber. I know it's, ah, probably unseemly, but I think we're past that, aren't we?"

Most definitely, but the request still unsettled her. He'd asked for her opinions in various rooms—selecting a new carpet and draperies for the sitting room to remove some of his mother's stamp, replacing the wallpaper in the dining room, which would be happening soon, again to delete his mother's influence.

In this case, however, because it was *his* chamber, it did feel rather unseemly. She wasn't his wife. Furthermore, she'd never even been inside his chamber.

"I'm not sure I'd have anything of import to contribute. It is, after all, your bedchamber."

"True, but I'd still appreciate your opinion. You've been instrumental in helping me make the house feel more like a home, such as adding plants. I wouldn't have thought to do that."

They'd added potted greenery to every room, including several palms, which Evie adored. She even had one in her chamber.

"Would you believe," Bran continued, "that my mother suggested I import plants from Barbados for the conservatory at Knight's Hall?" He shook his head as if *he* didn't believe it.

"That's an excellent idea."

"I've been considering adding a small conservatory here to the back of the house. It would take up a bit of the garden, but then it would just be an indoor garden. What do you think?"

It was likely the closest Jo would ever get to the home he and Evie adored. Hearing them speak of it, she found herself missing it almost as much as they did, and she'd never even been there. "Evie would love it."

"Especially if we could grow some of the fruit that she misses." He pushed away from the desk. "I'm going to do it. Perhaps Kendal or West can recommend an architect." He'd become rather friendly with Nora's husband and the Duke of Clare. Jo supposed he would also have befriended Dartford and Sutton if they weren't constantly traveling back and forth between their homes outside London. They were quite busy tending to their responsibilities in town while anxiously awaiting the arrival of their children, which were expected at any time.

He came toward her, and she flicked a gaze at the open doorway. Seeming to catch her silent cue, he paused before he got too close. Still, the air between them crackled with longing, as it always did. "Will you help me with my chamber?"

"I don't know what I can do. What do I know of a man's bedchamber?"

He considered her question, or seemed to. "Why are you so hesitant?"

Because it felt *too* intimate. She wasn't his countess, and while she currently harbored a fervent hope that might actually come to pass, she was afraid to overstep. Indeed, maybe because it *was* now in the realm of possibility, she was feeling a bit superstitious. Which was absurd. Nevertheless, she couldn't do it.

"I'm not sure it's my place. In any case, just add a plant or two and lighten the bedclothes. You did say the darkness is what bothered you?"

"Yes." He reached for her hand and twined his fingers with hers. "Perhaps if you came to see it tonight, you could offer more insight." His gaze sparked with intent.

Jo's insides melted, and despite knowing better, she leaned toward him.

Just as a maid stepped into the office and stopped short with a loud "Oh!"

Jo whipped her hand from his and pivoted from him. Bran backed up to the desk and leaned against it once more.

The maid dipped a curtsey to Bran. "My apologies, my lord. I came to light the fire for the evening. I didn't realize you were here."

"It's quite all right," Bran said, gesturing toward the hearth. "Please."

Jo stepped from her path and went to the door. Turning her head, she told Bran she'd see him at dinner.

As she made her way upstairs, her hand drifted again to her belly. One would think she would feel better with this potential turn of events, but until she knew for certain, everything seemed far more tenuous than it had yesterday. She had only to be patient.

And pray.

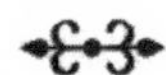

BRAN PAUSED IN the doorway to the drawing room where he was meant to dine this evening. The dining room was in disarray with new wallpaper being installed, so dinner for him and Jo would be served here. Normally Evie would join them, but she had gone to Becky's for the night.

Only, the room had been transformed. White linens that reminded him of the mosquito netting they used in Barbados hung from the ceiling. He'd no idea who had put them there or why. They'd added several plants to the room, but more—from other areas of the house—had been added. There were also drawings pasted around the room—of flowers from Barbados, birds, and, of course, a turtle. Clearly, Evie had drawn them. And perhaps Becky. They did like to draw.

A table was set near the center of the room, amidst several drapes of the white gauze. He belatedly realized that Jo was already seated.

He strode toward her. "What is all this?"

Jo looked up at him, her hands folded in her lap.

"The girls were here this afternoon. Evie wanted to recreate her home for Becky, so they enlisted Bucket and Hudson to help them. She asked Hudson specifically, since he's the only one of the staff that's actually been there."

"It's extraordinary." He kept looking around the room, enchanted. "It really does remind me of home. Of Barbados, I mean." He sat down opposite Jo at the small table.

"Do you think you'll ever go back?"

"I don't know." His chest tightened. He hated thinking he'd never see those beaches again. But leaving it a second time would be torture.

"I hope you do," she said softly. "It's so much a part of you."

The footman entered with the first course, which included cod and carrots as well as a soup. Bran poured wine—a madeira—as the footman served them.

They discussed their day while they ate and when the second course came, Jo laughed.

Confused, Bran asked why.

"There's pheasant." She looked up at the footman. "Do you know if there will be a dessert?"

"Trifle, madam."

Jo laughed again briefly. When the footman retreated, Bran said, "I'm very confused at what is so amusing."

"Evie and Becky quizzed me about my favorite foods the other day. I told them cod, carrots, pheasant, and trifle."

"I still don't understand. Is it your birthday?" He was going to feel horrible if he'd missed such an occasion.

"No. I'm not entirely sure what they're up to, but they're very dear."

He looked around at the room again. Barbados for him. Favorite foods for Jo. It was a stretch, but were they trying to play Cupid? No, that seemed preposterous. They were children for heaven's sake.

Bran shook the nonsense from his head and focused on his beautiful companion. "You look particularly lovely this evening. I admit I always look forward to seeing you at dinner." She dressed more formally than during the day when she was performing her governess duties. The gowns she wore exposed more of her, and he had to admit he enjoyed the view. But it was more than that tonight. There was something about her, an inexplicable sparkle that seemed to come from within her.

"Are you certain it's not your birthday?" he asked.

She laughed again. "I think I would know. My birthday is in September."

"Well, you seem in particularly good spirits."

She seemed to consider his statement before nodding with a smile. "I am, thank you."

"I think it's working out very well with you here, don't you?" It hadn't even been a month yet, but they'd settled into a pleasant routine, which included him visiting her chamber most nights.

He'd worried that the maid had seen him holding Jo's hand the other day in his office, but when he'd queried Hudson, his valet had assured him that there was no gossip amongst the staff. Bran had argued that he might not be privy to it, but Hudson said he was close enough with a few of them to know. Bran had accepted his reassurances.

When the dessert course came, Bran had an idea. "I think netting on my bed will remind me of Barbados. Yes, that may be just what my chamber needs." He was suddenly excited to order it. He finished his madeira. "I want you to come see it tonight."

She looked puzzled. "The netting? You won't have it."

He smiled. "No, my *chamber*. I want you to come tonight." He was afraid she was going to refuse. She hadn't wanted to help him with the refurbishment. Well, she had given him advice, but she'd declined coming to his room.

"All right."

Anticipation curled through him. "I think I'm finished eating. And that I'll retire early." He gave her a meaningful look.

Her answering stare was full of heat as she finished her wine and rose from the table. "Good evening."

He stood and bowed. "Good evening."

He waited a few minutes before he practically ran upstairs. Hudson wasn't even waiting for him yet. Bran summoned him, not necessarily because he required assistance, but so he could tell him that he didn't wish to be disturbed.

Garbed in only a silk banyan, Bran poured two glasses of rum and set them on a table near the bed. Then he paced until he heard a soft rap. He dashed toward the sound and threw open the door. Without speaking, he curled his arm around her waist and pulled her inside. He closed the door swiftly and then pressed her back against it, his mouth covering hers.

She clasped his back, and several minutes passed before he drew away. Her lips were full and reddened from their kisses, her eyes dark with desire.

Taking her hand, he led her toward the bed. "I've a special treat tonight." He let go of her and picked up the two glasses from the nightstand. "It's rum from my plantation. I thought you might like to try it."

She took the glass and held it up to study the rich brown color. "It's so dark."

"It's aged in barrels that contribute to the color. This one was aged for a few years." He took a sip. "Just take a very small taste to start. Actually, smell it first."

She did just that, inhaling the brew. Her nostrils flared, and she blinked.

He smiled. "It's a bit strong."

"Yes. I'm not sure I'll like it." She held the glass to her lips and took a small sip.

He waited anxiously for her reaction. She didn't visually flinch or otherwise reveal her opinion. "Well?"

"It's sweeter than I imagined." She gave him a wry half smile. "I daresay it's more than a 'bit' strong."

He laughed before taking another drink and setting his glass down. He took hers and put it next to his.

She looked around at the chamber. "It is dark in here. You should remove this wallpaper too."

He arched a brow at her. "But where will I sleep while they're doing that?"

She rolled her eyes. "You can't sleep in my chamber. Would you even want to? You rarely linger…after."

That was true. He'd done that in the beginning because it seemed as though he shouldn't stay. And he definitely didn't want to be seen leaving her room, or worse, caught *in* her bed. He realized he hadn't ever stayed because he'd never slept with someone before, and he wasn't sure he knew how, as stupid as that sounded. But he'd invited her here tonight. That meant he'd have to ask her to go or…leave it up to her.

He drew her into his arms next to the bed. "I've never slept with anyone before. Stay as long as you like."

She kissed him, her lips molding against his. She opened his banyan and ran her hands down his chest, her nails raking over his flesh. With a groan, he deepened the kiss, tangling his fingers in the length of her hair. She lightly skimmed his stomach and found his rigid cock.

With one hand, she cupped his sac and with the other she stroked his length. He closed his eyes and buried himself in her touch. She was quite good at this, having brought him to orgasm several times. He realized, however, that she'd never taken him into her mouth.

Gripping her head, he drew her lips to his again. After kissing her thoroughly, he pulled back just enough to whisper, "Take me in your mouth."

Her hand stopped, and he instantly recognized that something was wrong. His eyes came open. She was staring at him, her eyes stark with…fear.

Apprehension tore through him. "Jo, what's the matter?"

"I…I can't."

He cupped the sides of her head and looked into her eyes. "You don't have to. I…I'm an ass." He'd been caught up in the moment. Maybe she didn't know how or didn't like it. *Hell.*

She touched his chest, laying her hand over his heart. "You aren't. I'm just…a little broken, I think. I had to do that a lot. It was often the only way Matthias could reach completion. Not that he ever cared if I did.

"After I discovered that he preferred men, I concluded that it was perhaps the only way he could find pleasure with me." She looked away from Bran. "I know it was the only way—he told me so often. Well, not the only way. Occasionally, he would make me get on my knees. He liked it that way too. He always told me I didn't deserve to look at him." She shuddered.

Every muscle in Bran's body screamed with tension. "Your husband was a bastard. None of that was your fault."

Her gaze found his once more, and in it he saw gratitude. "I know that now. Thanks to you. I own I never expected to find so much pleasure in the bedchamber. You've shown me things I never imagined." She took a deep breath. "I trust you. I'd like to overcome this…problem or whatever it is." She reached for the rum on the nightstand. Lifting the glass, she took a hearty drink. She twitched as she swallowed, then repeated the act, except for the twitching.

She pressed her chest to his and kissed him, her rum-soaked mouth devouring his with heat and desire. Stripping his banyan from his shoulders, she let it drop between him and the bed, then she pushed him back onto the mattress, breaking the kiss. He had to hitch himself up slightly to lie back, but as soon as he did so, she grasped his cock once more. He went completely stiff, blood rushing to fill the shaft.

Then her mouth was on him, her lips and tongue gliding over his flesh. He cast his head back and closed his eyes, all his senses fixed on what she was doing to his cock.

"*Jo.*" He moaned as she expertly worked his shaft with her hand and her mouth. He didn't think he'd ever experienced such exquisite ecstasy. He pumped his hips up, and she clasped his backside, her fingers digging deliciously into his flesh.

God, he was going to come, and this was not what he'd envisioned. Plus, he didn't want to do that. Not this time, at least. He wanted this to be different for her. He hoped it was different.

He reached for her shoulder and tapped her flesh. "Jo."

She moved faster, her hand stroking and her mouth sucking furiously. His balls tightened, and he was afraid he was lost. "Jo!" He leaned up and grabbed her hand, pulling it away from his flesh.

She stopped and looked at him with dismay. Her cheeks were flushed. "Did I do something wrong?" She sounded so worried. Maybe even a little afraid.

Dammit. He winced. "*No.*" He sat up and tugged her onto the bed with him. "On the contrary. You were too perfect. I didn't want to finish like that. I want you beneath me. Writhing. Panting. Moaning my name."

Her lips curved into a saucy smile. "I like the sound of that."

With a growl, he tore her robe free and tossed it from the bed. Then he pulled her beneath him and kissed her, his tongue diving into her mouth. She clutched at his neck and shoulders and opened her legs, inviting him to settle between her thighs.

He moved his mouth to her breast, suckling her flesh as he found the wet sheath between her legs. She was hot and ready for him, so he didn't wait. He slid into her, and she wrapped her legs around his waist, urging him deeper.

He buried himself as far as he could go and devoured her breast. She moaned his name, just as he hoped she would. He withdrew, then plunged forward once more, driving into her with fierce precision. This was no mild coupling. This was wild and passionate. He wanted to erase any memory of her past and promise her a spectacular future.

They moved together, their bodies in perfect harmony. Her muscles contracted around him, and she let out a series of whimpers followed by a low moan ending with his name over and over and over again.

He let himself drown in the sounds and feel of her. The orgasm he'd managed to stave off before crashed into him. He cried out and buried himself deep inside her. He kissed her again pouring all of himself into her.

Minutes later—or maybe hours, he'd completely lost track of anything but her—he slowed and rolled to his back, throwing his arms over his head, panting.

She lifted the covers and slid beneath them, then snuggled into his side, her own breathing harsh and ragged.

He put his arm around her shoulders and stroked her arm. "You're amazing."

"So are you." She lifted her head and looked up at him. "Thank you for your patience."

"Thank *you* for your courage. Not just for tonight, but for the way you've given yourself to me. After everything you've endured, I can't imagine it's easy."

She stared at him a long moment, and he was sure she was going to say something else. She didn't, however. She laid her head back against his side and nuzzled him. He felt her yawn and then yawned himself.

"You don't mind me staying for a while?" she asked, her voice heavy with impending sleep.

"No." He continued massaging her bicep, his fingers gliding along her flesh.

With his free hand, he pulled the covers up. He brushed his hand along her head, smoothing her lush brown hair. He'd been certain she meant to say something else, and curiosity ate at him.

Could it be that she was going to tell him she loved him?

Idiot, why would you think that? What experience do you have with that emotion?

None, with the exception of his daughter. But this would be a different kind of love, the romantic kind. He'd felt deep affection for Louisa, but this was definitely not the same. Maybe he suspected Jo was in love with him because he was in love with her. How would he know? He'd described the love he felt for Evie as an emotion that, once experienced, had forever altered his soul. He realized that was precisely how he felt.

Tonight he'd envisioned a future with her, not some nebulous possibility, but a real future where she never left his chamber at night. He leaned his head down and kissed her forehead. "I love you," he whispered.

But he knew she was already asleep.

Chapter Seventeen

AFTER RELUCTANTLY LEAVING Bran's bed before dawn, Jo had returned to her chamber and fallen into a deep, satisfied slumber. She was so happy, so *content.*

So when she woke up to the feel of sticky wetness between her thighs, she panicked.

It could be from last night, she told herself, even as ice coated her flesh.

Anxiety lacing through her, she eased back the covers of her bed and looked down. Despair stole though every corner of her body, robbing her of breath and coherence.

Tears flooded her eyes, and she began to shake.

She'd no idea how long she lay there while every emotion—and every scrap of hope—drained from her. Eventually, she dragged herself from the bed and cleaned up. With Evie gone, she didn't have anywhere to be this morning, so she kept to her chamber. A maid brought her chocolate and toast, which she barely touched.

Around noon, she forced herself to get dressed so she could go to Nora's to fetch Evie, as they'd planned. She'd no desire to see her sister. She'd no desire to see anyone. Thankfully, Bran was not at home.

Her insides churned at the thought of him. Last night had been so perfect. The culmination of so many beautiful nights together. She'd come so close to telling him that she could be with child, but had ultimately decided not to. Now she was glad. He need never know of her foolishness.

She arrived at Nora's and sternly told herself to put on the brave façade she'd used all those years she'd been with Matthias. It was as natural as breathing, and yet today she found it unbearably difficult. Almost impossible.

And yet she did it, smiling at Abbott as he opened the door.

She went up to the drawing room to await Evie, bracing herself when Nora greeted her from the desk.

"Good afternoon," Jo said brightly.

Nora set a piece of parchment aside. "I just received a letter from Lucy. Still no baby!" Nora shook her head as she rose. "Both she and Aquilla should have delivered by now, poor dears."

Jo's entire body stiffened to the point of feeling brittle, as if a strong wind would blow her into a thousand pieces. "Is Evie ready?"

Nora came toward her. "Do you need to hurry off? I thought we could have tea or maybe even some luncheon. I'm starving all the time now." She rolled her eyes. "Soon I'll be as big as a coach."

Talk of babies and pregnancy had always made Jo uncomfortable, but today it was intolerable. She had to get out of there. "I really can't stay."

Nora's gaze turned assessing in that I'm-watching-you older-sister way. "Is something the matter? You don't look well."

"I'm fine," she said tightly. "Just…that time. I'd like to go home and lie down."

"Of course, I'll just ask Abbott to fetch Evie." Nora left for a moment, and when she returned, Jo was no more settled than when she'd gone.

"Why don't you sit while you wait?" Nora suggested.

"Please stop mothering me." Jo knew she sounded waspish but didn't care. It was all she could do to keep herself together.

"I'm not." Nora used the overly patient tone that always drove Jo mad when they were younger, when Nora had indeed been trying to mother her. "I'm trying to be helpful. But apparently you are not in the mood for that." Her voice grew cool.

Jo snapped. How dare Nora become irritated with her? "It's your fault. I've always said it wasn't, that you weren't to blame for how my life turned out, but you are. If you hadn't kissed Haywood, I would've had a Season, and I certainly wouldn't have had to marry Matthias."

Nora's eyes widened, and her mouth gaped open.

Jo clasped her hands together, squeezing her fingers as long-buried anger burned through her. "You ruined my life."

A tear fell from Nora's eye, tracking down her cheek. "I know. And I'm so sorry. I never knew that your marriage was so troubled. If I could go back and change things, I would."

"Would you? You probably wouldn't be married to Titus. You might not even be a duchess."

"That never really mattered to me—I only wanted to be happy. I wanted *you* to be happy."

"But you didn't think of me when Haywood came along." Jo knew she was hurting her sister, but she was hurting too. She'd never voiced the bitterness she'd felt when her entire future had been spoiled.

Nora was crying in earnest now. "I would go back and change things. I would gladly give up my happiness for yours. When I think of you suffering for all those years… Did he beat you?" She wiped at her cheeks.

"Not with his fists but with words. He said I was less than a woman because I couldn't give him children. When I found him in bed with a man, he told me that too was due to my failures."

Nora gasped. She brought both hands to her mouth and shook her head. She moved toward Jo, but Jo took a step back. "I don't want you to console me, and I don't want to console you. I know that would make you feel better, but I've always done things for other people, never for myself. For you, for Matthias."

For Bran. She'd warmed his bed—or allowed him to warm hers—and he'd reaped all the benefits. Now here she was, broken again, and she'd have to go on alone while he'd have his family.

She nearly doubled over at the thought. They'd been *her* family. She loved them—Evie and Bran. Oh yes, she loved him so very much.

Nora's tearstained voice broke into Jo's tormented thoughts. "Jo, I'm heartbroken. Please. Tell me what I can do."

All the rage in Jo dissolved into sadness and hopelessness. Her head dropped, and she stared at the floor through a veil of unshed tears. "I don't know. It's…it's all a mess," she whispered, feeling utterly defeated. She blinked, then looked over at Nora. "I am barren after all. I thought I might not be, but I am."

This time when Nora came toward her, Jo let her. And when her sister's arms came around her, Jo buried her face in her shoulder. She didn't cry, but she closed her eyes and thought of all the times Nora had held her after their mother had died. She might not remember their mother too clearly, but she remembered that.

Jo lifted her head and eased back. "I'm sorry. I guess I've been holding that in a very long time. I don't really blame you—at least, not anymore. I wouldn't want your life to be different. I'm so glad you have Titus and Becky and Christopher." She glanced down at Nora's gently rounded belly. "And the new baby." Her throat knotted.

"Did you think you were with child?" Nora asked.

Jo nodded, unable to voice any words.

"Oh, Jo." Nora hugged her again. "But maybe there's still hope. I didn't get pregnant right away with Titus."

Jo pulled back and summoned a wobbly smile. "Please don't. I can't bear to hope anymore. It's too hard. Anyway, Bran needs an heir, and if I can't give him one, he must find someone who can. I'm not sure how much longer I can stay with him."

"You mean you'd resign your position?"

"I have to." Jo's heart squeezed. "I don't think I can bear it."

"You love him," Nora said.

"Yes."

"I'm ready, Jo!" Evie bounded into the room with a gleeful smile.

Jo was glad she hadn't cried. She leaned down and swept Evie into a hug. "Did you have a fun time?"

"Yes! We stayed up very late and ate Shrewsbury cakes!"

Nora chuckled. "The cook sent a tray up. She can't seem to help herself from spoiling the girls."

As Jo and Evie turned to go, Nora touched her arm. She sent a worried glance toward Evie, who was thankfully oblivious. "Think about things before you make any decisions," she whispered. "I'm here if you need me.

Jo appreciated the support. "I truly am sorry for before."

Nora shook her head briskly. "Don't be. It was long overdue for you to let that out. I love you."

Jo found a small smile, then left with Evie.

Once they were settled into the coach, Evie snuggled close to Jo on the seat. "I missed you and Papa last night. I'm so glad you're my governess."

Jo's throat clogged with thick emotion as she pressed a kiss to Evie's head. Yes, she should leave, but she wasn't sure she could.

•ε•3•

BRAN STOOD IN the corner of the drawing room at the Kendals' town house while everyone else engaged in bright conversation. Well, almost everyone. He noted that Jo, seated on the opposite side of the room, seemed rather subdued. But then she'd been like that the past several days.

He'd barely spoken to her since the amazing night they'd spent together, and she'd informed him that she couldn't receive him because she was indisposed.

They'd arrived at the dinner party together, and aside from Evie being with them, the short coach ride had been fraught with tension—and not the kind he usually felt with her. Instead of being consumed with desire and the need to touch her, he'd been off-balance and unsure.

Upon their arrival, Evie had gone up to the nursery to be with Becky and to rehearse the puppet show they would give after dinner. Jo had moved away from him with alacrity, and he hadn't been close enough to talk to her since.

Lady Dunn came to his side, leaning rather heavily on her cane. "Why are you lurking in the shadows over here? The purpose of this party was to give you a chance to meet people and establish yourself."

It wasn't a terribly large party, but he supposed there were a few people of import here, and he'd already met them when the gentlemen had taken port after dinner. "I'm not lurking. I'm enjoying a few moments of solitude."

"I see." She followed his gaze and inclined her head. "I *do* see. How are things with Mrs. Shaw?"

"She's working out quite well. Evie adores her."

"Don't be obtuse. Have you given any more consideration to making her your countess?"

He'd done little else the past few days since realizing he was in love with her. "Yes. It may happen." Or not. Given her behavior, he had to wonder if she'd decided to end their affair.

"I shall continue to hope so," his godmother said. "You'll make an excellent match." She patted his arm, then doddered off.

Bran knew he should make an effort to talk to people, but it was difficult when all he wanted to do was tear off his coat and cravat. Then he would be more at ease. Damn Society and their stupid rules.

Just as he'd almost talked himself into going to talk to West, his mother approached him with another woman in tow.

"Knighton, have you met Mrs. Rollins?"

Bran eyed the woman. She was perhaps a few years younger than him—about Jo's age, he would guess—with velvety brown eyes and ebony hair. "No, I haven't had the pleasure." He offered a bow. "How do you do?"

She curtsied. "Well, thank you. It's an honor to meet you." She looked him in the eye and carried a confidence that had been absent in the frivolous young women he'd danced with at the Andover ball.

"Mrs. Rollins is Welsh—like us," his mother said. "She's also widowed—like us."

Bran had to give his mother credit. For a first matchmaking attempt, it wasn't terrible. He'd expected her to foist eager young debutantes on him. This was much better. "I'm sorry for your loss," Bran said.

"And I yours. It can be difficult raising children on your own. I understand you have a daughter."

"Yes, she'll be performing a puppet show in a while with the duke's daughter."

"Oh yes, the duchess told me about that before dinner. How wonderful."

There was a beat of silence, and Bran's mother rushed to fill it. "Mrs. Rollins also has a daughter. And she's six, just like Lady Evangeline will be shortly."

Bran threw his mother an incredulous look. How on earth had she found a woman who was "just like" him? If she'd spent time living in the tropics, he might have to seriously consider her.

Wait, wasn't he already seriously considering Jo? His gaze found her again, and he saw that she was watching him. Her expression was serene and completely inscrutable.

The duke called for everyone's attention and asked that they assemble themselves to watch the puppet show. He indicated a dais that had been set up on one side of the room with a wooden theatre with curtains.

"Allow me to introduce my daughter, Lady Rebecca, and her friend, Lady Evangeline."

The girls entered the drawing room on cue and curtsied to a round of applause. Bran's discomfort melted away as he watched his daughter's excitement.

She and Becky had written a short romantic play about a maid who becomes a princess and had been thrilled when the duchess had asked them to perform tonight.

As the girls made their way to the stage, Evie's gaze found Bran's. He smiled and winked at her, and she gave him a little wave.

"Is that your daughter?" Mrs. Rollins asked.

Bran noticed that his mother had moved away. Cheeky.

"Yes."

"She's lovely. How fun to do a puppet show. I understand she and Lady Rebecca wrote it. My daughter enjoys making up stories."

Just like Evie.

He turned to Mrs. Rollins. "Have you lived in England your whole life?"

"Since I married. Before that, I lived in Wales."

Bran exhaled, glad that he could cross "lived in the tropics" off the list of things they had in common.

The show started, and Bran was riveted. The girls had several puppets of varying genders, and they did voices for each one that were unique and, in some cases, hilarious. The maid's father was a comical fellow who kept tripping over everything. They finished to boisterous cheers and applause. Bran had never been more proud.

"That was marvelous," Mrs. Rollins declared, grinning. "Lady Evie is delightful. Perhaps she and my Margaret would like to meet one day."

Bran couldn't see why not. "That's an excellent idea. I'll have my secretary contact you."

Something flashed in her eyes, but she quickly disguised it with a smile. "That would be splendid, thank you. It was lovely to meet you." She curtsied again, and he bowed. Then she was gone.

Evie ran to him then, and he swept her up into a great hug. "You were brilliant!" he said.

"Where's Jo?" she asked. "Didn't you watch it together?"

"No, I watched it with a nice woman named Mrs. Rollins. And do you know what? She has a daughter your age, and we're going to introduce you so that you can make another friend."

Evie blinked. "Oh." She turned her head. "There's Jo. Put me down."

He set her down, and she took off to Jo who held her arms out and squatted down to give her a warm hug. Watching them together made his heart ache in a way he hadn't felt since Louisa had died. He'd been sad at her passing, but mostly because Evie had lost her mother, not because he'd lost his wife. Seeing Evie embrace another woman with such happiness filled him with joy.

"Did you like Mrs. Rollins?" His mother seemed to appear out of nowhere.

Startled, Bran turned to face her. "Yes. We had quite a few things in common."

"I know. That's why I introduced you. I met her the other day and arranged an invitation for her tonight. I told you I could be helpful."

Yes, but he wasn't going to give her the satisfaction of saying so. They may have reached a truce of sorts, but he wasn't ready to let her close to him—and he might never be.

"Well, I hope you'll pursue getting to know her. You need to get on with things."

She meant find a countess and produce an heir. His duty. It had been near the forefront of his mind since he'd read his father's letter. He'd been hopeful that Jo would fulfill that duty, but with each day that she pulled away from him, his doubt increased. And then there was the matter of the heir and whether she could give him one.

"Yes, I know," he finally said.

She smiled and patted his arm. "Good. I'm counting on you to lead as the head of the family now." Her gaze was filled with something he'd never seen from her before: affection. He shuddered as he walked away.

Moving to gather Evie and Jo to return home, he caught Mrs. Rollins's eye. She smiled at him and inclined her head. She was charming, self-assured, and clearly capable of having children.

Oh hell, what a tangle.

Chapter Eighteen

AFTER BARELY EATING any of her luncheon, Jo retreated to her chamber for a respite before giving Evie her afternoon lessons. How much longer could she go on like this? She was tired and defeated and paralyzed with fear.

She'd planned to talk to Bran last night, but then she'd watched him with that widow, Mrs. Rollins, and she'd been overcome with jealousy. She hated feeling that way, just as she'd hated the way she'd exploded with Nora the other day. She *couldn't* go on like this. She was tense and distraught, and it had to stop.

She tipped her chin up and straightened her spine, intent on going for a walk. That would lift her spirits. Walking into the corridor, she encountered Bucket. "I have mail for you, Mrs. Shaw." He handed her two letters.

"Thank you." She saw that they were from Lucy and Aquilla. Her stomach fell into her feet. Retracing her steps to her room, she slowly opened the missives and read the contents. Both had delivered their children yesterday. And both were sons.

And just like that, the courage that Jo had summoned went up in flames.

But just as quickly, it transformed into a different kind of courage. She knew what she had to do. It wasn't going to be easy, but it had to be done.

Surprisingly dry-eyed, she set the letters on her desk and strode from her room. She made her way to the nursery, where she asked Mrs. Poole to give her a few minutes to speak with Evie.

Conjuring a smile, Jo sat down and asked Evie to join her at the table.

"What is it?" Evie asked. "Did I do something wrong?"

Jo's smile widened, but there was a great deal of sadness behind it, which she was working to suppress. "Not at all. And you must remember that after what I tell you."

Evie sat down, her face registering confusion. "What is it?"

"I'm not going to be able to be your governess anymore."

Evie stared at her, and Jo wasn't sure she'd processed the information until she said, "You *have* to be."

"I'm afraid I cannot. This was always a temporary situation—remember when I said at the very beginning that we were going to try it?"

Evie's forehead formed deep creases, and her gaze was stricken. "Yes, but that means I did do something wrong. Why else would you leave?"

"Oh, Evie, you did nothing wrong. Being a governess just isn't…" She couldn't say it wasn't what she wanted, because it was—and so much more. So she lied. "I miss being able to have more freedom, to attend events with my sister. Going to the dinner party last night reminded me of that."

Evie's lip began to quiver, and Jo's heart ripped in two. She scooted her chair close to Evie and put her arm around her. "I'm so sorry, but we will still be friends. You'll see me all the time when you come to visit Becky." Until Jo determined what she was going to do next. The lonely cottage was beginning to look like her best option. Or, at least the one that might cause her the least misery.

Evie, silent tears now streaming down her face, shook off Jo's arm. "No, we won't. I don't want to be your friend. Friends don't hurt each other. I hate you!" She jumped up and ran from the room, passing a startled Bran, who watched her go and then swung his confused face toward Jo.

But confusion quickly changed to anger. "What the hell just happened?"

Jo tried to swallow past the lump in her throat but had great difficulty. She stood, her legs quaking. "I informed Evie that I wouldn't be her governess any longer. I was going to speak with you when you arrived home. I resign my position effective immediately."

"*Immediately*? You won't even give me the courtesy of staying while I find a replacement?" He shook his head and took a few steps farther into the nursery. "Never mind that. Why are you leaving?"

Jo clenched her hands together, squeezing, but not feeling a thing. "I can't continue in this manner. We behaved poorly, allowing our relationship to become too intimate. It's not good for Evie."

He stared at her, a muscle in his jaw twitching. "What changed? Things have been fine—better than fine—for weeks. Then a few days ago, you began acting strangely. Did I do something? You know I can be a thoughtless ass."

A hysterical laugh bubbled in her chest, but she didn't let it out. "You didn't do anything. I've enjoyed our time together, which is precisely why I have to go. Can't you see?"

He took another step toward her. "No, I can't. If things are good, why leave?"

"Because you need to find a countess, and I can't be here when you do." In her mind, she saw him with Mrs. Rollins last night. Her heart twisted anew. "I can't, Bran."

He moved nearly close enough to touch her. "I wanted you to be that countess."

"But I can't give you children. I'd hoped—for a few days—that I could. I was wrong. I'm *barren*, Bran. There wouldn't be more children, no heir." The pain of her lost dreams cut deep. She wrapped her arms around her belly, as if she could soothe the agony. But she couldn't. "You need to move on, and you can't do that with me here."

He opened his mouth but snapped it closed. A small piece of her had hoped he would tell her it didn't matter, that he'd ask her to stay.

At last, he spoke, his voice dark and brittle. "You broke Evie's heart."

Emotion pushed up through Jo's chest, and her eyes burned as tears formed. She didn't want to lose her composure here. Not now, not with Bran. "Unfortunately, I think our selfishness brought about many casualties, and now we have to live with the consequences." She stepped around him, giving him a wide berth. "I'll send for my things." And then she left, going straight downstairs and out the door into a bleak future.

BRAN STARED AT the empty doorway. Agitated, he threw off his coat and untied his cravat. What a blasted mess.

When he'd told Jo that she'd broken Evie's heart,

he'd really meant his. He loved her far more than he realized as he considered a future without her in it. He would make her his countess, but she'd refused him, citing her inability to have children.

Which could be a valid reason. Or not.

He didn't care. He wanted her any way he could have her. Yes, he wanted children. Yes, he felt a duty to provide an heir. But when all accounts were settled, he wanted her most of all.

A small, horrid voice in the back of his head called him Bran the Defiant—still putting what he wanted before everyone else. Maybe, but it was what Evie wanted too, he was sure of it. But was it what Jo wanted? He thought so, but he couldn't be certain.

There was only one way to find out.

First, however, he needed to talk to Evie, to soothe her.

He went down to her bedchamber, but she wasn't there. Puzzled, he went in search of Mrs. Poole, who was in her room, up on the same floor as the nursery.

"Have you seen Evie?" he asked.

Mrs. Poole shook her head. "I haven't, my lord. I left her with Mrs. Shaw. Perhaps they've gone for a walk?"

Almost certainly not, since he'd heard Evie tell Jo that she hated her. He winced at the memory. "I'll ask Bucket. Thank you."

The nurse's brow furrowed. "Please let me know if aught is amiss."

"Of course." He hurried downstairs, out of breath, when he reached Bucket's office in the basement.

"Bucket, have you seen Evie?"

"No, my lord."

"What about Mrs. Shaw?"

"She left a short while ago." Bucket looked as if he

wanted to say more, but was uncertain if he should.

"If you have something of import to share, please do so," Bran urged.

"Mrs. Shaw seemed rather distraught. She was, however, alone."

Growing worried, Bran paced for a moment. "I need to find Evie. Ask the staff to search the house immediately."

He went back up to the ground floor just as Mrs. Poole came down the stairs. "My lord," she said. "Do you think Evie went to Becky's? I don't know why she would, but it's not *terribly* far to walk and it is a rather nice day."

It wasn't far, and they'd walked there several times, typically only using the coach in inclement weather. Plus, he knew Jo was there, and if by some chance Evie had gone after her… It made more sense that she was still in the house—he hoped.

He joined the search, but a quarter hour later, Bucket informed him that every room had been searched. Evie wasn't there.

Bran dashed to the mews and had a groom saddle his horse in record time. He arrived at the Kendals' a short while later and tore up the steps to the door. Abbott admitted him.

"Where is Mrs. Shaw?"

"In the drawing room, my lord," Abbott answered, but Bran was already halfway up the stairs by the time he finished the sentence.

He burst into the drawing room. Huddled together on the settee were Jo and her sister. "Where's Evie?" he blurted.

Jo blinked at him and straightened. "What do you mean? She's not here."

He swore and ran his hand through his hair. "She's not at home either."

The duchess rose from the settee, her face pale. "Let's try to remain calm. She was upset, yes?"

Jo stood with her, her eyes red and her cheeks flushed. "Yes. This is all my fault."

Bran wanted to agree, but that would help nothing. And really, he was just as much to blame. They'd created a terrible situation where Evie was the one who would suffer for their actions. He'd invited Jo into his home and treated her like a treasured member of the family, like his countess, for heaven's sake. Of course Evie felt as though they were a family and that their family had just been split in two.

"I'll be right back." The duchess hurried from the room.

"I'm so sorry," Jo said, her voice ravaged from crying. "I handled that very poorly. I didn't know what else to do." She clasped her hands in front of herself and lowered her head to stare at them.

He stared at her as emotions careened through him—anger, fear, love. "I don't care if you're barren."

Her head snapped up. "What did you say?"

"I don't care if you're barren. I love you. I can't bear a future without you. Please don't leave us."

Before Jo could answer, the duchess came back into the room with Becky. "Tell them what you told me," she said sternly.

Becky, looking rather stubborn, pouted for a moment. "I might know where she is. But I'm not supposed to tell."

Bran felt a mixture of relief and frustration. He went to Becky and knelt before her. "I'm very worried about her. I want to make sure she's all right. Will you please tell me where she might be?" He only hoped it was more than a *might* and that Evie was safely ensconced somewhere.

Becky chewed her lip. She looked up at her mother, who nodded encouragingly. She returned her gaze to Bran, looking worried. "Please tell her not to be angry with me. We promised each other it would be our secret."

Jo knelt beside him and took her niece's hand. "It will be all right. Evie will understand."

"We have a secret hiding place at her house. It's in the attic. There's a narrow staircase behind a door in one of the maids' rooms—the smallest one, in the corner."

Bran leapt up, but Jo grabbed his hand and held him fast before he could run out. "Thank you, Becky," she said. "You were very brave and very good to tell us."

Bran patted the girl's shoulder, anxiety searing his insides. "Yes. Thank you." He looked at Jo, and she nodded.

They hurried from the room and down the stairs. Abbott just got the door opened before they fled outside. "I only have my horse," Bran said. One of the Kendals' grooms stood with it.

"You can go on ahead," Jo said, letting go of his hand.

"No, we'll do this together." He brushed a stray hair from her forehead and leaned forward to kiss her, his lips briefly touching hers. "We'll do everything together from now on."

She nodded, and there were tears in her eyes. "I love you."

"Good." He turned, slipping his arm around her waist and guiding her to the horse. He climbed up first, then asked the footman to give her a leg up. Bran pulled her in front of him. "It's a bit awkward, sorry."

"I don't care," she said, pressing back into his chest. "Let's go."

He rode the horse as quickly as he dared, and they arrived at his town house a few minutes later. He slid from the saddle and helped Jo down. Bucket opened the door. "Did you find her, my lord?"

"Not yet, but we will. See to my horse."

Bran ran up the stairs and heard Jo close behind him. Up two more flights to the servants' floor where the nursery was located. They passed that on their way to the corner. "Is this the right room?" he asked Jo.

"Yes, I believe so."

He opened the door. The chamber was small and sparsely furnished. It was also empty. A narrow door was nestled into the corner. He crossed to it and pulled, but it stuck a bit, and he paused. Turning, he looked at Jo, who was just behind him.

He pulled on the door a second time. This time, it gave way.

The staircase was indeed narrow and also dark. But there was a faint light coming from above. He started up, the boards beneath his feet creaking as he went.

"Who's there?" came a frightened voice.

Bran relaxed as he recognized his daughter's tones. "It's Papa." He came into the attic. It was cold and dusty, with a low ceiling that required him to stoop.

Evie sat on a blanket with a doll on her lap and a candle burning in a lamp beside her.

"May we sit down?" Bran asked.

Evie looked uncertain. "Who's with you?"

Bran hadn't heard Jo on the stairs behind him. He turned and called down, "Jo?"

The creak of the stairs signaled her ascent. A moment later, she joined them, her expression tentative.

"You came back," Evie said flatly. "Why?"

"Because I asked her to," Bran said, sitting.

"But she doesn't want to be a governess anymore." Evie sent her a mutinous look that tore at Bran's heart.

"No, she doesn't." He looked at her, remembering what she'd told him just a few minutes ago—that she loved him. Did that mean she would marry him? He didn't want to presume, nor did he want to encourage Evie's hopes only to have them be dashed. "I am hopeful she will still be a close part of our lives, however." He held his hand toward Jo, hoping she ascertained his meaning.

She came forward and sat down beside him. Hope unfurled in his chest as he gazed into her eyes.

Her lips curved up, and she faced Evie. "Instead of your governess, I'm going to be your father's countess. If it's all right with you."

Evie blinked, her gaze disbelieving. She looked from Jo to Bran. "Truly?"

Bran nodded, unable to speak through the joy clogging his throat.

Evie let out a long breath teeming with relief. "Becky and I tried so hard. We arranged that picnic and the dinner. I was certain you might be falling in love. But then I thought it was maybe just my imagination."

Jo reached out and laid her hand over Evie's. "It wasn't. I've been in love with your father for some time."

Bran snapped his head toward her. She had? Of course she had. And if he'd been paying attention, he would've known that.

Happiness bloomed in Evie's gaze. "We are going to be a family for real, then."

"Yes." Bran and Jo answered in unison. They looked at each other and joined hands.

Evie clasped Jo's hand and then reached for Bran's. He took her small fingers in his and gave them a squeeze.

Evie grinned. "I'm the luckiest girl in the world!" She launched herself forward and threw her arms around both their necks.

Bran heard Jo murmur, "No, I am."

Chapter Nineteen

TWO WEEKS LATER, after being wed by special license, Jo tucked Evie into bed and went to the chamber she now shared with Bran to await his arrival. He'd had a late meeting tonight—House of Lords business—and Jo knew he would need a massage, which would undoubtedly lead to other things.

Not long after she was settled in bed with a book, Bran strode into the chamber, slamming the door behind him. A dark cloud seemed to follow him as he moved farther into the room.

Jo set her book aside and climbed out of the bed. Without a word, she went to him and took his coat and cravat, which he'd already removed. One of the buttons of his waistcoat went flying as he hastily stripped that away as well.

"Bloody Talbot," Bran growled.

"Oh dear. What happened?" Jo accepted his waistcoat and deposited the garments on a chair. She'd deal with them later or Hudson would in the morning. Right now, she needed to focus on Bran.

Bran sat on the bench at the end of their bed and removed his shoes and stockings. "I simply can't abide his insipid tone. I'm afraid he pushed me too far. He compared me to John again."

This had happened a few times—Talbot bringing up Bran's eldest brother and how it was too bad he couldn't be the earl. He was careful not to outright insult Bran, but it was offensive nonetheless.

Jo climbed onto the bed and set to massaging his shoulders. He was stiff and tense. "Forget about him."

Bran grunted in response, hanging his head and allowing his shoulders to droop as she worked. A few minutes later he said, "I may have threatened him."

Jo lifted her hands and slid from the bed. She sat beside him on the cushioned bench and took his hand while she massaged his bicep. "*May* have?"

He swung his head about to look at her, his gaze sharp in the firelight. "I told him that if he mentioned John to me again, I'd call him out, and I demanded he show me—the rightful earl—the respect I deserved."

Pride welled in Jo's chest along with a bit of anxiety. She knew how Bran struggled to be comfortable in his new role, particularly when he had to interact with people who grated on his nerves. She stroked his cheek. "I doubt he'll bother you again."

Bran turned into her touch and kissed her palm. "Never mind him. He's not worth my thoughts, especially not when I'm finally here with you." He leaned back against the bed as she returned to massaging his arm. "This has been the longest day."

Yes, it had. Earlier that afternoon they'd entertained his mother for a brief visit, her first since they'd wed. She'd congratulated them and seemed to focus on the fact that Bran had done well to align himself to a duke, even if it was only by marriage.

"Thankfully, it's over," she said, standing and moving to his other side.

He succumbed to her ministrations for another moment before asking, "I'm afraid to inquire, but how did things go with my mother after I left?" He hadn't wanted to leave Jo alone with the dowager countess, but he'd had an appointment.

"Fine. She left shortly after you." She'd stayed just long enough to ask Jo if she could bear children given that she'd been married so long without issue. Jo had feared the question, but also expected it.

Bran grunted again as Jo rubbed his elbow. "Good. I made sure you'd be interrupted so she'd leave."

Bucket had told her that the cook required a meeting. "You were behind that?"

His gaze was alight with mischief when it found hers. "You're welcome."

Jo looked down as she worked her fingers into his wrist. "Thank you."

He pulled his arm from her grip and put his finger beneath her chin, tipping it up. "What did she say? Did she upset you?" His voice held a soft, dangerous quality, but it didn't frighten her. She was well aware of the lingering animosity he felt toward his mother and perhaps always would.

She considered keeping the truth from him, but she wanted their relationship to be completely honest. Besides, there was no one she would rather confide in. "I'm all right. She asked if I could have children."

Bran swore softly. "I'll speak to her."

Jo shook her head and put her arms around his neck. "There's no need. I told her that no one could say what the future holds and that if trying accounted for anything, we'd likely give her plenty of grandchildren."

Bran's eyes widened and he let out a laugh. His mouth settled into a grin. "Have I told you today how much I adore you?"

"I'm not sure. I'd much rather you show me, however."

He pulled her over his lap, settling her legs around his hips so she straddled him. He brought his hands up to cup the back of her neck then stroked his fingers through her loose hair. "You know I don't care if you give me a hundred children or none at all."

She nodded. They'd discussed it at length, and while she still hoped her dream might come true, she'd accepted that she was already living a life she absolutely cherished. "I'm so sorry I let it be a barrier between us."

He kissed her, his lips moving artfully over hers. A moment later he said, "You've nothing to be sorry for. We found our way here, didn't we?"

She nodded as she kissed him back. When she pulled away, she looked into his eyes and saw the love she felt reflected there. "We found our way home."

Epilogue

Knight's Hall, Wales, August 1822

JO WATCHED EVIE lead her two younger sisters down the hill to the stream that ran through the property. Barefoot, they were going to dip their toes into the cool water to relieve the heat.

Jo's feet were barefoot too, and she wore a gown that barely reached her calves. It was scandalous, but in the privacy of their own home or on their own estate, she didn't much care. Bran had taught her long ago that life was too short to be uncomfortable. Especially when one was excessively large with child.

This pregnancy had been particularly challenging, but then she'd never carried during the heat of the summer before. Not that she minded. When she'd been blessed to have one child, let alone three, she could never complain.

Four children, she amended, for Evie was every bit as much her daughter as Theodosia and Francesca. And Evie absolutely doted on them. Almost as much as their father.

Jo turned back toward the house to see if Bran had come to join them yet. He'd been working in his conservatory, which had surpassed hobby and become a passion. She saw a figure striding down the slope and lifted her hand to her forehead to shield the bright sunlight.

Her lips curved up as he neared. He was also

barefoot and wore breeches that hugged his familiar thighs and a loose, flowing white shirt that bared a V-shaped hint of flesh. Well, maybe more than a hint.

"It's almost like Barbados here," he said as he reached her. He slipped his hand around her waist and drew her close so that he could kiss her lips.

She sighed into the kiss, leaning on him.

He grasped her more tightly. "Careful. Don't knock me over."

She playfully smacked his arm. "It's your fault I'm in danger of doing that."

He laid his palm on her belly and was rewarded with a swift kick. "Our daughter is ready to join her sisters."

"It could be a boy," Jo said.

"I don't care. And I've gotten rather good at daughters." He gazed down the hill at the girls, who were now playing in the stream. Two-year-old Francesca was kicking her feet, splashing water on three-year-old Theodosia while Evie stood in the center of the gentle current.

He really didn't care if he had a son or not, and neither did she. They were both just very grateful for what they had since it was far beyond what they'd ever dared dream.

Jo laid her head against his chest. "You said this was like Barbados, but Evie said it's not quite the same. She wants to go to Cornwall again, but understands we can't with the baby coming soon."

"I'd love to go too. If she makes her appearance soon, we might be able to go in September. For your birthday." He brushed his lips along her temple, and a warm breeze stirred a wisp of her hair free. She tucked it behind her ear.

They'd gone to Cornwall after marrying five years

ago and had fallen in love with the seaside villages and the warm, temperate weather. Bran had purchased property and built a house for them, which they'd dubbed Knight's Plantation even though it wasn't a plantation at all. It was, however, modeled after his and Evie's house on Barbados and was even decorated in the same fashion. It was everyone's favorite place.

Suddenly, her belly tightened. She recognized that pain. But it was just a twinge. She'd wait and see if it happened again.

Bran continued to stroke her belly, seemingly oblivious to the contraction she'd just felt. "Someday, I'll take you to Barbados. Maybe we won't come back."

"You have to. You're the earl."

He shrugged. "We can fake our deaths."

"Only if our children are with us. I won't have them believing we're dead."

He pulled back with a gasp, then chuckled. "God, no. Who would be that cruel?"

He snuggled against her once more, but she began to grow hot and stepped away. "I'm going to melt."

He let her go. "I understand."

She flicked a glance down toward her belly and gave him a sardonic look. "I doubt that. How are your pineapples?"

"Beautiful. We'll have an excellent dessert tonight—trifle with pineapple slices."

Jo groaned. "Oh, that sounds heavenly." Her belly tightened again, and she gritted her teeth against the pain.

Bran frowned at her. "Is it the babe?"

She nodded. "I'd say we have plenty of time given how long Theodosia took, but since Francesca came much quicker, perhaps I should go inside."

Bran called down to Evie. "Your mother needs to go in. The baby's coming."

"I *think* it's coming."

The sounds of laughter and clapping that came from the stream made Jo smile. But it faded as another pain gripped her. She reached for Bran. "Will you help me walk?"

"I'd pick you up if I could."

She snorted. "You'd never walk again."

After an interminable waddle back to the house, Jo was soon situated in their chamber. A footman went to fetch the doctor while all the preparations were made. Jo had only given birth in London and hoped things went as smoothly here.

In the dark of night, she and Bran welcomed their fourth child—a boy. His hair was dark, his face red, and his ten fingers and toes absolutely perfect.

As she nursed him, Bran sat on the bed beside her, his long fingers stroking the lad's downy-soft hair. "What shall we call him?"

Jo still couldn't believe it. "A miracle?"

Bran laughed. "We're all miracles, if you think about it. *Life* is a miracle."

"How about Michael? It sounds a bit like miracle."

"Yes, it does. It's perfect. Just like him. Just like you." He kissed her, his lips lingering on hers. "Thank you for making my life a true miracle."

She looked up into his eyes and saw the love shining in their depths. "All I did was love you."

He smiled and kissed their son's head. "And for that, I will be eternally grateful."

THE END

Thank You!

Thank you so much for reading The Duke of Defiance. I hope you enjoyed Bran and Jo's story! I loved writing them.

Would you like to know when my next book is available? You can sign up for my newsletter, follow me on Twitter at @darcyburke, or like my Facebook page at http://facebook.com/DarcyBurkeFans.

The Duke of Defiance is the fifth book in The Untouchables series. The next book in the series is *The Duke of Danger.* Watch for more information! In the meantime, catch up with my other historical series: Secrets and Scandals and Legendary Rogues. If you like contemporary romance, I hope you'll check out my Ribbon Ridge series available from Avon Impulse and my latest series, which continues the lives and loves of Ribbon Ridge's denizens – Love on the Vine.

I appreciate my readers so much. Thank you, thank you, *thank you.*

Books by Darcy Burke

Historical Romance

The Untouchables

The Forbidden Duke
The Duke of Daring
The Duke of Deception
The Duke of Desire
The Duke of Defiance
The Duke of Danger

Secrets and Scandals

Her Wicked Ways
His Wicked Heart
To Seduce a Scoundrel
To Love a Thief (a novella)
Never Love a Scoundrel
Scoundrel Ever After

Legendary Rogues

Lady of Desire
Romancing the Earl

Contemporary Romance

Ribbon Ridge

Where the Heart Is (a prequel novella)
Only in My Dreams
Yours to Hold
When Love Happens
The Idea of You
When We Kiss
You're Still the One

Ribbon Ridge: Love on the Vine
So Good
So Right
So in Love

Acknowledgments

Huge thanks to Erica Ridley for critiquing and an epic weekend in the PNW! Thank you also to Elizabeth Wright for beta reading—I really appreciate your eyeballs!

I love all of the covers of The Untouchables, but this one is just extra gorgeous. Thank you Carrie for making it so purdy!

Thank you to Linda and Toni for editing and proofreading. I love working with you and some day I will stop inserting extra ofs.

I am especially grateful to Danielle Gorman for all the heavy lifting she does. Thank you so much for your creativity and support!

As always, I can't do anything without the love of my family and three very…interesting cats. Welcome, Banana, to our crazy family, we love you.

Praise for Darcy Burke's Secrets & Scandals Series

HER WICKED WAYS

"A bad girl heroine steals both the show and a highwayman's heart in Darcy Burke's deliciously wicked debut."

–Courtney Milan, *NYT* Bestselling Author

"…fast paced, very sexy, with engaging characters."

–Smexybooks

HIS WICKED HEART

"Intense and intriguing. Cinderella meets *Fight Club* in a historical romance packed with passion, action and secrets."

–Anna Campbell, *Seven Nights in a Rogue's Bed*

"A romance...to make you smile and sigh…a wonderful read!"

–Rogues Under the Covers

TO SEDUCE A SCOUNDREL

"Darcy Burke pulls no punches with this sexy, romantic page-turner. Sevrin and Philippa's story grabs you from the first scene and doesn't let go. To Seduce a Scoundrel is simply delicious!"

–Tessa Dare, *NYT* Bestselling Author

"I was captivated on the first page and didn't let go until this glorious book was finished!"

–Romancing the Book

TO LOVE A THIEF

"With refreshing circumstances surrounding both the hero and the heroine, a nice little mystery, and a touch of heat, this novella was a perfect way to pass the day."

–The Romanceaholic

"A refreshing read with a dash of danger and a little heat. For fans of honorable heroes and fun heroines who know what they want and take it."

-The Luv NV

NEVER LOVE A SCOUNDREL

"I loved the story of these two misfits thumbing their noses at society and finding love." Five stars.

–A Lust for Reading

"A nice mix of intrigue and passion...wonderfully complex characters, with flaws and quirks that will draw you in and steal your heart."

–BookTrib

SCOUNDREL EVER AFTER

"There is something so delicious about a bad boy, no matter what era he is from, and Ethan was definitely delicious."

-A Lust for Reading

"I loved the chemistry between the two main characters...Jagger/Ethan is not what he seems at all and neither is sweet society Miss Audrey. They are believably compatible."

-Confessions of a College Angel

Legendary Rogues Series

LADY of DESIRE

"A fast-paced mixture of adventure and romance, very much in the mould of *Romancing the Stone* or *Indiana Jones*."

-All About Romance

"...gave me such a book hangover! ...addictive...one of the most entertaining stories I've read this year!"

-Adria's Romance Reviews

ROMANCING the EARL

"Once again Darcy Burke takes an interesting story and...turns it into magic. An exceptionally well-written book."

-Bodice Rippers, Femme Fatale, and Fantasy

"...A fast paced story that was exciting and interesting. This is a definite must add to your book lists!"

-Kilts and Swords

The Untouchables Series

THE FORBIDDEN DUKE

"I LOVED this story!!" 5 Stars

-Historical Romance Lover

"This is a wonderful read and I can't wait to see what comes next in this amazing series..." 5 Stars

-Teatime and Books

THE DUKE of DARING

"You will not be able to put it down once you start. Such a good read."

-Books Need TLC

"An unconventional beauty set on life as a spinster meets the one man who might change her mind, only to find his painful past makes it impossible to love. A wonderfully emotional journey from attraction, to friendship, to a love that conquers all."

-Bronwen Evans, USA Today Bestselling Author

THE DUKE of DECEPTION

"...an enjoyable, well-paced story ... Ned and Aquilla are an engaging, well-matched couple – strong, caring and compassionate; and ...it's easy to believe that they will continue to be happy together long after the book is ended."

-All About Romance

"This is my favorite so far in the series! They had chemistry from the moment they met...their passion leaps off the pages."

-Sassy Book Lover

THE DUKE of DESIRE

"Masterfully written with great characterization...with a flourish toward characters, secrets, and romance... Must read addition to "The Untouchables" series!"

--My Book Addiction and More

"If you are looking for a truly endearing story about two people who take the path least travelled to find the other, with a side of 'YAH THAT'S HOT!' then this book is absolutely for you!"

-The Reading Cafe

Ribbon Ridge Series

A contemporary family saga featuring the Archer family of sextuplets who return to their small Oregon wine country town to confront tragedy and find love...

The "multilayered plot keeps readers invested in the story line, and the explicit sensuality adds to the excitement that will have readers craving the next Ribbon Ridge offering."
-Library Journal Starred Review on YOURS TO HOLD

"Darcy Burke writes a uniquely touching and heart-warming series about the love, pain, and joys of family as well as the love that feeds your soul when you meet "the one."
-The Many Faces of Romance

I can't tell you how much I love this series. Each book gets better and better.
-Romancing the Readers

"Darcy Burke's Ribbon Ridge series is one of my all-time favorites. Fall in love with the Archer family, I know I did."
-Forever Book Lover

Ribbon Ridge: Love on The Vine

SO GOOD

" ...worth the read with its well-written words, beautiful descriptions, and likeable characters...they are flirty, sexy and a match made in wine heaven."

-Harlequin Junkie Top Pick

"I absolutely love the characters in this book and the families. I honestly could not put it down and finished it in a day."

-Chin Up Mom

SO RIGHT

"This is another great story by Darcy Burke. Painting pictures with her words that make you want to sit and stare at them for hours. I love the banter between the characters and the general sense of fun and friendliness."

-The Ardent Reader

" ...the romance is emotional; the characters are spirited and passionate... "

-The Reading Cafe

About the Author

Darcy Burke is the USA Today Bestselling Author of hot, action-packed historical and sexy, emotional contemporary romance. Darcy wrote her first book at age 11, a happily ever after about a swan addicted to magic and the female swan who loved him, with exceedingly poor illustrations.

A native Oregonian, Darcy lives on the edge of wine country with her guitar-strumming husband, their two hilarious kids who seem to have inherited the writing gene, two Bengal cats and a third cat named after a fruit In her "spare" time Darcy is a serial volunteer enrolled in a 12-step program where one learns to say "no," but she keeps having to start over. Her happy places are Disneyland and Labor Day weekend at the Gorge. Visit Darcy online at http://www.darcyburke.com and sign up for her newsletter, follow her on Twitter at http://twitter.com/darcyburke, or like her Facebook page, http://www.facebook.com/darcyburkefans.

Made in the USA
Monee, IL
15 May 2022